SOLDIER OF DEATH

A DARK, MAFIA ROMANCE

SHADOWS OF REDEMPTION

AJME WILLIAMS

DESCRIPTION

What's my last resort to getting out of an arranged marriage?
Selling my V-card to the highest bidder...
Who freaking knocks me up.
Throw in a kidnapping and you'll understand the mess I'm in.

Don Niko Leone paid $100,000 to own me for the first time. And I succumbed, telling myself it was only to escape my gilded cage, but knowing deep down the chemistry between us was unmatched.

But when I find out I've ended up pregnant *(with twins)* after our illicit encounter and my dad finds the cash, I'm forced to marry Niko's enemy... until Niko himself shows up at the wedding.

And kidnaps me.

Even though I know I'm just a pawn in his game, handsome and authoritative Niko is damn hard to resist. And when I'm faced with the ultimate choice to stay or run...

I know both could lead to my death... or the sweetest darkness of all.

1

ELENA

My time is running out. If I don't make a move soon, I'll be doomed to a life of degradation and abuse by a husband with no honor or morals. Leaving is dangerous for so many reasons. I have no money of my own and few skills. My father and would-be husband would see my leaving as an act of betrayal punishable by death.

On the outside, I appear to have it all—wealth, beauty, charm—but I'm a prisoner.

I first learned of the term *gilded cage* when I was about ten years old and overheard two of our family's servants talking about it in terms of me and my older sister, Lucia. It didn't sound positive, so I looked up the term and discovered it referenced a wealthy person's prison. At the time, I didn't understand why the servants would think Lucia and I were in a gilded cage. I didn't feel imprisoned. While my parents weren't affectionate, my nanny was. I spent most of my day playing, reading, and enjoying my life.

It wasn't until I turned twenty and I watched my father ship my sister off to Italy to marry a Don who was older than my father that I finally understood what living in a gilded cage meant. No matter how much my sister begged my father, she had no say in the matter. It was punishment for thinking she had a choice in the man that she would love. The young man she'd been caught with who prompted my father to send her away was found dead just before she left.

I understood then that while I lived in the lap of luxury, I had no agency. I also discovered the type of man my father truly was. He wasn't just a ruthless businessman. He was a Don, and no one, not even his children, had any power in the Family.

In the three years since my sister was sent away, my powerlessness has become more and more evident. My father doesn't care about my interests or my goals. I've been groomed to be a Mafia wife. I know everything about being submissive to a man... well, everything except pleasures of the flesh. I find it odd how men want a virginal woman for the purposes of sex. Worse, virginity is a commodity for my father to barter with or sell. My sister's actions not only brought shame to the Family, but they reduced her value in my father's eyes. His grip on my life tightened, determined to keep me innocent and at top price.

My life is the very definition of living in a gilded cage. Today, I spend all my time and energy figuring out how to escape my prison. I live in a family with wealth, but I have no assets, no money to survive on my own. My only escape at the moment is through the classes that I take in computer science. Of course, I had to lie to my father to get the money to take the courses. I told him I was taking cooking and other homemaking classes so that I can be a good wife. What I really want is to learn a skill that will allow me to support myself.

But my time is running out. In two months, my father is marrying me to Romeo Abate, a man who is known to take pleasure in hurting women. It's rumored that at least two of the women in his life have disappeared, and everyone suspects they're dead. I can't live a life like that, but I'm not prepared to leave. I haven't been able to save enough money for everything I need to escape. I need funds to travel, including getting a passport. I'll need money to change my name. It takes money to eat and find shelter. My plan so far is to get to Italy and pray my sister and her husband will protect me. It's probably naïve. More likely, her husband will ship me back home. But I have to hope that Lucia can help me.

I walk out of class, realizing I didn't catch any of today's lesson because my mind is filled with the terror of becoming Romeo's wife. Desperation is consuming me. I have to find a way out.

I stop by the coffee kiosk before leaving campus. Caffeine may not be the right thing to have when I'm already feeling anxious, but I need a moment to think.

I stand in line behind two women I've seen around campus but haven't ever had a class with.

"Look at this." One woman pulls out a flier from her bookbag and hands it to the other woman.

The second woman scans the page and rolls her eyes in disgust. "Just when you thought women had earned equal standing with men, here they are, dragging us back down."

I lean to the side a little to see what has sparked her comment. The page is a flier for a club in New Jersey that is auctioning off virgins. I may have been sheltered, but I understand sex. In particular, I understand that men value virginity, although I can't fathom why.

"Why would a virgin want to prostitute herself?" the second woman finishes.

"I heard the last time they did one of these, one of the women made $20,000."

My jaw drops.

"It's still prostitution."

"I thought you were all for women's freedom. If that's what she chooses to do, shouldn't that be her choice? Her body, her choice, and all that?"

The first woman has a point. In my current situation, I have no choice. My life, along with my virginity, is being given by my father to Romeo. I don't know the terms, but I know there's some benefit for my father.

However, I can take charge of my life and get the money I need quickly by selling my virginity myself.

"Are you even a virgin?" the second woman asks.

The first woman shrugs. "I don't know that they check you for those things. All you gotta do is act like you don't know what you're doing. Look innocent and confused. Let them fuck you and walk out with thousands of dollars."

"I think I'd rather knock off a liquor store."

The first girl laughs. "You're such a prude sometimes."

When the girls finish ordering, I step up to order my coffee and then hurry to my best friend's apartment. Kate, like my studies, is outside the Mafia world, or "The Family", as my father refers to it. To hide what I'm really studying, I store my books at her place. It's also near where I pick up a to-go meal and repackage it at her place to bring home as an example of something I made at school. Today, I skip the stop at the restaurant and head straight to Kate's.

"Hey, girl, how was class today?" Kate asks as I put my bookbag in the corner where I normally leave it.

"Do you know anything about virgin auctions?"

Her brows shoot up. "Why are you asking about something like that?"

"Two girls at school were talking about one at a club in New Jersey."

"Yeah, so?" A tinge of worry laces her tone.

I shrug. "We're about the same size, right? Can you to lend me something really sexy?" I own nice clothes, but nothing that would be considered sexy. Romeo once told me that he'd fix that when we were married. "I want my wife to show off her tits and ass. I want men to see what great pussy I'm getting." I cringe at the memory.

"Oh, God. You're not thinking of selling your virginity, are you?"

I nod, even though hearing my friend say aloud what I'd been thinking sends a shiver of doubt through me.

Kate moves toward me, taking both my hands and squeezing them as she stares at me. "That is stupid and dangerous. I know you're trying to save up money, but surely, there's another way."

I appreciate having Kate as my friend. She doesn't know the details about my Family. Even so, the Fiori name is known. It's like how everyone knows the name Gotti. Most people outside The Family who learn my last name get nervous and shy away. But Kate doesn't. I'm not sure whether that's because she doesn't care or she just doesn't realize who my Family is. Perhaps it's selfish of me not to find out for sure, but she's my best, my only friend and the only link to a world outside of my Family. All she knows is that my family is strict and is forcing me to marry. She doesn't understand how that can happen. Sometimes, she suggests going to her father for help. But the last thing I need is to bring someone in law enforcement into my Family. That would be a death sentence for us all.

"I don't see how I can make the amount of money I need in the two months that I have."

"Look, Elena, I'm not a prude, so I'm not going to tell you to wait until marriage to give away your virginity. But you should wait to give it to somebody who deserves it. Selling your virginity... that seems like a horrible sacrifice just to make money."

"Either I sell it myself, or my father is giving it to a man who won't be worthy. I value my freedom more than my virginity. And at least this way, I am in charge of my life. I'm making the choice to sell my virginity." I know I'm working hard to justify this decision, and at the same time, it makes perfect sense. I am desperate to avoid marrying Romeo. I'm desperate to leave the life that I was born into, the life my father is planning to sell me into.

"What happens if it doesn't work? What if you can't get away or your father hunts you down?"

It's something I have to consider. My father married my sister off to an old man in Italy. He could do the same to me. Maybe he'd have me killed. I imagine selling my virginity is worse than what Lucia did with the man she loved. What I know for sure is that Romeo won't want me if I'm not a virgin. At this point, the other consequences are worth the risk.

"This is my only shot. Will you help me?"

She releases my hands with a sigh. "Yes, fine. Come on." She leads me to her bedroom and opens her closet.

I step up to it, going through the various dresses hanging there. I pull out a blood-red dress that looks too small to cover a body. It's definitely a dress designed to lure men.

I hold it up. "How about this one?"

She shakes her head, taking the dress from me and hanging it up. "You're selling your virginity. You need to look like a virgin. On you, that dress would make it look like you can fuck your way through the whole club."

Kate pulls out a cream-colored dress. "This is the dress of a virgin. The shade will match your skin tone perfectly."

The dress reminds me of a style I wore as a little girl with a square neckline, short sleeves, and a high-waisted skirt that flares out from a tighter bodice. The fabric is plain. No embellishments. No texture.

"It looks like something a child would wear."

"It's called a baby doll style. Men don't just want virgins. They want young ones. It's creepy."

I take the dress to try it on. It's short, reaching almost to mid-thigh. The bodice is snug enough to hint at cleavage without actually showing it.

"I look—"

"Like a virgin. See how crazy this is? Seriously, Elena, there has to be something else you can do. Move in with me."

I love her for her support. "I can't. I'd just be forced home, and then you'd be dragged into my family drama." I turn back to the mirror. "How should I wear my hair?"

For a moment, she only stares at me, and I think she's going to stop helping. "Down. And not too much makeup. Here." She leads me to her bathroom and helps me finish getting ready.

When she's finished, she studies the results. "I have some heels that would work. That's the one area where you might consider looking sexy. I think I wear a half-size bigger than you, but try these." She hands me a pair of high-heeled sandals with thin straps the same color as the dress.

"Thank goodness I recently had a pedicure," I quip as I put them on. I stand, studying myself in the mirror. Does this convey a sexy virgin?

"The only thing you have to do now is look innocent, which in your case, won't be too hard."

I frown. "What does that mean?"

Kate leans against the wall and crosses her arms. "You're smart, and you're not afraid to be assertive when you need to be, but you are a virgin and you're sheltered. This could be really dangerous."

"It can't be any more dangerous than marrying Romeo." As I watch myself in my mirror, my courage grows. This is my way out. I'm sure of it.

2

ELENA

My resolve wanes as I sign up for the auction and am led to a room where there are other women, some who are chatting together and others who are primping themselves at makeup tables along one wall of the room. They're all beautiful and have an air of seduction around them, which makes me wonder if they're really virgins. Perhaps all this is just about role-play.

My stomach rolls, and I'm seriously thinking about abandoning this idea. Kate is right. It's stupid and possibly dangerous. I bypass the primping and stand in the wings of a stage where I see women, one at a time, saunter on stage to the whooping and hollering of men.

"She'll be lucky if she gets $3000."

I turn my head to the tall, redheaded woman standing next to me. "What makes you say that?"

"Her tits are too small, and her ass is too big." The woman adjusts the bodice of her dress so that the pink of her nipples is nearly showing. One wrong move and her breasts will pop out of her dress.

"You sound like you've been to something like this before." I can't believe she's a virgin.

She casts a glance at me as if she's suspicious. "I'm a virgin. Just like you." Her hazel eyes take me in, and she smirks. "Well, maybe not like you."

I look down at my dress and then back at her. I came here needing money, but what if I'm not appealing enough?

"Don't sweat it, honey. I bet you'll get five or ten thousand. Maybe even fifteen if you keep up that wide-eyed innocence."

"The woman who made twenty thousand—"

The woman laughs. "Don't get your hopes up."

I bite my lip. Will this be worth it if I don't make enough to leave home?

"God, you're not just a virgin, you're completely innocent. Did you grow up in one of those strict families?"

I nod.

"Well, don't you worry. You'll do okay. Better than most people here. And when it comes time to do the deed, think of your favorite crush. Do you have a crush? Maybe some movie star you would love to whisk you away and fuck you? Think of them in a sexual way. You know, fantasize, so at least you get a little bit wet down there. That way, it won't hurt so much."

I swallow the lump in my throat and look at the other women in the room and then back to the redhead next to me. "Is there anyone else here who is a virgin?"

She looks over my shoulder toward the room and then back at me. "Most of us are born-again virgins."

Is that a thing?

"But yeah, there's always a few. But most of them have made out or watched porn. Have you watched porn?"

I shake my head. "The men don't mind if you're not a virgin?"

She rolls her eyes. " All they want is to fuck someone who isn't their wife. You just need to act subservient and innocent. Let them do whatever they want to get their rocks off."

"Why do you do it?"

Her eyes narrow. "Why are you here, honey? For the money, right?"

I nod.

"Nadine," a voice calls from the curtain.

She plasters on a smile. "That's me. Wish me luck."

I watch as she struts onto the stage and the other woman comes off. I wonder how much she made. More than that, I wonder if Nadine is right and that I can get fifteen thousand dollars? And is prostituting myself worth it? What if I don't make enough to leave?

For long moments, I stand paralyzed at the edge of the stage. Kate is right. This is a crazy idea. I'm aware of the concept of sex. A man sticks his penis into a woman. But I have no clue beyond the logistics. Why did Nadine say it would hurt? Does it normally hurt, or are the men here rough?

I take a step back as Nadine comes off the stage with a big smile and a swagger.

"Ten K and the dude's not half bad, even if he is old enough to be my father. Men like that, you know. That's why I bet you'll do well. Men like to imagine fucking little girls."

God, that's disturbing.

"Alice!" the voice calls from the curtain.

I glance down at my dress and remember how I looked younger than my twenty-three years in the mirror. What am I doing?

"Alice, you're on," the voice calls again.

Nadine nudges me. "That's you, Alice."

Oh, yeah. I gave a fake name so nobody would know who I was.

Tentatively, I put one foot in front of the other. As I come from behind the curtain and stand on the stage, a bright light nearly blinds me.

"That looks like some true-blue pussy virgin."

I flinch, but I keep moving toward the center of the stage.

"Don't be scared, honey. I'll take real good care of you."

I come to the center of the stage and stand, closing my eyes, wishing I were anywhere but here. This was a mistake.

"Three grand."

"Five."

"Six."

The voices of the men ricochet off the walls around me. The price slowly rises. When it hits $10,000, I remind myself that this is why I'm here. Ten thousand dollars will go a long way toward helping me escape not only Romeo, but my father as well.

The bidding continues upward. Fifteen, twenty, thirty... and suddenly, freedom feels closer. The sacrifice I'm making feels worth it.

"$100,000."

A gasp echoes through the room. My head jerks toward the voice, but the light is so bright I can't see who made the bid.

For a moment, I stand as a murmur floats through the audience. I can't hear specifically what people are saying, but it's clear the bidding has gone up too high. It hits me, a hundred thousand dollars.

I can't help but smile. One hundred thousand dollars is definitely freedom.

"Don't smile too much, girly. Knowing Niko, he's going to get all hundred thousand dollars' worth of pussy out of you."

The words bring me back to reality. I've just sold my virginity. A man I don't know is going to touch me, do nasty things to me.

I swallow the bile that threatens to rise. I don't have a crush to think about, like Nadine suggested. I've thought men were handsome, but I'd never felt a desire to touch them or be touched. Instead, while he does whatever he's going to do to me, I'll think about leaving my cage, my prison. About making my own choices. Making my own way in the world. With a hundred thousand dollars, I can free Lucia too.

I'm escorted off the stage and up a long hallway. I'm guided through a door and then up some steps.

"You lucked out," the large, gruff man says as we reach the second-floor landing. "The Boss never joins in on the auction."

The use of the word Boss has me stalling. What sort of boss is this man who bought me?

The man who is leading me opens the door to the room, putting out a hand to guide me in.

"Boss?" I ask, stopping outside the door.

"Yeah. He owns the place."

I let out a sigh of relief. The man who bought me isn't a Boss in organized crime. He's a businessman. The owner of the club.

I move into the room and look around. It reminds me a little of a hotel suite with a bed, sitting area, and even a bar.

"It means you get the nicest private room too. Wait here. He'll be up in a minute."

After he leaves, I'm once again struck by what I've just done. And what I am about to do. My knees shake, and I wonder if it's too late for me to change my mind. I take a step toward the door, but before I reach it, a body fills the space. I gasp and step back.

He smirks as he steps in, his gaze inventorying my body as if he's searing it into his memory. "Having second thoughts? It doesn't matter. You're bought and paid for. I plan to get every penny's worth."

Freedom. Freedom for me and Lucia. I run it like a mantra in my mind. "Where is my money?" My voice trembles, but I won't hand over my virginity until I have my money.

"You'll have your check as soon as you've delivered the goods."

I flinch at his referring to me as goods. But of course, that's what I am. I just sold my virginity.

Wait? A check? I can't take a check. To cash a check, I'd have to give my real name. There's no way I can cash a check without my father finding out. Surely, that's not how these auctions work. I might be sheltered, but I know checks leave a money trail. I can't believe any man in this club is willing to write a check. It would show up as having bought sex.

I shake my head. "I need cash."

He crosses his arms and leans against the doorjamb. An amused smirk fills his face. And by amused, I don't mean he finds me charming. It makes me think of a Cheshire Cat. Or the amusement a cat might have as it watches a mouse trying to escape before it finally pounces on its prey.

"If you're concerned about a check being traced, I can recommend a bank. It takes care of all our customers' business."

The hairs on the back of my neck stand up. There are only a certain few types of people who have the sort of power to control a bank. Politicians, tycoons, and organized crime bosses. I peg this man as a tycoon because he clearly isn't a politician, and I can't bear the thought of having sold my virginity to a Don.

"I need cash. Cash or the deal is canceled."

His mouth continues to smirk, but his eyes narrow in a way that makes him look dangerous. "No refunds, no returns, *cara mia*."

3

NIKO

I don't have time for this. I'm not here tonight to fuck. I'm supposed to be checking on the club. It's been a month since I've stopped by, and while I've hired top-notch people, I make my presence known at all my establishments. I trust no one. The closer they are to me, the less I trust them. I didn't become the youngest Don in the Leone Family—hell, any family—by trusting people. I did it through brute strength fueled by revenge and anger. It still drives me today, so I'm fucking pissed off that my dick has been distracted by a woman.

I've had my share of pussy. So much pussy that fucking doesn't have the appeal that it once had. Fine. I'd rather take care of business, and my enemies, without the hassle and complications of women or hard-ons. So why the fuck did this woman stop me in my tracks as I entered the club?

I've never participated in the virgin auctions. The truth is that most of these women aren't really virgins. Carlo, my manager, reports it doesn't matter. It's all an illusion that our patrons are willing to pay for. While some of the so-called virgins clearly have fucked, others might be technically a virgin in that a cock has never passed their pussy lips. But they're far from innocent. A cock has passed their other lips.

But this woman on the stage with the long, dark hair, child-like dress, and innocence pouring out from her... good God, I doubt she's ever seen a cock in real life. Hell, probably not in a book, either.

I never pegged myself for the lusting after virgins type. I like women who know what they're doing in bed and better yet, understand that fucking is all about getting me off. Tonight, however, it appears I'm in lust for a virgin. A virgin with wide, innocent eyes, the dress of a girl, and tits made for fucking.

With my bid, I make sure she is mine. I don't know what to expect from her, although her demand to be paid isn't it. She's over her head here, and yet, she has enough sass to assert herself. I wonder if fucking her will be the same. Uncertainty, and yet, talking back. The idea makes my cock thicken.

I'm an asshole and a brute, but something about her has me hesitating to take what is mine. I don't want to scare her. In fact, I want to make her come. Hard. I want this first time for her to be a memory that lasts until her dying day. I want her to always be disappointed in the men she's with next because they can't satisfy her like I can.

I go to the bar and pour myself a double whisky on the rocks. "Want a drink?"

She shakes her head. I wonder if she's never had alcohol either. She looks young, but not underage.

Even so. "How old are you?" I don't normally have scruples about anything, but underage girls aren't my thing. I think pedophiles and people who abuse animals should get the death penalty.

"Twenty-three. When do I get my money?"

"When my cum is dripping from your pussy." Or at least fills the condom I brought with me.

Her breath hitches and her eyes widen, but it's not fear I see. She's intrigued.

"You understand what's happening here, right?" It would be just my luck if one of my enemies like Tiberius Abate or Giovanni Fiori would force a woman to sell herself to me and get me arrested for sexual assault.

I down my whisky at the thought of Abate and Fiori. It won't be long now before those two fuckers are six feet under. They're going to pay for killing my mother and little brother. Nothing they can do, including joining forces against me, will save them. I will crush them and everyone close to them.

She nods again. "Why do men like virgins?"

I pour another drink. "I suppose in history, it was to make sure the firstborn was actually the man's kid."

Her brows pull together.

"What. You think I'm not smart?"

"We're not procreating, though. Don't men like virgins for other reasons?"

Is she trying to delay the inevitable? "Tight pussies. Knowing they're the first." I shrug.

"Why did you buy me?"

Good question. "I like your tits. I want to see them. Take your clothes off."

"What about my money?"

"I told you. You'll have your money when I'm satisfied. Now take your clothes off," I snap.

For a moment, she stares at me. Normally, I don't tolerate obstinance or hesitation, but there's something about her that prevents me from getting angry. Her eyes are an unusual brown... light like amber or my whisky. It makes me think of fire. Fire in a woman turns me on.

Finally, she undoes her dress, letting it drop in a pool around her shapely legs. Legs I imagine wrapped around my hips as I pump into her.

"Bra and panties too," I tell her as I come around the bar toward her.

She complies and crosses her arms over her tits.

"Don't do that. I want to see you." I step up to her, slowly, to keep her calm. I reach into my glass, pulling out a cube of ice. I rub it over her pink nipple. Her breath hitches again, and she lets out a moan.

I let a slow smile spread. "You like that, eh?"

"It's cold."

I put the ice cube in my mouth and then take her nipple between my lips. I run the cube over it with my tongue. She lets out another moan and her hips rock. My virgin is turned on.

I pull away. "Where did you feel that?"

She looks at me in confusion. "My breast."

"No. Not just there. Did you feel it here too?" I slide my fingers between her thighs, and holy hell, she's sopping wet. "You did feel it there. Feels good, doesn't it, *cara mia*?"

She bites her lip, and I get the feeling she thinks she shouldn't enjoy it. Normally, I don't care how much women enjoy sex, but tonight, she's going to enjoy this. And I am too. Perhaps the appeal of a virgin is teaching and watching a woman come for the first time.

That thought makes me wonder if she's ever touched herself. "Have you ever come?"

She looks at me blankly.

"Had an orgasm? Have you touched and given yourself pleasure?"

She shakes her head, and now my cock is straining in my slacks not only to be the first in her pussy, but the first to make her cry out in pleasure.

I set my glass on the bar and walk over to the table. "Come here. Sit on the table and spread your legs."

She glances at the bed. "We're not—"

"I don't like to repeat myself," I snap.

Most women would flinch, but she sucks in a breath and almost looks annoyed. I wonder if she has other asshole men in her life who boss her around.

She complies, sitting on the table, but her legs aren't nearly open enough. I push her thighs apart and drop to my knees to study her pussy. I see it glistening from her essence. A part of me wants to eat her out, but my dick is too greedy.

I rise and undo my pants, freeing my cock. Her eyes round when she sees it. I like the shock and her wondering if it will fit that I see in her eyes.

In the back of my mind, I'm telling myself to cover up. I don't need little Nikos running around. But this situation calls for a bare ride. I'm about to have an innocent virgin for the first time. I don't want to dull the excitement by rolling on a rubber. I just have to pull out when the time comes. It shouldn't be hard. I find that most women come way before me, giving me plenty of time to withdraw. Maybe I'll have her suck me off to the end.

I rub my cock through her pussy lips. She sucks in a breath and tenses. I continue to rub her clit, up and down, round and round, until she relaxes. Her breathing quickens. Her hips rock. Her moan is one of need. She's ready.

"I'm going to fuck you now. Hard and fast."

She looks at me, and for a moment, I feel like there's trust in her eyes. I don't like that. I'm no hero. Why ever she sold her virginity is not my business. We'll do this, and she'll take the money and use it to run away or whatever she needs. I'll go on with my life without a second thought about this moment.

I thrust in hard, and her look of trust vaporizes into shock. She cries out and grips my shoulders. My instinct is to drive in and out, in and out, but I hold for a moment, letting her adjust. After all, I want to make her come.

"Lay back," I demand.

She does as I ask, and as I hold myself seeped inside her, I lick my thumb and rub her clit. With my other hand, I pinch her nipples. They're dark pink and hard as rocks. Maybe when I pull out, I'll fuck those round tits of hers.

Soon, she's relaxed again, her hips gyrating. I pull out and plunge in, making her gasp. Holy hell, is she tight, and it feels so fucking good.

I am a man of control. Always. But for a brief moment, I let go. I give in to the sensation. I close my eyes, letting the friction of her pussy take my pleasure to new heights. I guess there is something to virgins, after all.

"Oh!" She cries out again, and her body bows off the table. Her pussy clamps down on my dick like it plans to never let go.

Instantly, my cock thrusts in and releases. "Fuck!" I withdraw and wrap my hand around my dick hard enough to stop the flow. "Get on your knees."

She seems dazed, not understanding what I'm demanding.

I tug her hand, pulling her off the table. "On your knees."

She drops to her knees.

"Open your mouth."

The moment her lips part, I'm stroking my cock like it's the end of the world and this is the last orgasm I'm ever going to have.

My cum shoots out, hitting her on the face, her tits, and finally, I slip my tip over her lips and slide into her mouth.

"Fuck!" I groan as my release rolls through me like thunder.

When I'm done, my legs shake, and I don't like it. I look down at her, wondering again if she was sent by my enemies to fuck me up somehow.

She wipes her mouth, but I don't see any sort of smugness in her expression. In some ways, that's worse because I have this over-whelming urge to keep her around. Not for long. Maybe just tonight.

But I'm a man of control. I gave into the urge by buying and fucking her. It has to stop now.

I step away, pulling up my pants and going to the bar to finish my drink. "There's a bathroom to clean up. Get dressed." I keep my gaze away from her, unsettled by the pull she has on me.

Finally, I hear her exit the bathroom and I turn toward her. She's standing in the middle of the room, fully dressed and still looking innocent. Heaven help me, I want to fuck her again.

I stalk toward the door. "I'll send your money up now."

4

ELENA

I hurry from class to Kate's apartment, skipping the coffee kiosk. I'm a week away from my forced marriage to Romeo, so I have all my fingers and toes crossed that today will be the day my passport shows up in the mail. In the nearly two months since I sold my virginity, I've been putting my plan of escape into action. I've run into challenges and obstacles along the way. I didn't know I would need my birth certificate to apply for a passport. For most people, it's no big deal to go to the clerk's office for a birth certificate. For me, it's not possible. My father has eyes everywhere, and I can't afford to have anyone noticing what I'm doing. So, I ordered my birth certificate online by sneaking onto my mother's computer in the middle of the night and had it sent to Kate's. Once I had the birth certificate, I applied for my passport, paying extra for the expedited service. Even so, I was cutting it close. Right now, I can't buy my plane ticket until I have the passport, and if it doesn't come in the next few days, all this effort will be for nothing.

Although I'm still not sure what to make of my encounter with the man who bought my virginity, the hundred thousand dollars makes it easy to be grateful. The truth is, although I was scared to death to have sex and that first moment of penetration hurt a lot, the experience wasn't all that unpleasant. As he moved in and out of me, he also touched me, evoking feelings that were a mixture of pleasure and torment that built until it was like a dam broke and sweet sensations flowed throughout me.

He had cursed and forced me onto my knees as he stroked himself and his release splattered over me. His words and his expression made it seem like he was in pain. But that couldn't be right. Men liked sex, right?

I wasn't sure what to make of how abruptly he ended things with me, but I didn't complain. A few moments after he walked out, the man who had led me up to the room appeared with a bag filled with cash. I returned home excited and hopeful, but also knowing that I wasn't home free yet. Until I have my passport and a plane ticket, I'm stuck here. I also have to figure out when exactly I'll make my escape. Do I try to leave late at night? Everything I've done up to now has been dangerous, but the closer I get to leaving, the more dangerous my situation becomes. I can feel the stress of it weighing on me. I'm tired and stressed out, hardly able to eat.

I arrive at Kate's place, and as I set my book bag in the corner, she's holding up an envelope, waving it at me. "I think your freedom is here."

Elated, filled with energy for the first time in weeks, I rush to her and take the envelope. I rip it open. Inside is a dark blue passport. My eyes well with tears as emotion floods me. I'm not normally one to be overcome with emotion, but this little book is a symbol of my freedom.

"Just in time, right?" Kate says.

I nod, sniffing from the tears.

She rubs my back. "I hate to see you leave, but I understand that you have to go. Do you think you'll be able to stay in touch with me?"

Up until this moment, I haven't thought too far ahead once I make my escape. I know that I want to change my identity and not give my father or Romeo any chance to find me. As long as he never finds out about my friendship with Kate, maybe I could stay in touch with her.

"I hope so. I need to buy a plane ticket."

Kate grabs her laptop from her tiny dining table. "We can do it now."

"Did I give you enough money to cover all this?"

I've given Kate the money I need, and she's made the payments so there's no trace of it to me. When I first handed her the five thousand dollars, she was resistant to taking it knowing where it came from. But I told her this was my freedom money, and eventually, she gave in.

"You have given me more than enough. So, when do you plan to leave?"

A part of me wants to leave right this moment, but I need to go home and pack. That is one thing I haven't done in advance because I can't afford for anybody at home to notice a packed suitcase in my room. As it is, I had to be clever in hiding the bag of money I got from the club. It's stored in my closet, under a floorboard, hidden by carpet.

I'm only seven days from having to get married, so I need to arrange my flight soon, but I can't rush things. I need to do everything right.

"Tomorrow. I don't think I can get out of my house when everyone is sleeping, so maybe I can do it when they think I'm going to class. Is there a plane in the afternoon?"

"Let me look."

The best we could manage is a flight from New York to Rome leaving tomorrow evening. I have to hope that my parents don't notice I'm gone until I'm on the flight. Ever since the evening I was at the club, I feel like they've been watching me more closely. Like they're suspicious of something. It's probably just paranoia on my end because if my parents knew what I was planning, they wouldn't hesitate to lock me in my room or maybe send me away like they did with my sister.

Once the ticket is bought, Kate prints it out since I don't have a smartphone. All I have is a small burner one I've been saving to call my sister when I'm ready to flee. I can't wait to see Lucia. I haven't spoken to her since my father sent her away. I begged my father to invite her to the wedding, but he didn't want the taint of her to ruin my day. At least that's what he said. I know what he really meant was that he didn't want the Abate Family to have a reminder of what my sister had done.

"Here, have some tea. You sure you're alright?" Kate said, handing me a mug of tea as we sat on her couch.

"I'm nervous, of course, but I'm doing alright."

She cocked her head to the side. "You look like you've lost weight. And you're pale."

I nod. "It's probably the stress. It's wreaking havoc on me. I'm not really hungry, but when I do eat, I feel nauseous."

She arches her brow at me. "Nauseous as in you throw up, or just feeling queasy?"

"Mostly queasy. Maybe I've been sick once or twice."

She takes a sip of her tea, but her eyes are watching me over the rim. I'm not sure what to make of her expression.

"How long have you been feeling like this?" she asks.

"The closer I get to the wedding or running away, the worse it gets."

"What about your period?"

I find her question odd. But as I think about it, I realize I haven't had my period in a while.

I shake my head. "I guess the stress and weight loss have caused me to stop having one."

"Or you're pregnant."

My jaw drops. "Why would you say that?"

"Well, you're exhausted, you're feeling nauseous, and maybe the big point is that you had sex."

"Yeah, but—"

"I never asked you about the details because you seemed okay and wanted to move on. But... did he use a condom?"

"No, but he... you know... none of the stuff went in me." My cheeks flush. Kate is my best friend, but I still don't want to discuss what happened that night. Not because it traumatized me, because it didn't. It's embarrassing to talk about.

Kate arches a brow. "Are you saying his penis wasn't inside you, or that he didn't come in you?"

Moments like this make me feel so stupid. They highlight how sheltered and ignorant I really am. "He pulled out."

She reaches out and takes my hand. "That's not foolproof, Elena. I'm sorry, maybe we should've talked about this more before you did this."

I'm trying not to panic but it's difficult. "He didn't finish in me."

"But sometimes before that happens, there's still a little bit of semen. It helps lubricate everything."

Humiliation and embarrassment mix with my panic.

"Listen, I picked up a pregnancy test because I was worried about you. You should take it."

I shake my head. "No. I don't want to."

"Then take it with you. Once you're away from your family, if you don't feel better, take it. Just to be sure."

She rises from the couch and disappears down her short hallway. She reemerges a few moments later with a box. "All the directions are there. You just need to pee on it and wait a few minutes."

"I'm not pregnant." Still, I take the box.

I head home wondering how I'm going to get a passport and a pregnancy test into the house. No one goes through my things when I get home as a matter of course, but it is something my father could order to be done at any time. He'd done it to my sister.

Before I walk in the house, I remove the test and instructions from the box and shove it into the package that my passport is in. Then I hide both under my shirt, held in place by the waistband of my jeans. I'm glad I wore a tunic top today to cover it up.

I make it to my room and hide the items under the mattress of my bed. This time of night, anyone can check on me and I don't want to be caught hiding them in my closet. I go to the bathroom and find the phone I'd hidden behind my toilet, deciding to keep it and money separate. If I lost one, I'd have the other. With the door closed, I turn on the shower and then sit in the corner and with shaking hands, call my sister.

"*Pronto.*"

"Luce?"

There's a pause. "Elena?"

"Yes, it's me."

"Oh, God. Are you okay? How are you?" Her voice is a mixture of happiness and worry.

"I'm going to run away. I have a ticket to Rome leaving tomorrow night. Can I come to you? Will Giuseppe—"

"Yes, of course. Me and Giuseppe will protect you. But God, how are you going to manage it? Did something happen?"

"I'm supposed to marry Romeo Abate in a week. I can't, Luce."

"That monster? How can you manage it?"

I tell her my plan.

"Be careful, Elena."

Once off the phone, I vacillate on whether to trash it or keep it just in case. If my father finds it, he'll know who I called and that could cause problems for Lucia. Then again, my showing up in Italy will cause problems. I second-guess my decision to run to her. But her husband, while old, is more powerful, especially in Italy. I can't see my father wanting to take him on.

I turn off the shower and step into my bedroom when my bedroom door flies open. My dad's right-hand man enters the room. "Your father demands your presence."

Fear skitters down my spine. The rules of the house have always been that employees are not allowed to enter my room without knocking. The only exception is if I'm in trouble and my father wants to see me. I have a sense of déjà vu from when it happened to my sister.

I work to make my face impassive and lift my chin, wanting to show an air of superiority even though I know that at my father's command, this man could punish me. I give a curt nod and head out of my room, downstairs to my father's office.

I take a breath and walk in, standing in the middle of my father's office. I wait and give a whole new meaning to shaking in my boots, or in my case, flats. I'm terrified.

My father stands behind his desk, his scowl deeper than I've ever seen before. He picks up a bag, my bag, and turns it on its end. Out falls my money. In that moment, I see my freedom evaporate. And quite possibly, my life.

Sheer terror paralyzes me, stopping me from running. Of course, there's no reason to run. I have nowhere I could get to before my father or his men would catch me.

I'm not sure how I'm still standing as my legs are wobbly. My world is tilting off its axis.

"Where did you get this?" he bellows at me.

I try to think of a reasonable excuse. Maybe I can say Romeo gave it to me, but he probably won't back me up. Or if he does, he'd expect something that I'm sure I'm unwilling to pay.

Perhaps I can say my mother gave it to me in preparation for the wedding, but I know she won't back me up. My mom is a perfect Mafia wife. She had to be because she didn't give my father a son, so it won't take much for him to decide she isn't worth anything. My mother supports him, and everything she does is to make him look good in front of the other Families.

My father comes around the desk, and I flinch as he grabs my chin, jerking my head to look up at him. I keep my gaze on his because I know from experience that looking away is seen as a sign of guilt.

"The only way I can think of a woman being able to squirrel away this much money is that she's been opening her legs to men. Have you been whoring yourself, Elena?" He releases my chin with a sharp push. "No. Don't tell me. I don't know what the fuck you're planning, but from now on, you're confined to this house. You're going to marry Romeo Abate next week. For your sake, I hope to hell you're still a virgin. And if you're not, you'd better hope he can't tell. If you fuck up this deal for me, Elena—"

The door opens and my mother walks in. I feel like I'm going to be sick, and it takes all my effort to hold myself together.

"Is she still pure?" my mother asks.

"I don't want to know, and you don't either. We act like she is. We need plausible deniability in this." My father glares at me. "I can't believe you did this. I trusted you. I thought you were like your mother. A little fiery, but dutiful, obedient. If however you got this money comes back to bite me in the ass, you're going to have a real problem."

I'm shaking visibly. He dismisses me and has my mother escort me to my room with instructions to keep me there until the wedding.

"I thought you were smarter than this, Elena," my mother says as she takes me to my room.

One of my father's men is standing outside the door. My mother pushes me in and then slams the door behind me. My legs are like jelly, but they manage to get me to the bathroom where I heave and empty out my stomach.

After I brush my teeth, I take the phone I've hidden. I vacillate on whether to call someone or destroy it. Lucia can't help me. I should call her and let her know I'm not coming, but who knows if someone is listening? Kate can't help, either. If the phone is found, my situation will be even worse than it is already, so I break the phone into small bits and flush them.

I go back into my room, looking out my window. Outside, my father has stationed another man. There is no way to escape now. I sink onto my bed feeling defeated. Hope of freedom is lost.

Or is it? Could I make an escape during the wedding?

I shake my head. My father will have men on me twenty-four, seven, and at the wedding, Romeo's father's men will be there.

I wonder what I did that prompted my father to have my room searched to the point that they lifted the carpet in my closet and found my money.

I remember the passport and the pregnancy test under my mattress. I decide to hide the passport in my box of tampons. I don't know that it's a good hiding spot, but it's the best one I can think of at the moment. As far as the pregnancy test, I'm about to break it and flush it when I decide that maybe I should take it. Now that Kate has planted the seed of possibility, I'll worry until I can confirm that it's just stress that is impacting my body. Once I know for sure that I'm not pregnant, it will be one less thing weighing on me.

I quickly read the instructions and follow them. Then I sit and wait. God, if I am pregnant, I am in deeper trouble. I don't know if Romeo will be able to tell whether I'm a virgin or not. But if he finds out I'm pregnant, I'm as good as dead. Then again, I imagine Romeo will want to sleep with me on our wedding night, and maybe I'll be able to pass a baby off as his. God, I can't deal with this extra burden weighing me down.

When the time is up, I pick up the stick to read it.

Pregnant.

5

ELENA

The last week has been a new sort of misery. My cage isn't gilded. Oh, sure, I'm in my opulent room, but I'm not allowed to leave. Not even for meals. They're brought up to me by servants who look at me like I'm a spoiled brat. I remember seeing a movie, or maybe it was a book, in which two people from opposite ends of the financial spectrum meet and after discovering they're identical, they switch places. I'd do that in a minute if I wouldn't feel guilty for having another person locked up in my place.

Despite being imprisoned in my room, I'm not bored. My mind is a raceway of thoughts, my heart a torrent of emotions. I'm going to be married to an abusive man in a matter of days. I'm carrying another man's baby. If Romeo finds out, I'm dead for sure. If he doesn't kill me, my father will for ruining whatever arrangement he has with Romeo's father, Tiberius Abate. It must be something more than just a show of solidarity, a partnership between Families.

Then again, my father has wanted to align with the Abate Family after the murder of the head of the Leone Family's mother and brother. I don't have details because women, especially daughters, aren't privy to such things. But being passive and quiet, I often over-hear conversations among my father's *capos* and soldiers. Rumor was that Tiberius wanted to take over the Leone Family, or at least their territory, and my father was there to help, including some involvement in killing the head of the Leone Family's mother and brother. It was a shocking revelation at the time, but now I fully understand my father and the savage life he leads.

"It's war," my father's *capo* had said. "*Il Soldato Della Morte* won't rest until the deaths are avenged."

"Is it true he killed his cousin to take over the family, making him the youngest Don ever?" the soldier had asked.

"It is true. Don Leone lives up to his name, Soldier of Death."

What all that means for me, if anything, I don't know. I'll likely never know. But locked in my room, there's little else to do but ponder the world I'm in. The savageness of it. As far as I can tell, the regular world doesn't have this level of fear and violence. I so desperately wish I could be in that world, but facing reality means accepting the world that I'm in. I need to tow the line and be a good wife.

"Don't give him a reason to be angry with you, Elena, and you'll be fine," my mother is telling me during one of her daily visits to me. I want to think it's because she's worried about me, but I know she's preparing me for my marriage to Romeo. Not to help me cope, but to make sure Romeo is happy so that my father looks good in the Abate Family's eyes.

"Always look pretty. Make sure your staff keeps the house clean and good food on the table. And when he wants to force himself on you, you lie back and take it. It only hurts for a moment."

I think back to the club and how the man who bought me had touched me. How it had hurt but then felt good.

"Does it always hurt?" I ask my mom.

She sniffs, like she finds the topic unsavory. "If you're lucky, once you give him a son, he'll spend his time with his *goomah*."

"You don't mind him having other women?"

She shakes her head. "Not at all. I don't know why such things are so popular among young women today. It's a dirty, messy, feral thing."

I can see her point. My night with my mystery man had been

messy and somewhat feral, but it wasn't icky, as my mother seems to be suggesting.

"Why do they want that?"

Her head tilts to the side. "The fact that you ask tells me you're still pure. That warms my heart. Men are sexual and violent beasts. It's their nature." She takes my hand, and it's an unusual gesture from her. "When he wants you, he's going to put his *peesche* inside you."

My mother always uses Italian when she doesn't want to say the word in English, like *peesche* for dick.

"It's very uncomfortable but doesn't last long. When he's done, he'll be on his way. You might tell him how big he is or praise him. Men are weak and need their women to make them feel confident and strong."

I have a feeling my father wouldn't agree with that assessment, but I nod.

She gives me a smile. "You'll make me and your father proud, won't you, Elena?"

I nod again. What choice do I have?

SEVERAL DAYS LATER, I leave my room, and despite how much I hated being locked up there, I don't want to leave. Stuck in my room is better than what is awaiting me once I marry Romeo today.

I sit in the bridal room of the Catholic church as my mother and the other ladies in my wedding party primp and fuss. My mother is angry at me because my dress doesn't fit the way it should. The words sink into my foggy brain, and I wonder if she can tell that I'm pregnant. But then I realize she's upset because I've lost weight.

"I knew we should've had an extra fitting," she snaps.

"Mrs. Fiori, the wedding is going to be perfect. Don't worry," the maid of honor says. I have no clue who she is. Perhaps she's part of the Abate Family.

I lose myself in my mind again, unable to cope with what is happening. Before I know it, I'm standing in front of the priest with Romeo. I don't remember walking up the aisle.

I briefly glance around, and no one around me is smiling. Not Romeo. Not his family. Not mine. Not the attendants. Not the few guests. Weddings are supposed to be joyous occasions, but for all the pomp and circumstance, the reality is that this is a business deal. The wedding is just the transfer of ownership from one family to another.

Deep inside me, a wail of agony wants to burst through, but I know if I do anything to embarrass or bring shame on my family, I'm a dead woman.

"Mr. Abate, repeat after me. I, Romeo Tiberius Abate, take Elena Antonia Fiori to be my wife," the priest says.

How am I going to say these vows? God knows, they're not true. There will not be any having or holding or faithfulness. And death do us part can come to me at any time.

Romeo is finishing his vow, and I'm dying inside as my turn is next.

The doors of the church burst open, causing us all to flinch and look. A hail of gunfire echoes through the nave. It's pure instinct that has me dropping to the floor and covering my head. Chaos surrounds me. Women scream. Men shout.

I glance up, seeing my father, Tiberius, and Romeo looking confused. They've taken refuge in the sanctuary.

"How the hell did they get in? Is this your doing?"

My father glares at him. "Why would I do this?"

From my place on the floor, I look up toward the aisle. I see a single man walking up, a gun in each hand pointed toward the sanctuary.

I should try to run, but instead, I close my eyes and cover my head again.

"Sorry to ruin such a joyous occasion." There's something about the voice that seems familiar.

"You have some nerve, *Giovane Re*. You really think you're going to walk out of here alive?" Tiberius bellows. I wonder who the *Giovane Re*, the boy king, is. From the tone, the term is mocking, not complimentary.

"I don't care if I do. But I'm taking you to hell with me." I'm trying to place his voice. Who had they killed? Is he one of my father's men who is mutinying? Or Abate's? And how did he get in and so close to us? Where are my father's men? The Abate Family's men?

"What do you want?" my father calls.

"Ah, Fiori. I knew you were both cowards. You think you're big men to kill a woman and her son. Look at you cowering in the altar of God," this man sneers.

There must be more men than this one man, but I'm not going to lift my head to find out. If I keep my head down, maybe I'll survive. I try to make myself smaller, but a few moments later, I can feel him near me.

I peek open my eyes to see his shoes next to me. "Good God, you have no honor, do you? Hiding while your daughter, your bride, is left here."

Cold metal rests on my temple, and I know this is it. I'm done. Dead.

"Talk about feeling like a big man, attacking a defenseless girl," the priest says. Not my father. Not my would-be husband or father-in-law.

"You're right. You know what? On second thought, maybe I'll let you live just a little longer. I think instead, I'll take this pretty little virginal bride of yours and make her my plaything for a little while. And then I'll do to her what you did to my brother and my mother, right before I kill you both. Donovan?"

"Boss."

There are other men.

"Deal with them while I take my spoils." A moment later, I'm hauled up and tossed over the man's shoulder as he strides out of the room.

6

NIKO

I'm fucking brilliant. Tiberius thinks he's insulting me by calling me *Giovane Re*, Boy King. But it's a compliment. I'm already feared and revered as the youngest Don, and that reputation is going to grow when it comes out that the Leone Family took down both the Fiori and the Abate Families in one fell swoop.

The plan worked perfectly. My men had been uncertain, fearing my need for revenge blinded me to the dangers of this mission. But when I'd read that Fiori was marrying off his daughter to Romeo Abate, I knew this was the moment I'd been waiting for. The two men responsible for my mother and brother's deaths, and possibly my father's with the help of my cousin years before, were going to be at the same place at the same time. Perfect.

When we'd arrived at the church, a distraction was all we needed to divert Fiori and Abate's men outside. I was shocked at how few men there are inside the main part of the church. It proves I'm smarter than Fiori and Abate.

I strode up the aisle, ready to take both men out and anyone else who tried to get in my way. I relished the way the men scattered, along with Tiberius's asshole son, Romeo, hiding on the altar. But neither God nor Jesus nor Mother Mary could save them.

The wedding had been small, and all of the wedding party had scattered to other areas of the room. They cowered too, knowing they were all still at the mercy of me and my men. Power like this is beyond any feeling I've ever felt. It fills the empty part of me, if only for a moment.

I hadn't noticed the woman in a protective ball on the ground at the base of the altar until I was nearly on top of her. Romeo Abate's bride. Fiori's daughter. Revenge coursed through my blood, and I reveled in the thought that they would watch me kill the innocent woman. Just like they'd killed my mother and my older brother.

The priest hinted that killing her would make me the same sort of man who had killed my family. That didn't bother me. My thirst for vengeance was greater than any concern for what somebody thought about me.

What had me changing my mind was the added humiliation I would bring on Fiori and Abate before they met their end. They would walk out of this church today, and everyone would know that Niko Leone had bested both of their Families and walked off with their prize.

Now, I have said prize tossed over my shoulder as I stride toward the exit of the church.

"What are your orders, Boss?" Donovan took my position holding the two Dons hostage on the altar.

"The women and children won't be touched. Fiori and Abate walk out of here looking like the losers they are. But if anyone tries to come after me or any of you, take them out. Meet me at the regular spot."

I'm on top of the fucking world. Tiberius Abate is an idiot if he continues to try and infringe on my business. Not that I don't think he won't try to retaliate. Of course, he will. I've just humiliated him. But he's no match for me.

It's been awhile since I have felt this strong, this invincible. The woman over my shoulder must feel it too because she's quiet, making no attempt to escape. She's not even begging me to let her go. Then again, perhaps she's happy not to be marrying that fucker, Romeo Abate.

To be honest, I don't know what I'm going to do with her. The biggest revenge would be to take her, ruin her. But my interest in sex disappeared as quickly as it rose two months ago at the club. Even now, I'm confused about what it was about that woman that had me spending a fortune for a single fuck. Not that it hadn't been worth it, because it had been spectacular. For a few days afterward, I woke in the middle of the night with a hard-on so fierce, I had to take matters into my own hand, conjuring up the memory of the woman in my mind as I jerked off until my cum splattered over my chest.

Afterward, the feelings I'd had that night also turned up. Feelings of protection and damn near compassion for the woman. That isn't me. I don't care about people except for my men and my sister. Nothing in my life gets the better of me. I'm the very definition of control in all areas. My anger. My passions. I'm not a man led around by his dick. And now, two months later, after being blindsided by my virgin beauty, I'm back in total and absolute control. I've just taken on and beaten the Fiori and the Abate Families. Life is fucking awesome.

In the vestibule, I make a right-hand turn, heading toward a side exit where my car is waiting. I know Catholic churches because until my mother died, we'd gone to services regularly. She was the epitome of devoutness. I remember the day I understood the line of work my father was in, a *capo* for his Don uncle's family, and wondered how she reconciled that.

"There's more war than love in the Bible. But the love is stronger," she'd said. My parents were different among the other made members of the family. My mother was traditional in her love and support, but she had a genuine caring that other mothers around me didn't have. She spent a great deal of time supporting children and animal charities. I'm a heartless man, but to this day, I send her favorite charities money.

My father was strong, second in command of the family should something happen to my uncle. But his love for his wife and children made those around him feel he was weak. His murder was never solved, but I was certain my cousin was involved. He wanted to take over from his father, my uncle. He was also known to be indebted to establishments owned by the Fiori and Abate Families, which in my mind made him vulnerable. My uncle wasn't gone a week before I killed my cousin and took over the Family. It was another week of challenges from my uncle and cousin's men. Those who survived now served me.

I step outside, first glancing to make sure everything is as it should be. My driver is waiting and straightens when he sees me coming out of the building.

"Pop the trunk," I order him.

The trunk opens, and I trot down the steps to the back of the car. "You've been well-behaved up to this point. You continue to do that. Everything's going to be alright," I tell the woman over my shoulder. "Right now, you're about to take a ride in the trunk. Continue to behave."

"Not the trunk, please. I'm not going to try anything."

Something about her voice makes the hairs on the back of my neck stand up. But I don't have time to figure out why. Nor do I have time to argue with this woman.

I lift the trunk lid and hoist her off my shoulder into the trunk. The billowy white dress covers her head, exposing her shapely legs. Again, my neck tingles. Her arms flail around, pulling the skirt of her dress down off her face. She starts to talk, but then her mouth snaps shut while her eyes round. It's only then that I realize I've just kidnapped that sweet little virgin from the club.

For a moment, I consider taking her out of the trunk, but I chastise myself. Stick to the plan. I've broken that rule already by letting Fiori and Abate live and taking the woman. I'm arrogant, but I can't get cocky. Not now.

I slam the trunk lid shut and get into the back of the car. Once we're out on the main street, I look like any rich businessman being driven by his chauffeur.

"Was there trouble?" the driver, Little Tony, asks.

"No. Went like clockwork. Those fuckers probably pissed themselves."

Little Tony laughs. "They deserve it." He glances at me through the rearview mirror. "I don't remember the woman."

"Slight change of plans. You're still taking me to the switch off." This time, instead of moving the bodies of Fiori and Abate, we're moving my virgin. What is her name? Alice? No. That was fake. The priest called her Elena. It fit. Classic. Beautiful. Innocent. Yet with fire.

Fucking hell, why am I thinking that?

When we get to the new location, we wait until Donovan shows up in the dark SUV.

I exit the car and meet him. "Everything okay?"

"There's a lot of threats, but they knew they were outgunned. It's war now, *mio amico*."

"Just as we knew it would be."

"What about the woman?"

"I want you to take her home." I give him instructions on what to do once she gets there.

He arches a brow, but he knows enough not to ask. At least not now. We're far from out of trouble.

"Where are you going?"

I nod across the street from the alley. "I'm getting a pizza. As planned. No one will possibly think I was involved when I've been here all afternoon having pizza." Plus, I know that Donovan likely dropped off one of Fiori or Abate's men we'd taken from the wedding. I plan to get as much info from him about Fiori and Abate's plans against me.

Donovan nods. "Bring me a slice?"

"I'll bring home a few pies." I pat him on the back, knowing he'll take care of my virgin Elena... or no, she's not a virgin. Not since I filled her sweet, innocent pussy.

A shiver runs down my spine. It's not fear. It's not worry. It's lust.

7

ELENA

The trunk slams shut, encasing me in darkness. My heart pounds as the engine roars to life and the car begins to move. I'm torn between relief and terror. Relief that I'm not married to Romeo, but fear about what my new captor intends to do with me. Not just a captor, but the man who bought my virginity. Is that why I'm here?

No. His expression was surprised before he shut the trunk. The realization hits that I'd been wrong to assume he was the boss of the club, or more accurately, *only* the boss of the club. He is the head of a Family. The club is likely a front, a way to launder whatever bad deeds he's into.

I've gone from one prison to another. But is my new one worse, better, or the same as before? Not knowing is terrifying.

Think, Elena, think. If I'm to be free, my only window for escape is now while I'm on a public street. Once I'm taken into my captor's lair, I'll be guarded or killed, so now is my only chance to get away.

If I can get the trunk open, I can hop out and run. The streets are busy with people and cars. Surely, I can manage to elude him long enough to disappear. Perhaps someone will help me. As long as they don't know my family or him, maybe they'll be receptive to assisting my escape. Or perhaps I can go to a homeless shelter. I have no money. All I have is my passport hidden in the bodice of my wedding dress.

I feel around inside the trunk, looking for a latch. I decide that I'll release it when the car stops at a stoplight. I have to hope that my dress doesn't catch or slow me down. Maybe I should take it off. I have a slip on.

But as my fingers slide along the back and edges of the trunk, groping for a release mechanism, I don't find any. No latch. No buttons. Likely, it's been tampered with. I'd bet I'm not the first person to be in this space. I shiver at the idea of all the bodies that were here before me. Many, if not most, were likely dead.

The car stops at what I think is a traffic light. Panic rises in my chest. I have to get out of here. Now. I pound on the trunk lid and call for help. Moments later, the car accelerates. I blow out a breath. I'm trapped.

The vehicle halts. Doors open, and I can sense the weight of bodies shifting. Men's muffled voices filter through. I want out, but the terror of what awaits me when the trunk opens makes me want to stay hidden.

All is quiet for a moment and then the trunk pops open. Blinding light floods in, and I shield my eyes.

"Time to go, Princess."

The voice is different. My pulse races as for unknown reasons, I feel more in danger than I did with my captor.

He pulls me from the trunk like I weigh nothing.

"Where are we going?" I scan the area. It's still New York, but I can't find a landmark. We're in another alley with no one around.

He leads me to an SUV. "Boss says you behave. Keep it up. Hands out."

I do as he asks. "Who is your boss?"

He doesn't answer. He simply zip-ties my wrists and then my ankles. He lifts me into the backseat of the SUV and buckles me in. For some reason, I see that as a good sign. Why bother putting on my seatbelt if he's going to kill me?

He gets into the front seat and we move again.

"Who are you? Where are you taking me?"

The man doesn't glance at me. Doesn't speak.

"What do you want from me?" My voice trembles despite my resolve to appear strong.

Still, no comment from the driver.

"Please, say something. Who was the last man? What Family are you with?"

His shoulders roll, the only sign that he's not an automaton.

"What does your boss want with me?" *The Boss.* The man I'd let touch me, whom I gave the most intimate part of me to. I should feel repulsed, but mostly, I feel lost. I'm nobody. Nothing. Not to anyone except maybe Kate and Lucia, but they have no power to help me.

"Are you going to kill me?"

The partition between us begins to rise, cutting off my view of him, and I suppose, his ability to hear me.

Again, I think this is the only moment I can get free. My fingers brush against the door handle as I glance to the front seat. My driver's eyes are on the road. I pull, but the door stays latched. Of course, it does. Deep down, I knew this attempt to escape was futile. Sighing, I slump against the seat and stare out the tinted window at the passing streets.

The SUV slows, then turns down an alley and descends into an underground parking garage. The man, still silent, pulls me from the car.

"Don't try anything." He pulls out a knife, and my heart stops in my chest. Why has he brought me here just to kill me? He could have done it back in the alley and tossed me in the trash.

He leans over and cuts the zip-tie around my ankles. He rises up, gripping my arm hard. "Let's go." He drags me toward an elevator as his phone rings. "*Pronto.*"

I can't hear who is on the other side. Finally, he says, "Yep. Got it." He hangs up and smirks at me as he presses the button for the penthouse.

"Who is your boss?" I ask again.

He shakes his head like he's annoyed with me but doesn't respond.

The elevator doors slide open, revealing a world of opulence that takes my breath away. I grew up in wealth, but my family home is filled with traditional décor. This one is modern, brighter than I'd have thought for such a dark man.

I'm led through a stunningly grand foyer and to an open room surrounded by windows. It's like floating among the clouds.

The man guides me to a lavish bedroom, giving me a nudge to enter. "Behave." The door shuts behind me. ——

"Wait... my hands..." But when I open the door, he's gone, replaced by another man who steps forward into my space, his eyes menacing.

I swallow hard and hold my hands up. "Can you cut me free?"

"No." He pushes me back into the room and shuts the door.

I blow out a breath and sit on the edge of the bed. At least the accommodations are nice. I'll be in luxury in my last moments.

A few moments later, the door opens again. I stand up, ready to confront whoever is coming for me. A woman walks in dressed like she works for the family. A maid or a servant. She has more power than me, but not enough to help me.

She's no-nonsense as she carries in some clothes and cuts my hands free. "You can get cleaned up. The shower is over there." She nods toward a door. "Here are some clothes. They should fit close enough."

I take the clothes. "Please. Can you tell me who your boss is? Why am I here?"

She isn't swayed by my plea. It would be dangerous for her to be. "You will learn all you need to know when the Boss wants you to know." She moves to the door but looks over her shoulder at me. "My advice is to do what you're told."

Tears prick at my eyes as the door closes behind her. I feel like I'm in a type of purgatory. Not living, but not dead yet, either.

With that said, I'm happy to be able to wash away the wedding and the ride in the trunk. I undress, the passport I'd hidden falling out. A new wave of panic slides through me as I worry someone will walk in and find it. I shove it under the mattress and pray it's not found.

Then I go into the bathroom to clean up. I step into the steaming shower, letting the water cascade over my body. I have light bruising, mostly from the ride in the trunk.

I let the hot water cascade over me, letting my mind go for a moment. I'm afraid, and yet, I'm also aware that I'm being treated differently. Why? Is it because of our night together at the club?

I shake my head. A man like this doesn't care about a woman. It was odd that he recognized me at all, considering how little care men like him have for others. But I know it doesn't mean anything. My value is in getting back at my father and Don Abate.

As my hands wash over my breasts, it occurs to me that my captor may plan to touch me again. What better way to humiliate my father and Romeo and Don Abate than to defile their daughter and fiancée? But he's already done that. Will he do it again?

The memory of how his fingers pinched my nipples or rubbed that secret spot between my legs sends warm sensations through me.

I curse myself for that. The man kidnapped me. He'll likely kill me. Why am I thinking about the pleasure he'd given me?

8

NIKO

The door to my penthouse clicks shut behind me. The scents of garlic and tomatoes waft from the box of pizza I discard atop the marble countertop in the kitchen. The pizza is delicious, but the revenge is sweeter. Blood still pumps hard through my veins, the aftermath of my victory today.

I stride toward my office and head straight to the bar, pouring myself a scotch.

Donovan appears in the doorway, his presence unannounced yet expected. "The woman is in your room as requested. Maria brought her clothes."

"Did she give you any trouble?" I pour a drink for him, handing it to him.

He smirks. "She asks a lot of questions, but no. She wasn't any trouble."

My memory flashes on the night in the club. She'd asked questions then too, but she never resisted. Then today in the church, she was frightened, protecting herself, but she didn't scream or beg when I snatched her.

Unsettled by the uninvited memory, I take a long pull of my drink. I should be thinking about her value to me in this war. She's a prize to exploit, a way to humiliate her family further. But something about her distracts me, which isn't good. I need total control and focus to run the Family and take revenge on my enemies, something she could threaten with the way she can divert my attention.

And there is the matter of why her father was really marrying her off to Romeo Abate. I look at my knuckles, still red and raw from the beating I gave Fiori's man we held captive in the basement of the pizza restaurant to get the information.

"Get someone to guard the room. No one goes in or out."

"Already done. You planning to keep her long?" Donovan sips his drink as he sits on the couch. He's my right-hand man, but also my confidant, my friend. I don't have total trust in anyone, but if I did, it would be in him.

"As long as it takes." I down the rest of my drink. "She's not going anywhere."

The door to my office opens, and Liam Rostova saunters in, a smirk on his face. "Stealing brides now, Niko?" Liam is another friend, nearly a brother. We grew up together. It's a friendship that should have never happened since his father was a Russian mob leader until he was killed when we were kids. Liam's life took a right turn when he decided to go into the FBI. My men think I'm nuts to keep Liam close, but what they don't know is that while Liam is technically a good guy, he was instrumental in helping me take out my cousin. I got information to kill him, and Liam got evidence to put my cousin's supporters in prison. Liam has my back, that I know. But I also know he has limitations in what he can do and concerns about my business.

"Word travels fast. Or did they come crying to you?" It would be a cold day in hell before Fiori or Abate would go to the FBI. Then again, it was a cold hell in the church today for them.

"Please. Like they'd admit to being humiliated. But shooting up a church during a wedding? Taking the bride? Only one sort of man has the balls for that kind of statement. Only you have a hard-on for Fiori and Abate."

More like for his daughter, but I held that bit of information back. "Flattery will get you nowhere."

He pours himself a drink. "You're playing with fire here."

"Fire cleanses, purifies." I grin at him, knowing it irks him when I don't heed his warning.

"Or it burns everything to the ground, including you. You know this isn't a game."

"Isn't it?"

"Revenge is one thing, but this... I understand how you think, but Jesus, she's someone's daughter, not just a pawn."

My humor fades. "Everyone's a pawn in this world, Liam. If you don't think she was a pawn in that wedding, then you're naïve."

"I think she was relieved," Donovan quips from the couch.

"What?" Liam turns to him. "You should be helping me here. You know this is foolish."

"I'm just saying, she didn't try to fight him. Didn't cry or beg. She asked a bunch of questions, but... I don't know, I think she's glad not to be Mrs. Romeo Abate."

I nodded. "No one wants to be Mrs. Romeo Abate."

"Christ, Niko. What's the endgame here?" Liam is like a dog with a bone sometimes.

I shrug. "Justice has many faces."

"Justice or vendetta?"

"Sometimes, there's no difference."

"God help us all, then."

"Let's leave God out of this. He turned a blind eye a long time ago. He definitely wasn't in that church or I'd have been smote down." I frown. "Smited? What's the word?"

"Fuck the word. I can't help you. Not when you go this far." Liam downs his drink and pours another.

I glare at him. "Then why are you here?"

"Someone's got to keep you from crossing lines even you can't come back from."

"Lines? There are no lines. You know that."

He lets out an exasperated sigh as he shakes head. "Is she here... the bride?"

"Yes. She's safe and well-taken care of." I don't care about the opinion of many people. For a long time, it was just my mother. I don't consider Liam's opinion, but I can't deny that sometimes, it matters. I try not to look too closely at what that means. I've taken on the persona of *Il Soldato Della Morte*. I like it. Except at times when Liam looks at me like I'm a monster.

"Well-taken care of? God, is that innuendo for you've taken advantage of her?"

"I didn't have to take advantage of her."

His eyes narrow. "What the fuck does that mean?"

"He hasn't been back long enough to do anything," Donovan adds.

"Please don't tell me you're going to, though. God... I've accepted that you're a lot of things, Niko, but that poor woman—"

"She's Fiori's daughter." My jaw tightens, but my issue is inside myself because that protective, compassionate feeling for the woman is trying to take root again.

"And you know she has no power."

"She has value."

"And so you're going to fuck her and ruin her life? God, why didn't you just kill them when you had the chance? Surely, that was your plan."

Liam is right. I should have. I didn't. Because of her.

Liam's expression softens, turns more understanding. "Look, I know what they did to your family—"

"Then you know why I'm doing what I'm doing. My mother was innocent. They didn't flinch to kill her. Fiori and Abate are lucky I didn't kill Fiori's daughter on the altar today."

"This is a mistake," Liam says bluntly. "Taking her like this will only escalate the war with the other Families. She's a person, Niko."

"Stay out of it," I snap. "She's mine. I paid for her, fair and square."

"What?" Liam looks at Donovan, who shrugs.

"Her father and Tiberius won't let this go."

"I know." The blood is pumping again as I imagine how they're planning to come after me.

"You're risking everything for some misguided vendetta and a quick fuck—"

"Watch yourself." My voice is lethal. The way he sucks in a breath tells me he knows it.

"Alright. I've said my piece." Liam turns to Donovan. "You know he's going to get you killed. All of you."

"It's what I've signed up for." Donovan, always the jokester.

I give Liam a look that tells him my men know my mission and are all on board. I wish he would be too. It's not like Liam doesn't have a beef with the Fiori and Abate Families.

"I'm heading out." He sets his glass on my bar. "You should think about redoing your will. Your ass is writing checks it can't cash." He strides out.

"He's not necessarily wrong," Donovan says.

"No. But I'm ready to die as long as I bring those motherfuckers to hell with me."

Donovan holds up his glass. "To motherfuckers going to hell."

I lift my glass and drink, then set it down. "Pizza is in the kitchen. I'm heading up to check on my prize."

I make my way upstairs, surprised when I realize I took two steps at a time. Like I was eager. Excited.

"Everything okay?" I ask my man at the door.

"Quiet."

"You can take off. I've got it from here."

He nods and heads toward the stairs.

My hand pauses on the doorknob as I wonder what I'll find. Most women in my life have been easy to figure out. My mother, loving, compassionate, loyal. My sister, sweet, a romantic, innocent. All others want sex and money. Other Families have tried to use their daughters to garner my favor, to which I've refused. Women don't have personal power in my world, but they can be used to ruin the men who control me.

But what is this woman's story? If she didn't want to marry

Romeo, why didn't she take my money and run? Why did she even sell her virginity knowing it could cost her life if her father or the Abates found out?

I push the door open but find emptiness. I'm annoyed. Where is she? Why isn't she waiting?

Then I hear it—the spray of the shower. Images of her naked under a warm spray fill my mind. My dick twitches. This is not welcome. I don't like this feeling, this pull, the way my body responds to the mere thought of her.

I enter the bathroom, the glass shower filled with steam so I can't see anything but a silhouette of a lovely female form.

I lean against the vanity, arms crossed over my chest, like that will somehow protect me from the way she draws me in.

The shower stops. Moments tick by until finally, the shower door opens. She emerges, and I'm enraptured again by the soft, graceful curves and lines of her body. She's like a fucking sculpture.

At the sight of me, her eyes widen. She grabs the towel, clutching it to her body.

"Didn't realize you were shy," I say. "You weren't at the club."

A beat passes as she watches me. I can see she's assessing the situation. Determining whether she's safe. She draws the towel tighter around her.

I arch a brow, and my lips twitch upward in amusement. "You don't have anything I haven't already seen."

"What are you going to do with me?"

God, what a loaded question. "What is your name? I assume it isn't Alice." The priest had said Elena, I think, but I want to know for sure. I'm filled with questions now. Why did she sell her virginity? Why didn't she resist when I took her from the church? Why hasn't she tried to escape?

"Elena."

Just like the priest said.

"What's your name?"

"Niko Leone."

Recognition flickers in her eyes, as well as fear. "*Il Soldato Della Morte.*"

It's awesome and annoying at how pleased I am that she knows who I am. "That's right. Are you afraid?"

She purses her lips in an expression that says I should know that she is.

"I'm guessing your dear father and Romeo don't know about our little encounter. I can't imagine you'd still be getting married if they did."

She gives a single head shake. "They don't know."

"Has anyone else touched you?"

She swallows but again shakes her head.

A surge of desire envelops me. It's unwelcome even as it's insistent. Powerful. Too powerful for me to resist. Without thinking, my finger catches the edge of the towel, tugging it free.

She lets off a soft mewl of fear.

"You've lost weight, *cara mia*. No doubt from the stress of marrying into the Abate Family. They're very bad people."

She nods.

It's then that I notice the engagement ring on her left hand. "You're not Romeo's woman. Take his ring off." I take her hand, sliding the ring off and slipping it into my pocket. "You're mine, *cara mia*. Bought and paid for."

Her breath hitches, but she doesn't shy away. Doesn't attempt to flee. She's nervous, for sure, but I suspect it's more out of concern that I'll kill her than that I'll touch her.

"Do you understand?" I ask.

She nods again.

"Good." My gaze takes in her smooth skin. Untouched except by me. "Let's not pretend this is anything but what it is. You're a pawn in a much larger game. You didn't ask to be a part of it. That's your father's fault. But make no mistake." I lean closer, inhaling my soap on her body. "I play to win."

This close, I can see her eyes, and I remember how they'd made me take notice when I met her. The color of whisky. Her pink lips part slightly, and an urge to kiss her blooms. I pull back slightly, fighting the lure of her mouth.

My gaze drops to her tits, full and round with pink nipples, hard. Is that from the cool air or me?

I rub my thumb over one. "Remember how it felt when I touched you, Elena?"

She nods, and I wonder why she's not talking. Not even questions.

"You liked it, didn't you?" I slid my hand over her belly and down to the dark curls guarding her pussy. "You came when I touched you. It was the first time, right?"

She nods again.

"Tell me the words," I demand, and inwardly, I chastise myself. I don't need confirmation from her. I'm Niko-Fucking-Leone.

"I liked it." Her voice is soft, but clear.

"I'm going to make you come again." My hands are firm, possessive as I turn her toward the mirror. "You're going to watch. Watch yourself come."

Standing behind her, I reach around, one hand pinching and rubbing her nipple.

"Oh." She gasps, and her eyes close.

"Open your eyes, *cara mia*." I want to see them fill with desire, passion as I touch her.

She opens her eyes.

"Don't close them again." My voice is harsh, demanding. I slide my other hand over her belly. I remember how I'd fucked her bare at the club, and I yearn to do it again, except the last thing I need is to get her pregnant. Then again, doing so would be the ultimate humiliation for Fiori and the Abates.

I find her clit. It's hard too, and her pussy is wet. My little innocent captive is turned on. "Did you think of me over the last few months?"

"Yes," she gasps as I flick my finger over her clit.

"Did you touch yourself when you did?"

She shakes her head.

"Why not?" I'm a little disappointed. After all, I'd had to jerk off several times to her.

She shrugs.

"Someday, I'll teach you." I slip a finger inside her.

She moans, and her head drops back against my chest. She's trying to keep her eyes open, but I can tell it's hard for her.

"Go ahead and close your eyes. Just feel. Let the pleasure take you."

Her lids drop, and her head arches back, exposing her neck. I feel like a fucking vampire the way I want to suck on it.

"Oh!" She calls out, her body tensing and then shuddering.

"That's right. Feels good, doesn't it? And only I make you feel that, don't I?"

She's breathing hard through the orgasm.

"Don't I?" I demand again.

She nods.

I turn her around and make her look at me. "Say the words!"

She flinches. "Only you make me feel that."

"Good. Now get on your knees."

She does as I ask. I undo my pants, pushing them and my underwear down. My aching dick springs free.

I rub my tip along her lips. "This time, you'll drink it."

She looks up at me, and I see uncertainty, and maybe fear. Or perhaps it's resignation.

"Open your mouth."

Her lips part, and I sink my cock into her hot, innocent mouth. For a moment, I regret not kissing her. It doesn't feel right that my dick gets the taste of her first. But I push it away. This isn't some love story. This is sex and power and pleasure.

"That's right. It's like a popsicle. Suck and lick it."

I gently rock as her tongue slides along my cock. Her lips suck, and for a moment, I simply watch and savor the pleasure building, expanding. I let the sensations wash over me.

"Like that... yes." There's a rhythm to it. It's natural, primal, or maybe she's just made for sex. I watch her, the way she gives herself to this act, and something twists inside me, a knot of something dark and possessive that should feel right but instead feels a little out of control.

She makes a soft mewling sound and pulls back.

I thread my fingers through her hair and guide her to me. "Keep going." I think about how I'm the only man she's wrapped those pretty lips around. *Mine*. It filters into my brain again, and pleasure spears hard through my body.

"Fuck! Yes!" My hips buck as my release overtakes me. Her hands grip my thighs as I hold her to me and pump my cum into her mouth.

When I release her, she sits back on her heels, my cum dripping from the side of her mouth, which she uses her hand to wipe away. Her eyes stare up at me. She looks a bit stunned. That feeling in my chest twists again, this time feeling a little bit like guilt followed by compassion for the situation she's in.

I step back wondering if I have it all wrong. Maybe this innocent thing with her is an act. Perhaps she's manipulating me. Have I fallen into a trap? A trap set by her father? And does it matter? She's here now. In my home. Under my protection. *Mine*.

"Stand up," I demand.

She rises, staring at me with those amber eyes of hers. I catch her chin, lifting her gaze to meet mine, ensuring she sees the truth of my words. "Never forget who you belong to."

9

ELENA

Not long after I'd met Kate, she made a comment about feeling like she was in *The Twilight Zone*. I had no clue what that meant. She explained to me that it came from an old TV show and meant feeling like being in an alternate world. That is how I feel right now. I've been kidnapped by a rival family, the leader of which is referred to as the Soldier of Death. I'm a prize he will likely use against my father and the Abate Family. A prize who will likely be killed before all is said and done.

For all intents and purposes, I should be terrified. I should be repulsed by the man who is going to kill me or have me killed. So why did my body get warm and tingly when his gaze took in my naked body? Why did his words and his touch make me ache inside?

I can tell myself that I gave in to him because what choice did I have, anyway? Men like him take what they want, whether it's offered or stolen. But it would be a lie to say that I opened to his touch simply because I was his hostage. What is wrong with me that I so freely, willingly, gave in to his touch? I let myself enjoy the sweet torment and the delicious aftermath. And when I was on my knees, his manhood in my mouth, I felt a surge of power I'd never felt before. I realized that my actions controlled how he felt at that moment. His pleasure was coming from me. It was stupid to think of it like that, but I did. The salty essence filled my mouth, and I had the thrill of being the one who made it happen.

But the feeling subsides quickly because I can't be sure about Niko's demeanor. I wouldn't say he was necessarily gentle or kind, but he isn't rough or cruel as I would expect. Is he trying to pacify me? Does he want me to put my guard down so I don't do anything to cause trouble?

I realize I must guard myself from thoughts or feelings that would suggest I was anything more than a pawn in his war with my father and the Abate Family. If I'm going to get out of this alive, I need to play it smart. I need to be obedient and yet observant and figure out how I can get out of this mess.

I don't respond to his demand that I don't forget to whom I belong. I'm sure he won't let me forget, anyway.

He studies me for a moment and then says, "Get yourself cleaned up. I'll arrange for food."

I shake my head. "I'm not hungry."

His eyes narrow, darken slightly. "You are under the misguided impression that you have a choice. You are my prize, *cara mia*. You will not waste away under my control."

I give a short nod, indicating that I will obey. I step back into the shower and wash myself again. When I get out, I see a robe hanging on the back of the door. I decide I want more coverage than a robe offers, so I put on the clothes the woman had brought me.

I exit the bathroom and find him sitting at a table near the window doing something on his phone. A few moments later, there's a soft knock on the door.

"Come in." He doesn't look up from his phone until the door opens.

The servant who'd brought me the clothes enters carrying a tray.

The scent of pizza enters along with her. It smells delicious while at the same time, my stomach rolls over, reminding me that I'm pregnant with this man... my killer's... child. I purse my lips shut, hoping to keep whatever is in my empty stomach from trying to come up.

"Set the tray here, Maria." Niko motions for her to put the tray on the table. He sets his phone down next to it and then rises from his chair. "This is Maria. She will be taking care of you while you are here. Whatever you need, she's authorized to help you." He arches a brow at me. "Within reason, of course. For now, you are confined to this room. Do you understand?"

I was beginning to recognize that while Niko's tone could be smooth, even calm, underneath it, there is a hint of darkness. His words are the law. I have no input, no say in the matter, so I simply nod again.

Niko studies me for a moment. "You have grown awfully quiet. You have no questions?" This time, there's a hint of amusement in his tone. I'm reminded that I am the mouse and he is the cat who will enjoy toying with me.

"Just one."

"And it is?"

"Are you going to kill me?"

At that he does smile, and I hate that he finds pleasure in my fear. It's a reminder of why I should hate him, why I should be repulsed by him.

"Not right now." He pulls out a chair from the table. "Sit. Eat."

I do as he asks, taking a bite of pizza and hoping it stays down at least as long as he sticks around. I pick up my napkin to wipe my hands and mouth, and I note that his phone is lying next to the tray. I nonchalantly set my napkin over it, at the same time telling myself I'm an idiot if I think I can fool him.

I take another bite of pizza and then look up at him to find him watching me. Did he notice what I did?

"That will be all, Maria," he tells the woman who quickly leaves the room.

"I have business to attend to. Enjoy your meal. I will likely be late, but when you are tired, you will sleep in this bed."

"Will I have a nightgown or pajamas?" I ask.

He smirks. "You won't need those."

I hate the thrill that rushes through my body at the sensual promise of his words. Why is my body betraying me?

He exits the room. For long moments, I sit and wait. I pick up the napkin and move it to the tray so if he re-enters the room, he doesn't believe I was trying to hide his phone under it. But as the moments tick by, he doesn't return.

My hand shakes as I reach for the phone, but I'm too terrified to pick it up. I stand and go to the door, opening it to see if he's outside waiting to catch me in an illicit act.

A man looks up from his own phone from across the hall. "Do you need something?"

"I wanted to ask Don Leone something. But it will wait." I pray to God that my guard doesn't contact Niko to tell him I need something.

"He's busy. Get back in the room."

I shut the door and sag against it. My legs are shaking, but I inhale a deep breath and rush to the table, picking up the phone and then hurrying to the bathroom. My first stop is the toilet where I empty out the couple of bites of pizza. This time, I sure it's the fear that has me getting sick and not the pregnancy.

I rinse my mouth out and then, with phone in hand, move to the farthest corner of the bathroom and hope there are no listening devices. For moments, I sit and wonder whom I should call. My father is out of the question. Chances are he's planning to get me back anyway to hand me over to Romeo. Niko isn't my savior, but I feel certain that in Romeo's control, there would be no pleasurable touches. If the wedding had gone through, I'd probably be bruised and feel violated by Romeo.

I consider calling Kate since her father is a cop, but involving her would put her in danger. I realize there is no one I can call to rescue me. But there's one person I can reach out to who can give me advice.

I dial my sister's number. It rings for a long time, and I realize it's probably the middle of the night in Italy. I'm about to hang up when the call is answered.

"Who is this?" My sister's voice is a mixture of angry and frantic.

"It's me, Luce."

"Oh, my God, Elena. Are you okay? Where are you?"

"I'm sorry... I was caught and locked in my room—"

"Oh, no. So... you're with Romeo?"

"No. During the wedding, *Il Soldato Della Morte* ambushed and... he has me now."

"Are you okay?"

"I'm not hurt."

She let out a breath. "We had gotten word that Leone made a move on our family and the Abates and the bride had been taken. I've been worried sick. How are you able to call me?"

"Niko left the room without his phone."

"Oh, God. If he finds out..."

She doesn't need to finish the sentence. I know that what I'm doing is speeding up my demise.

"Has he hurt you?" she asks.

"No. I mean, he made me ride in the trunk and tied me up, but he has me confined to a room in his house. I'm not tied up and locked away somewhere. So there's that."

There's a long pause. "Did he touch you?"

I vacillate on what I should say. It's not that I want to lie, but I also don't want to give the impression that I've been forcibly taken. Then again, had I shown any resistance, he might've done just that.

But two months ago, I had handed myself over willingly in exchange for $100,000. If taking me from my father and Romeo didn't give Niko a sense of entitlement to my body, the hundred thousand dollars certainly did.

"Oh, my God, Elena. I'm so sorry."

"It's okay. He wasn't rough. He didn't hurt me." I decide not to share that I liked it. "But just because he's not being openly cruel doesn't mean I'm safe. I just don't know what to do. I can't imagine that Dad isn't finding a way to get me back, but only for his pride. And if he does, he'll turn me over Romeo. I don't want that, either."

"No, you wouldn't. Right now, you just need to do what you can to not make him angry. Toe the line, but pay attention. I'll see if there's something I can do on my end."

I appreciate that she wants to help me, but I also know that I can't have a lot of hope and faith that she'll be able to. I don't completely know about her marriage to Don Giuseppe, but I know she has no power. My father essentially sold her to him. And even if she had some sway, I couldn't imagine he would care about me all the way in New York.

I finish the call and put the phone back on the table next to the tray. Was it upright or face down? I can't remember, and not knowing sends my nerves into a tizzy again. I don't want to leave any hint that I touched it, much less used it.

I leave it and then go over to the window to look out at the view. I'm in a city filled with millions of people. Below on the streets and sidewalks are people driving and walking by. In the apartments around me and across from me are more people. But I am all alone. There's no one here to help me.

Over time, my fear and despair turn into boredom, and just when I'm about to go ask the guard to get Maria to see if there are books or something for me to do, the door pops open and she walks in. She goes over to pick up the tray and sees the phone. She looks up at me with suspicion.

I shrugged. "He left it there."

She looks at it again, and I get the feeling she's trying to decide whether she should take it or leave it there. If he had left it there on purpose, she could get in trouble by taking it. But if it had been an accident, she could get in trouble for leaving it where I could use it.

Apparently, she decides to leave it as she takes the tray and heads to the door.

"Maria? Do you have any books or anything? Is there something I can do to fill the time?"

"I will bring you some books."

She leaves and fifteen minutes later returns with a basket filled with books. There is a mixture of classics and mysteries. I thank her and pluck a book from the basket and sit on the bed to read.

Hours later, feeling tired, I go to the bathroom to get ready for bed. I really don't want to get naked as I know he wants me to. But I also know it is unwise to defy him, taking his phone notwithstanding.

I compromise by undressing and putting on the robe hanging on the back of the bathroom door. I climb into bed and curl into a ball. Exhaustion and fear don't mix. I desperately want to sleep, but all I can think about are Niko's words when I asked him if he was going to kill me.

Not right now.

Not now, but when? I wonder how much time I have left.

10

NIKO

I leave Elena and stroll to my office. The scent of her lingers on me, around me. The image of my cock in her mouth and the look of triumph in her eyes have my dick twitching in my pants.

Taking a deep breath, I sit behind my desk, reminding myself that I have more important things to do than to fuck Elena Fiori. But fucking hell. What is it about her? My enemies, even those around me, think I'm ruthless, that I don't feel a damned thing. They're wrong. Elena makes me feel. Too much.

What I can't figure out is why she sold her virginity. The obvious reason would be to escape from under her father's thumb or the marriage to Romeo. But she didn't. Why? There's a part of me that wonders again if this is an elaborate plan on Fiori's part. But would he really sell her virginity, which in our world was her most important asset? And he had no way of knowing I'd show up at her wedding, a wedding that wouldn't occur if the Abates knew she wasn't a virgin. It doesn't make any sense.

I have to believe that her father and the Abates believed she was as pure as snow, even though she wasn't. That thought fills me with glee because they know that she's no longer pure now. They know that part of my revenge will be to take that from her. I wonder what they'd think knowing she's already sold her virginity to me. That comes with some satisfaction too. Maybe I'll tell them.

I'd considered taking a picture of her while her mouth was around my cock and sending it to Fiori and Romeo, but I can't stand the idea of anyone seeing her luscious naked body, which brings me back to the unsettled protective feelings I'm having about her. She's a pawn. She's my key to ruining her father and the Abates until the time comes to eliminate them from this earth.

I shake off thoughts of Elena and focus on the matter at hand—Fiori and Abate's humiliation and eventual deaths.

My phone buzzes. It's the one that only Donovan has the number to. The one that I'll dispose of and replace with another before the week is through. A precaution recommended by Liam to prevent prying eyes—or I suppose, ears—of law enforcement.

"What have you got?"

"Abate and Fiori are sniffing around, getting bolder," he says. "They've sent goons on little field trips past your places. "

"Stupid." I scoff. "They think they're hunters, but they're my prey."

"Mostly, they seem to be scouting. They've got at least two men watching the penthouse. Want us to take care of them?"

I briefly consider having Donovan and a few men take Fiori's men out and put their lifeless bodies on Fiori's doorstep. "Give them a message, but make sure they get back to Fiori to tell him and Abate that they can't sneak up on me."

"Got it."

"Actually, when you're done, meet me at the office," I say referring to the pizza restaurant that acts as our office.

"An hour?"

"See you then." I hang up and leave my home office. "I'm heading out," I say to my butler.

"Yes, sir. Do you need anything while you're gone?"

"Just make sure the woman doesn't do anything stupid. I need her alive."

"Yes, sir."

I remember her asking if I'm going to kill her. Not now, I'd told her. God, what a waste it would be to have to kill her. I hope I don't have to. Inwardly, I kick myself for such a thought. This woman has gotten under my skin, and I don't like it.

My driver takes me through the busy streets to the pizzeria. I walk in, and the regulars greet me. Others are tourists who are preoccupied with having New York Pizza. I make my way back and down to the office.

My men straighten as I walk in. "We didn't expect you," one says. Good. I like keeping them on their toes.

"Donovan will be here shortly." I inspect their work, trying to keep it relaxed and cool, while I make sure they're not trying to skim off me.

Thirty minutes later, Donovan enters with a large slice of pizza in one hand and a beer bottle in the other. "Nothing like pizza after kicking someone's ass."

"I take it Fiori and Abate's men made it home safe."

"Safe, although maybe not sound."

Good.

"So, what's the plan?" Donovan sits on the couch and takes a long swig of his beer.

"We're going to burn them all down. But first, we'll make them swim in humiliation."

"The woman?"

My gut clenches at Donovan's mentioning Elena. I don't like his tone, even though he's right to think she's the key to furthering Fiori and Abate's downfall.

I nod.

"Fiori and Abate, Romeo *and* Tiberius, will want her back, or at least retribution," Donovan reminds me. "I know you know that, but—"

"I do know that. They'll have more than a few goons out next time. That's why I want to fortify. I don't want a shadow to get past anyone into my places."

"Already on it, Niko."

I nod, knowing Donovan is always on pace with me, sometimes

even a step ahead. But I begin to second guess staying in the city. It's crowded and public, but that also makes it easy for my enemies to slip through. My compound out on Long Island is easier to protect and monitor for enemy advances.

"I want Elena out of the city by tomorrow morning. Take her to the compound."

Donovan arches a brow. "You're on a first-name basis with her?"

I scowl. "What do you expect me to call her? Mrs. Romeo Abate?" Like that would ever happen. It won't. Not while I'm alive.

Donovan shrugs and smirks. I don't like the smirk. It's like he can see through me, see that she's getting to me.

"I want more men on Fiori and Abate as well."

Donovan nods. "On that too."

I stand and roll my shoulders. "Good. I'm heading down to New Jersey tomorrow. Tour the clubs, act like all is normal while you head to the compound with El... the woman."

"Will do." Donovan holds up his beer like he's cheering me.

I leave the pizzeria and head back to the penthouse. I have my driver weave through the city, watching for any of Fiori and Abate's men. Finally, I return to the penthouse, my driver dropping me off in the garage.

I take the elevator up to the penthouse and make my way to the kitchen where I believe Maria and my cook staff will be.

"How is my guest?" I ask when she rises from her chair upon seeing me.

"She requested books, which I brought her. She didn't eat much."

I wonder if Elena is on a diet or if it's just stress that has her not eating and losing weight. "We're going to the compound tomorrow."

Maria nods her understanding.

"Keep an eye on her meals. Make sure she eats."

"Of course, Don Leone."

It's good to know that she's not causing any trouble, but I can't help but feel a twinge of concern. Elena is a wild card, one that I can't quite figure out. And I don't like not being able to predict someone's actions.

I go upstairs to my bedroom. With each step I take, I imagine Elena warm and naked in my bed. It makes my blood heat.

When I reach my room, the guard at her door straightens. "Everything quiet?"

"Like a tomb, Boss."

"I want her quiet, not dead."

"Yes, sir, I meant it was quiet. Maria brought her books."

"Good. You can go." I push the door open and step into dimmed light from the moon shining through the window. I look to the bed and see her shape beneath the covers, a silhouette of sexy curves and vulnerability that pulls at something primal in me.

I disrobe, noting the phone I left on the table. It appears to be exactly where I left it. Is it possible that she didn't use it? Did she pass my test? Or is she clever and simply put it back as I'd left it? I find that I don't want to know the truth. At least not tonight. Another sign that she may be my downfall.

I slide behind Elena, my body curving to hers—a puzzle piece finding its counterpart. Her breath hitches slightly as I pull her closer, spooning her with an arm that has felled men but now holds a woman with a careful, possessive touch. I realize she has a robe on.

"Didn't realize a robe was part of your wardrobe now," I murmur in her ear.

"Was cold." The warmth of the room belies her words.

"You know I can punish you for lying, don't you?" I say, my voice low and dangerous as I let my hand drift down to her thigh, feeling the heat of her skin through the thin fabric of her robe.

"I know." Her voice is flat, lifeless. It perturbs me. This isn't the woman who questioned me even as she succumbed to me in the club. Where's the fire? This is someone else—a shadow of Elena Fiori.

"Have you given up?"

"I have nothing to give up. Nothing is mine." She turns her head to look at me. "It doesn't seem to bother any of you, does it?"

"What?" I ask the question even though I don't want the answer. I don't like the feeling that she can see or sense something in me that makes me weak.

"Sure, you have power. You own me until you kill me or I'm returned to my father."

"That's right."

"No one around you is here because they want to be."

Her words are like needles in my heart. "They like my money."

"They work for you. But they'll work for the next guy if they live."

"What is your point?" I snap.

"Just as I said. You have no one here because they care for you... you as a person, not you as the Don."

Her words cut me. She's saying no one loves me. If I didn't have power and money, I'd be alone. But I know I'm alone. I've been alone since my mother and brother died. I had my sister, but I sent her to Europe.

"Are you saying you'd rather be with Romeo?"

She turns back to her side, her face no longer looking at me. "No. I'd rather be free."

"Then why aren't you? I paid you $100,00 dollars. That's plenty to leave."

She doesn't say anything.

"Since you didn't leave, I can only assume you agreed to marry Romeo." I wonder why. Does she know the truth of the agreement her father made with Tiberius Abate? Does she love her father and agreed to the marriage to protect him?

Elena's body tenses. "I didn't have a choice. No woman in our world has a choice."

"It's not so different for me."

She scoffs, and it makes my blood boil.

"What?" I demand.

She turns her head to look at me, and I see derision in her eyes. "You have choices, Niko. You could walk out of here. You can decide what to eat. What to wear. Whom to marry."

I know she's right. My comparison is stupid, and yet, I don't have a choice, not if my family is to be avenged. I had to kill my cousin for his part in my father's death. And I have to kill Elena's father and Don

Abate for my mother and brother's deaths. I have no choice. It is my duty.

"So, why not take the money and run when you could?"

"My father found it." She turns away again, and I hate it. It feels like being dismissed. No one dismisses me.

"If you had it now, would you run?"

"You'll kill me."

"What if I didn't?"

"If I could escape and live free, I would."

I know I'm in trouble because her words bother me... hurt me. She'd leave me. She was right. No one is here because they want to be with me, Niko the man. They want what Don Leone can give them.

My anger seethes. I want her to pay for pointing out that I'm not loved. That I'm alone. I brush Elena's hair away from her neck, my fingers gentle but with warning, caressing the soft curve of her throat.

"Romeo wouldn't have been as gentle as I am with you," I say, my voice low. "He wouldn't care whether you had an orgasm or not."

Elena turns to look at me, her eyes wide with fear, but also, the fire. My cock fills to aching levels.

"You're right. But you'll likely kill me, anyway. If you don't, Romeo will."

Her words hit me like a punch to the gut. I know she's right. I can't keep her forever. For a moment, I wonder if after I kill her father and the Abates, I could send her to be a companion with my sister. It wouldn't be freedom like she wants, but it would be greater freedom than she's had.

"I have no plans to kill you, Elena, unless you give cause."

She scoffs again. "You mean like trying to leave and live freely? Telling you no if I don't want to be touched? Your definition of cause is anything I do that displeases you."

She's not wrong. I want to prove it to her, not by killing her but by showing my power and strength. At the same time, I can't stop myself from feeling compassion for her situation. She's trapped in a world she never asked to be a part of, and she has zero way out.

"You are the one who sold yourself to me, remember?" My voice is low, but lethal. It's fucking with my head that she's comparing me to her father and the Abates, even though she's right.

"I know." She's defeated again, and it stirs up my anger.

"I need to collect on the money I paid for your virginity."

Her breath hitches, but I'm not sure if it's fear or anticipation.

"Are you going to tell me no?" I lap my tongue along the curve of her neck as my fingers brush over her nipples. Nipples that have hard peaks... aroused.

"Ah... *cara mia*, you like my touch." My hands roam over her body, feeling the curve of her hips, the swell of her breasts. I want to consume her, possess her, claim her. The need is like a beast inside me. My fingers find her pussy wet, her clit hard. "Tell me no and I will stop." I rub her clit, knowing the truth. Maybe she doesn't want this in her mind, but her body does. I know by the way her hips rock. By the way she moans.

"You want me to fuck you, don't you?" My voice is rough and raspy in her ear.

She moans in response.

"Tell me. Tell me you want me to fuck you." I insert my finger inside her, rubbing the one spot that makes women go wild.

"Niko." She gasps, and I decide that's good enough.

I grip her, turning her over underneath me, and push away the robe until her smooth skin is bared for me. "Don't ever defy me again."

I spread her legs and position my cock at her pussy. "Look at me."

She opens her eyes, staring up at me, her gaze filled with a mix of fear and desire. I thrust into her, hard and fast, burying myself to the hilt. She cries out, her nails digging into my back as her body arches.

Mine. The word is like a mantra running through my head as her tight pussy squeezes around my dick. Fucking hell. I swear I see stars. I move, fucking her with a primal, feral urgency. My hips piston. My cock slams into her over and over again.

She's crying out, and I don't know if it's pleasure or pain, and frankly, at this moment, I don't care. All that matters is that her body is mine.

11

ELENA

Oh. My. God.

Up until this moment, I've been wondering what the hell I'm doing. This man is my family's enemy. He kidnapped me. No doubt, he's touching me as an insult to my father and the Abates.

And then he was inside me, and everything, all thoughts, all questions, all concerns vanished, replaced by pleasure beyond any I've known. Yes, I enjoyed it at the club and even this afternoon in the bathroom, but there's something different this time.

Maybe it's because we're in bed. Or maybe it's because this time, he's over me. I feel consumed by him. It fills my chest with a powerful warmth.

"Come for me," he demands as he drives into me. "Come now... fuck..."

His words are my undoing. Pleasure rips through me, shattering me.

"Yes!" he growls. He thrusts in again, grinds against me. I watch him, amazed by the power of his release, the way his face is contorted in a mixture of pain and pleasure.

I reach up, pressing my palm against his cheek. A wave of emotion overcomes me, and I lift my head to kiss him.

He jerks back, staring at me in shock. Like he's wondering what I'm doing. "That's not what this is."

I don't know what he means, but I know I feel his words like a slap in the face.

He moves off me, quickly exiting the bed. It's bad enough that I'm attracted to the man who kidnapped me and will very likely kill me, but it is beyond crazy that I feel his actions as a rejection. If I do survive this, I'm going to need some pretty intensive therapy to deal with how messed up all of this is.

He strides naked into the bathroom, and a moment later, I hear the shower going. I'm feeling vulnerable and want to put the robe on as if it would protect me. But I don't want to anger him. So far, he hasn't hurt me physically, but it's not out of the realm of possibility. Or he could lock me up somewhere with fewer comforts. Things are bad enough. I don't want to make them worse.

I pull the covers up around me tightly. When he comes out of the bathroom, he dresses and then goes over to the table, picking up the phone I used earlier. Panic flashes through me. Will he be able to tell that I used the phone? Of course, he can if he takes time to look. But maybe he won't look.

He turns to me, watching me, but I can't decipher his expression. "Tomorrow, Donovan is going to move you out to my compound. I expect you to behave."

For a moment, I wonder if that behaving simply means to not resist Donovan when he takes me to the compound, or does it mean something more? Will he want to touch me too? I've heard of stories where that happens. Where several men touch a woman. I've heard my father's men say how they've taken a woman one after another.

He cocks his head to the side and studies me. "Not to worry, *cara mia*. You are still too valuable to me to kill."

It seems like I should be relieved by that, but I'm not. "Will he want from me what you want?"

His brow furrows into confusion, and then finally, he says, "No. I don't share." His dark expression softens only slightly. "None of my men will touch you like I do. You have my word."

He didn't say his men wouldn't hurt me, only that they wouldn't touch me in the intimate ways that he had. At least now I know if his men do touch me, it will be for the purposes of killing me and not to have sex with me.

"Get your rest, and then tomorrow, you need to eat a good breakfast. You lost too much weight."

My insides respond by warming, as if his words suggest that he cares for me. Fortunately, at the moment, I have control of my brain, and while I don't know why he cares about my weight loss, I know it's not because he cares for me.

"Where are you going?" I figure even mob bosses need to sleep sometimes, so why is he leaving?

"I'm going to do a little more work. I'll sleep elsewhere."

I wonder if he would have stayed had I not tried to kiss him. There was something about that kiss that seemed to unsettle him. At the same time, there's a relief that he won't be in the room with me. I'm tired and sore and want to be alone.

I'M AWAKENED the next morning by Maria entering my room. She sets a new pile of clothes on the table.

"Your breakfast will be up in fifteen minutes." Then she exits the room, leaving me alone.

I know from experience growing up in my family that when any of my father's men or staff tell me to do something, I'm expected to do it. They are an extension of his orders, and so I assume it's the same with her. She's telling me to do something Niko wants me to do.

I exit from bed and head to the bathroom where I shower and then put on the clothes Maria left for me. The dark jeans are a little loose, as is the top. The sneakers are a half-size too long. But at least nothing is too small.

I remember that Nikko said I would be moved today, so I pull my passport out from underneath the mattress and attempt to hide it in my clothes.

Maria returns with a tray with a full breakfast of eggs, toast, bacon, milk, and juice. It smells delicious except for when the scent reaches my stomach and it rolls over.

"I'm not really very hungry."

"You are expected to eat."

I decide I'll wait until Maria leaves and then flush the breakfast down the toilet to make it look like I ate it. But she begins to straighten the room and every now and then looks over in my direction, as if she's checking to make sure I'm eating.

I have a baby growing in me, so I should at least make an attempt to eat. I get one egg down when my stomach revolts. I bolt from my chair, rushing to the bathroom, making it to the toilet just in time for my stomach to empty its contents.

I sit by the toilet, feeling exhausted and overcome with chills. I hear talking in the bedroom, and a moment later, Maria enters the bathroom along with the man who had driven me back here last night. Had it really been only last night?

The man scowls as he looks down at me on the floor. "Are you really that revolted by the Boss?" He shakes his head. "All you Don princesses are spoiled. He gave you his fucking room, and look at you."

Maria murmurs under her breath, and while I don't hear everything that she says, I do hear the words *morning sickness*.

The man next to her smirks. "Those things don't happen overnight, Maria. And what are the odds here that Princess Fiore didn't walk down the aisle as a squeaky-clean virgin? Nah, she's just spoiled and not appreciating how much worse things could be for her."

He makes it sound like I'm getting special treatment. I suppose maybe I am since I expected to be locked up in some dingy, dark place and tortured. I wonder why Niko is treating me differently? Is it just the sex? It has to be.

"Okay, Princess, we've got to get on the road," he says.

"The Boss wants her to eat, and she hasn't finished," Maria says.

"She can eat when we get there. I don't really want her puking in the car." He makes a face.

Maria shrugs and leaves the bathroom, presumably to go back to work.

The man comes over and hooks his hand underneath my arm, hoisting me up off the floor. "Get yourself cleaned up, and then we're going."

I make my way to the basin to rinse my mouth out and brush my teeth with the toothbrush that had been left for me. When I finish, I exit the bathroom, and the man is standing by the window, his arms crossed as he looks out over the city.

"Where are we going?"

He turns. "To the compound. I guess you don't have anything with you to pack. We've already trashed that wedding dress." He watches me like he expects me to be upset about that. But I'm not. "Come on, let's go."

"What do I call you?" I ask as we take the elevator down to the garage.

"Donovan."

I arch a brow. "You're Irish?"

"Irish mother. Italian father. Ricci is my last name."

I'm sort of surprised that he is sharing so much with me. Then again, what's the big deal that I know his name?

When the elevator stops, we step out, and immediately, I scan the basement garage. If there's a chance for me to get away, this is the moment to do it. But of course, the garage is closed, sealed up tight. I see two armed guards by the garage doors, and I suspect there are some outside them as well. Some might call it paranoia, but men like Niko aren't always the hunter. Sometimes, they're the prey. I imagine my father and Don Abate are planning how to retrieve me. If only it was because one of them actually cared about me.

A hand wraps around my upper arm, fingers squeezing tightly. "Don't even think about it, Princess."

"My name isn't Princess." I want to jerk my arm out of his hand but resist the urge. I don't want him to misinterpret the move as resisting and trying to run away. I know that men like him aren't beyond using violence against women, and while Niko said none of them would touch me in a sexual way, I don't think they've been ordered not to hurt me if they deem it necessary.

He leads me to an SUV, opening the back door. "If you're going to behave, I won't have to restrain you."

I climb into the back seat. He shuts the door, and I settle in even though I'm not sure how far it is to the so-called compound. My guess is it's out of Manhattan, which means we'll likely be in the vehicle for an hour, likely more.

Donovan starts the car and inches up to the garage door, which opens. The guards are on alert and then motion for him to pull out. We merge into traffic and start our way toward wherever we're going.

I lean my head against the window, watching the city pass by. All the hundreds of people on the street don't notice me, a kidnapped woman. It's odd to have so many potential good Samaritans just outside the vehicle, but none can help me.

"You're quiet for once, Princess," he quips.

"Do you want me to talk?"

He laughs. "Hell no. It's just nice that you've finally come to terms with the situation. It's smart. The Boss can be generous, but he'll kill you in an instant if you become too much trouble."

I swallow as fear slides down my spine.

Donovan's phone rings, and he answers it. "Yeah, Boss."

I know it's Niko, but I can't hear what he is saying. The only thing I notice is Donovan's gaze looking at me through the rearview mirror before returning to the road.

"Sure thing." He hangs up and then works to change lanes, taking us in a different direction.

Everything inside me goes on high alert. "What's going on?"

"Change of plans. Boss is unhappy. What did you do, Princess?"

12

NIKO

I was already agitated, unsettled after Elena attempted to kiss me last night. Why did she do that? Why did it make me feel weird things in my chest? And why the fuck did I want to kiss her back?

And now, I'm pissed. I'd told myself that Elena understood her position, accepted the situation. I'd even considered giving her more freedom. Because of that, I didn't need to check my phone to see if she'd used it. Finally, as the issue gnaws at me in my office at the pizzeria, I decide I have to know. I'll be a putz if I put my faith in her. Sure enough, staring back at me is a call to Italy, to the Conti Family, no less.

I gave her my fucking room. Treated her with more care and respect than anyone else. And she betrayed that trust.

The disappointment in her surprises me, and I don't like it. I'm pissed that I'm disappointed. I'm especially pissed at myself for thinking I could trust her. I don't trust anyone. Why should she be different?

After discovering the call, I spend the next few hours learning all I can about Elena Fiori. For all I know, she's playing a deadly game with her father. What I learn doesn't shed much light. Why did she call her sister in Italy rather than her father or Romeo? My sense is she doesn't care much for them, but she knows them. It's true that people prefer the devil they know over the devil they don't.

I toss my phone on my desk and gather my thoughts as I wait for Donovan to bring her to me. In the meantime, I call out for my men to join me to discuss more important issues than Elena Fiori. I need to focus on the task at hand, which is making sure that the Fiori and Abate Families don't get the retaliation I know they're seeking.

My men crowd into my office, ready and willing for whatever command I intend to give them.

"I've gotten word that Fiori is looking at taking action against one of the clubs, probably in New Jersey. But I want extra men and diligence on all of them."

"You got it, Boss. What about Don Abate?" says Marco, one of the few men who was smart enough to switch allegiance to me after I killed my cousin.

"I'm not hearing anything." And that bothers me. I know neither Tiberius nor Romeo is going to let go that I took something of theirs.

"We've seen some of Fiori's men staking out your various properties. But no sighting of the Abates," Lou, a longtime soldier with the family that Donovan brought in, says. "But we did see Romeo out running his mouth about popping you in an upscale titty bar."

Paulie, the oldest man on my crew because he had worked with my father, rolls his eyes. "Romeo Abate is too stupid to realize the humiliation he incurred when his bride was kidnapped from the altar while he ran and hid."

We all laugh at that.

"Tiberius is smarter. He might not have shared any of his smarts with his son, but we need to stay diligent." I know I'm smarter than them all. But I'm also smart enough not to underestimate any of them.

"I don't know why we just don't kill them all," Mikey, one of the newer members of the family, says. I like him because he takes orders well, but I'm a little concerned that he is overenthusiastic. Sometimes, impulsiveness can be dangerous in this game we play.

"In due time, Mikey. And when that time comes, I'll be the one to take them out." My eyes are hard as I look at him, wanting to make sure he understands that Giovanni Fiori and Tiberius Abate are mine. Mine to kill in return for taking my mother and brother from me.

I hear a commotion outside my office, and my men immediately tense, reaching for their weapons.

"It's okay. It's just Donovan." I can hear Elena, her voice pitched up. She's asking Donovan what's going on. The fear I hear in her voice makes me glad. I'd been nice to her, and she repaid me by going behind my back. Now she needs to know who she's dealing with.

But even as I feel the satisfaction from her fear, somewhere deep inside, I feel like an asshole for it. Jesus, am I growing a conscience?

The door opens and Donovan ushers Elena in. My men step aside to make room for them as Donovan brings her to my desk.

Elena's eyes dart around the room before settling on me. I lean back in my chair, tenting my fingers together in front of my chest as I study her.

She opens her mouth to speak, but I bring my finger up to my lips to shush her. "You will not speak unless I tell you to."

Something crosses her face. I think it's understanding and resolve. A recognition that she has no power here. If she'd realized that sooner and not used my phone, we wouldn't be here.

"First of all," I speak to my men. "She is not to be touched. Do you understand? She's mine."

All the men nod, including Mikey, although he looks a little disappointed. I don't blame him. I know firsthand that Elena has a body made for fucking.

I rise and walk around my desk to stand in front of Elena. I see terror in her eyes. Her hands are clasped together, but they're shaking.

I pull my phone from my pocket and hold it up in front of her. "If or when Lucia Fiori Conti arrives in New York, you are to bring her to me."

"No!" Elena stares at me with a frantic expression.

I turn to my men. "You all know what you need to do. Go do it. Donovan, you stay."

He nods, but he steps back, giving me the space I need and respect I deserve.

"You brought this on yourself, *cara mia*." I really want to punish her for making me feel such disappointment. "I saved you from having to marry Romeo Abate. I brought you into my home, clothed and fed you." I step closer to her, practically nose to nose. "I am *Il Soldato Della Morte*, but I was gentle with you. And how do you repay me?"

"I... I..." She's trembling, and I like the power it gives me.

"Did you really think your sister could save you?" I ask in a tone that suggests she's naïve, because she is.

Her head shakes. "I was afraid and alone. I didn't know what to do."

"You do what I tell you to do."

She looks down. "I just wanted her advice."

I put my finger under her chin to lift her face, forcing her to look at me. "You seem to be under the misguided impression that you have any control in the situation. The only advice you need is to do what you're told and don't fuck with me."

"I just wanted to talk to her. She's not coming. I know she can't help me."

"You're right about one thing. She can't help you. Whether she's coming remains to be seen. If she does come, she'll be brought to me, and whatever happens to her is going to be on you."

Her eyes flash with heat, with defiance. "She's married to Giuseppe Conti."

"So?" Disappointment fills me again that she doesn't recognize my power. "He's a million years old. Rumor is he's on his deathbed." I know this because in truth, I know him. Respect him. The Conti Family and I have no beef with each other. "I just fucking humiliated Don Fiori and Don Abate. Do you really expect me to be afraid of Giuseppe Conti?"

"His son—"

"Luca. Yes. I know him well."

The defiance in her eyes vanishes, replaced by defeat. Good.

"Please don't hurt her."

I step back and lean against my desk. "Should I hurt your friend Kate instead?"

Her head jerks to me, her expression one of surprise.

I cross my arms over my chest. "I know everything there is to know about you. I know that you were taking classes. I know about your friend who helped you." I cock my head to the side. "I find it hard to believe that your father didn't know about what you were up to. Clearly, he wasn't keeping a very good watch of you. Well, of course, we know he didn't because you sold yourself to me."

From across the room, Donovan arches a brow in surprise.

"I have to be honest, that part I don't understand. A hundred thousand dollars for your virginity and you do nothing with it."

She stumbles back, sitting in a chair, covering her face with her hands as her tears come. For a moment, I have an urge to comfort her, but I push it away.

"I wanted to be out of this life. This is no way to live."

"Poor Elena. Growing up in wealth. Protected from—"

"You don't understand anything," she snaps in derision.

"I understand that you have no respect for authority."

She sags back and shakes her head. "Authority has no respect for me. I'm just a commodity. If you're going to kill me, just do it already."

Her words tangle in my gut and I don't like it. "I'm not going to kill you yet. There's no satisfaction in that. The satisfaction is in watching the fear and the terror. Of seeing the knowledge in your target's eyes that their life is in my hands."

She actually lets out a laugh. It startles me, and I look at Donovan, his brows are arched in surprise as well.

I turn back to her. "You think it's funny?"

"You're under the misguided impression that I don't know any of this. I know I have no control of my life. I never have. Whether it's my father or Romeo or you, it makes no difference. It's all the same. You're all the same."

Fury surges through my blood. I grip her by the arms and haul her off the chair, holding her up until my face is in hers. "I am nothing like your father or the Abates."

She startles, but then I see in her eyes that she's resolved to her fate. "Aren't you? They take joy in terrorizing others. You take joy in terrorizing others. They kill, you kill. They feel entitled to whatever or whomever they want." Her gaze goes to where my hands are gripping her tight. "You do too."

I release her and turn away, pissed off that I've proven her right. "Someone needs to pay for your betrayal."

She glances at Donovan, and I wonder if she thinks he'll save her. She turns back to me. "You can make me pay. I'll do whatever you want. Just please don't hurt my sister and my friend."

"I'm sorry, but that's not how this works." I cup her cheek, wishing things could be different. The feeling startles me, so I abruptly turn away. "Take her to the compound."

"No!" She reaches for me, but Donovan has already moved and gripped her arm.

"Put Paulie on the sister. If she comes, she's to be brought to me."

"No. Please... Niko."

"Come on, Princess." Donovan tugs her toward the exit.

"Please don't." She's straining to turn and look at me as Donovan drags her through the door.

"So much for doing what you're told," Donovan quips as he finally gets her through it. "Can I restrain her if I need to?"

"Of course," I say flippantly. "Shut the door behind you."

Donovan shuts the door, but it doesn't prevent the sound of him taking Elena away or her begging. I sit back in my chair, feeling agitated and unsettled again. This moment should be filled with satisfaction. Instead, I feel guilty. Guilty! What the fuck! The only guilt I've felt in my life is over failing my mom and brother. What is it about this woman that is messing with me? Whatever it is, it has to stop. My concern is that the only way to stop it is to end her.

13

ELENA

"No, please, let me go back. I need to stop him from hurting my sister and Kate." I'm resisting Donovan's dragging me up the stairs from Niko's office. I'm pretty sure my arm is about to come out of its socket.

"Not a chance."

"Please. I promise I won't cause any trouble if you let me do this."

He stops, turns, puts his face right in front of mine similar to what Niko had done. "I suppose you think his making accommodations for you means that he likes you. But Niko likes no one. He trusts no one, especially someone who goes behind his back. That means that he won't care about begging for your sister's life. More likely, he'll revel in it."

I know Niko isn't a good man. The man I saw today was the epitome of the Mafia Don. But before that, there was something softer about him. Donovan says he made accommodations for me. Why? Is it possible for me to remind him of why so he won't hurt those I care for?

"Please, I have to try."

"You don't know what it means to behave, do you? You said you would. And now look at you. You're having a temper tantrum like the spoiled princess you are. I have my orders and I'm going to carry them out. You can come along, or I'll throw you over my shoulder, restrain you, and you can ride in the very back of the SUV. Your choice, Princess."

It's a losing proposition. He must see that I've given up as he turns and heads up the stairs, dragging me with him.

I was quiet and compliant until he put me in the SUV. Once we were on the road, I said, "My sister can't come to New York."

He glances at me through the rearview mirror but doesn't say anything. It has me wondering if he knows something I don't.

"Is she coming?" I imagine she would want to come, but I don't believe her husband would allow it. Then there's the fact that being in New York would put her in danger. My father sent her away with instructions to never show her face in New York again.

"Please, you have to tell me."

He laughs. "I don't have to do shit for you. How long is it going to be before you stop acting entitled?"

Interesting that it's what I said Niko was. I'm not entitled, though. I'm desperate.

"Please, Donovan. If she comes to New York she'll have a target on her back." I use his name to appeal to his humanity, but he's Mafia. He doesn't have any. None of them do. That's what I need to accept.

"Why?"

It's a basic question. It even makes sense to ask it. But I'm not sure I should tell. I don't feel the need to protect my father, but sharing my family secrets may possibly endanger my sister, and I can't have that.

But then it occurs to me that I am the daughter of Niko's rival. I have dirt on my family that could be useful to them. I don't want to help Niko, but perhaps I can use what I know to protect my sister, maybe even gain Niko's trust, and he'll let down his defenses and give me an opportunity to escape.

I start to reject that thought, knowing that it's a foolish plan that will likely only get me killed. But I've spent my life under one family's rule. Plus, I'm likely dead, anyway. I don't want to give up. I don't just want to lie down and accept my situation. I have to fight until I can't fight anymore.

"You have nothing to say?" Donovan says from the front seat.

I turn my head to look out the window, leaning against it as the city drifts away. It appears that we're heading out to Long Island. Knowing it will take some time, I close my eyes to rest.

When I open them again, we're pulling up to the security gate entrance of a very tall brick wall.

"My next new prison," I murmur.

Donovan arches a brow at me through the rearview mirror. "Sleeping Beauty awakens."

Guards approach, and when they see Donovan, one waves and the gates open. We drive through toward a large mansion. The home has a Gothic feel with its gray stone construction. It's impressive and beautiful. Too bad it's probably where I'll die.

Donovan pulls to the front of the house and parks. He gets out, coming around the car to open my door. I unlatch my seatbelt and start to get out, but he blocks me.

"Here's some advice, Princess. Don't mistake anything that the Boss does to mean that you're anything more to him than a way to get back at your father or the Abates. I'm sure your father raised you to be obedient, subservient, and to take care of her man's needs. Niko has decided to treat you decently."

I arch a brow. While I know that he means compared to how Romeo would have treated me, Niko has been better, but there's nothing decent about it.

"So you get to stay here in the main house. But don't ever forget that one false move will have you buried so deep that no one will find you. And then he'll kill you." Then he smiles and winks. "Welcome to Villa Leone."

He helps me out of the SUV, keeping his hand on my arm as he leads me up the steps to the front door. It opens before we reach it, and a man dressed in black welcomes us into the home.

A middle-aged woman scurries into the foyer.

"This is Rosa. She'll be looking after you," Donovan informs me.

She smiles and extends her hand toward a massive staircase. "Let me take you to your room."

I follow her up the stairs and down the long hallway. She opens the door to a room filled with sunshine coming through a large window that overlooks the massive yard and garden below. The room is cozy, with a window seat encased by bookshelves, a large canopy bed, and a sitting area by a fireplace. The room is bright and sunny, the opposite of how I feel and the man who owns the place.

Rosa is friendly and animated as she shows me about the room. "You're welcome to try out any of the books. I'm told that you like to read."

I nod.

"Back when this was built, this was the mistress of the house's room. And through that door there" —Rosa motions to a large, ornate door on the other side of the room— "that is Don Leone's room."

I turn away from Rosa so she can't see me roll my eyes. Of course, I'm in the room next to his. But then I wonder what it means that he had me in his room back in Manhattan, but a separate room now. Had that kiss effectively chased him away? Or maybe it was that I used his phone. I realize that in some ways, being in a separate room is a relief. I'm a prisoner, but at least I have my own space.

"And over here is the ensuite bath. Do you enjoy taking baths?" Maria walks toward another door.

I follow her into the bathroom with a very large garden tub.

"You'll find bath oils and salts, and of course, bubbles. Or if you prefer, there's a shower. I think you will find everything that you need."

It's surreal the way she's giving me a tour as if I am a guest of honor at a resort and not a prisoner, a pawn in a dangerous game Niko is playing with my father and Tiberius Abate.

"This is all very lovely. Thank you."

"Of course." We reenter the bedroom. "You have clothes in the dresser and closet." She opens the closet, and I'm surprised by the amount of clothing hanging in it. "Don Leone arranged for clothes. I hope they fit, but if not, we'll provide new ones."

"How is it that he has all these women's clothes?" Are they left over from other women he has taken? If so, what happened to them?

"Some of them I believe were Aria's. But a delivery came in today. I have put them away here in the dresser and hung them in the closet."

I frowned. "Aria?"

Rosa nods. "Yes, she's Don Leone's little sister." She shakes her head as she looks down. "Poor man. She's all he has left."

She says that like Niko is capable of love. "Where is she?"

"She is safely away from all this business."

I don't know what to think. Everyone in Niko's life is a pawn but also a potential target in this life. Is it possible that he cares enough about his sister to get her away from his world? If so, he recognizes the terrible toll the Mafia life takes on the members of the family, particularly the women. Perhaps that's the key for me to deal with him. If he does care about his sister, would he want another man to treat her the way he's treating me? Would he see the correlation? Would he care?

"Ah... Carmena. Come set that here."

I turn to find another woman entering carrying a tray of food. She sets it on the table where Rosa indicates.

"Maria indicated you didn't have a chance to finish breakfast. So we brought you lunch. She said that she thought you're under the weather, so we've brought soup and toast. But if you'd rather have something else—"

"Thank you, but I'm not hungry."

"You should try to eat something. It's important that you eat."

She doesn't say it, but I get the impression that Niko has told her, as he'd apparently told Maria, that I needed to eat more.

"We will leave you to eat and settle in. I should warn you, though, that Don Leone has asked that you stay in this room. If there's anything you need, just let me know." She smiles, and the two of them leave the room.

I'm not hungry, but knowing that I have a baby growing in me, I sit down to attempt to eat the soup, hoping it's gentler on my stomach than the eggs were.

I manage to eat half the soup and a piece of toast before my stomach revolts. I'm on the floor of the bathroom when Rosa finds me.

"Oh, dear. You are sick. I'll go call the doctor."

I shake my head and wave my hand at her. "No, you don't have to do that." I don't know why, but I don't want Niko to learn about the baby. I suppose it's because if I get away from here, I want the baby to grow up in a different world. Not one surrounded by violence. Not led by men who only care about power and control and see their children as pawns. If he doesn't know about the baby, then I have a better chance to keep him out of my life.

Then again, if he kills me, he kills our baby too. I probably should consider that being pregnant might be a way to save myself, at least until the baby is born. But that would assume that Niko would be interested in being a father. I shake my head. There's nothing about Niko that suggests he wants to be a father. Up until the mention of his sister, I didn't think he was capable of love. Maybe he isn't. Maybe he sent her away to get her out of his hair.

Rose's eyes turn sympathetic. She helps me off the floor and to the sink where I wash my face and brush my teeth with a new set of toiletries.

"Perhaps you should rest." Rosa guides me to the bedroom. "You will be expected for dinner tonight, but in the meantime, lie down."

The minute I lay down, fatigue overcomes me. I'm exhausted emotionally and physically.

As Rosa is about to leave the room, another man enters carrying a garment bag. "The Boss asks that she wear this to dinner tonight."

Rosa takes the bag from him. "I'll see to it." She turns to me. "I'll hang this in the closet. It looks like there's a note, though." She pulls the tag from the hanger and hands it to me. While she goes to hang the garment bag in the closet, I open the small envelope.

Don't disappoint me again, cara mia. *You wear this, or nothing at all.*

14

NIKO

I sit alone after Donovan hauls Elena out of my office, my thoughts a swirling mix of frustration and confusion. If I were smart, I'd send her to one of my other *capos* to watch over so I didn't have be around her. But I'm not smart, I suppose. I tell myself I need to keep her near me because she's the prize. I can't risk her father or the Abates rescuing her. While I trust my men, only I have the power and authority to protect her.

I can't get over the way she looked at me as I confronted her about using my phone. She had fear, and I'm glad she recognized it even as something deep inside me hates myself for causing it. What the fuck is that about?

But then she also showed defiance and determination when I brought up her sister and her friend. It shows she's loyal. But also, she's vulnerable. The best way to stay safe and keep from being vulnerable is not to care about anyone or anything. Now I know how I can control her.

A thrill runs up my spine as I consider that. I don't want to break her, but I do want her to know who is boss. Her naked curves flash in my mind. The way she responds when I touch her. The way her pussy wraps around my cock like a glove.

Holy hell. Why the fuck am I thinking about her like that? Yes, I like sex as much as the next guy, but I have more important matters to deal with, like taking down Fiori and Abate for their part in the deaths of my family and trying to infringe upon my business.

I run a hand through my hair in agitation. This attraction to Elena is dangerous. Any distraction could lead to my downfall. She is a pawn in this game between their Families, a means to an end. I can't forget that. I need to regain control of myself because I can't afford distractions now, not when so much is at stake.

My watch alarm beeps, telling me it's time to go meet Liam. To help keep Liam's involvement with me on the downlow, we always meet on the other side of the city, far away from any of my known businesses. I take two men, Lou and Marco, with me for added protection, but they keep their distance once I enter the coffee joint where Liam is already waiting.

"*Ciao.*" I smile and act like I don't have a care in the world, mostly because I know it annoys him. Liam is the Scrooge of the underworld. I sit in the chair across from him, but at an angle so I can still see the door.

Liam glares at me over the rim of his mug. "You know you're fucked, right?"

"I know I did fuck, but not that I am fucked."

His eyes close for a moment, and when he opens them I see disappointment. "I guess I shouldn't be surprised. You are more like the rest of them all the time."

His comment stings, especially since Elena made the same accusation. "I'm nothing like them."

"Fucking a woman to get back at her family, her fiancé... yeah, that's what they'd do."

I lean forward, not liking feeling defensive. It if were anyone else, I might kill him for that, which I suppose would prove his point. "She's come more with me than she ever would have with Abate."

"I don't need the details. Fucking hell, Niko. You've taken on two Families. Humiliated them. Taken what's theirs. It's a fucking miracle you're not dead. Or your establishments torched."

I smile in a way I hope looks menacing. "They know I'm not one to fuck with."

"But they will, my friend. They will come for you. I don't know that I can protect you."

A server comes, and I order a double espresso. I still have a long day ahead of me.

"I know what I'm doing."

"Do you? Because what was going to be two murders of the heads of Families became a kidnapping of one of their women. From what I heard, that was an in the moment decision. Why?"

I shrug. "Death didn't feel like a big enough payment. I'll kill them. I just want them to live in their cowardice, really wallow in their knowledge that I took from them. And it was easy, Liam. I basically walked in and walked out."

"It's not just you, though. This game impacts us all."

"Do you really think that had I simply killed Giovanni and Tiberius that we wouldn't be having a similar conversation? That their Families wouldn't be after my head?"

"No. But Giovanni's Family is weak. It's probably why he's trying to align with Tiberius. And Romeo... well... he's all hot air and no substance. It's a miracle he's not dead already."

I agree with Liam's assessment. I sit back so my server can set my drink in front of me. "Who is your guess for who follows Giovanni?"

Liam shrugs. "No clue. He has no sons. One daughter is married to Giuseppe Conti, but they're in Italy. It's believed the son Luka is mostly in charge now. Maybe they'll take over."

I shake my head. "No chance. I know them."

Liam arches a brow. "Do you now?"

"I do." But I don't go into details. "Speaking of Conti, his wife could be coming to town. Elena was able to call her."

Liam was unable to hide his amusement. "Your little prize got one over on you?"

I shift, hating the feeling of betrayal that resumes. "A test. She failed."

He watches me as he sips his coffee. "Test? Why?"

I don't know why. It was stupid. More proof that this woman should be kept far away from me. "Let's just say, she's not fond of her father or Romeo."

"What does that mean?"

"She didn't call either of them. She called her sister. I don't think she wants to be saved."

He laughed. "You think she'd rather be with you?"

I grin. "She seems to enjoy parts of our arrangement."

He rolls his eyes.

"The point is, her sister may be on the way. I have someone looking out for this, but I'd like you too as well. If she enters the country, I want to know about it and I want her brought to me."

"You do know the world doesn't revolve around you, right?"

"Oh, I think it does. That's not all."

"Fucking hell." He shakes his head.

"I want you to get eyes on Kate Emerson."

"Who?"

"Kate Emerson."

He thinks for a moment. "Emerson as in New York City's police chief?"

I nod. "She's his daughter. She's also friends with Elena Fiori."

"What? How? Is he dirty?"

I shake my head. "If he is, she isn't aware of it. Elena seemed to have befriended her while taking classes. How she managed that, I don't know. Fiori seemed to keep a loose tether on her." So loose that she showed up in a New Jersey night club and sold her virginity for one hundred thousand dollars. Money her father took. Perhaps I should kill him for stealing her freedom from her. Yes, I understand the irony that she's not free with me. But I paid for her.

"You know what, Niko? This is crazy, even for you."

"Who better to keep tabs on her than the FBI? It would be safer for sure. I don't want you to do anything except make sure she doesn't get into trouble. Keep her away from Elena and my business."

He blows out a breath. "I'll see what I can find out."

I smile and nonchalantly hand him an envelope filled with cash

—payment for services rendered. For someone receiving enough money to support a family, he doesn't seem very happy.

"If you weren't my best friend, you'd be rotting in federal prison right now because death would be too merciful." He begrudgingly stuffs the envelope into his jacket pocket and stands to leave.

"*Ciao*, my friend."

He ignores me, and I laugh. What a grump. I leave a few bills on the table and head out. My men flank me as we make our way to my waiting car. I survey the area just in case. My gaze stops on a car across the street with a person looking my way holding up his phone as if he were snapping a picture. When he lowers the phone, his eyes are wide, as if he's surprised I've spotted him.

"Romeo-Fucking-Abate." I hold up my middle figure to him and laugh as he almost mows someone over as he peels away from the curb.

"Want us to go after him, Boss?" Lou asks me.

"Nah. He'll get his soon."

I get in the car, and we head back to the pizzeria where I let Marco off. Lou stays with me to drive me to Long Island. During the trip, I entertain myself with all the ways I can toy with Romeo Abate. But then I wonder how he knew where I was. I wasn't in my territory. The coffee shop isn't Abate territory, either. It's Fiori. One of his fuckers must be reporting to the Abates. It surprises me some. Why is Giovanni so accommodating to Tiberius and his son? I remember hearing the truth about Elena's marriage to Romeo and decide that her father must be in some deep, deep shit with the Abates. I wonder how much of it Elena knows?

And as if on cue, thoughts of her fill my mind. I'm glad they're thoughts of resentment because that is the type of feeling I'm used to. I think about how I've tried to be nice, at least for me, and yet, she went behind my back. Maybe I should threaten to hand her over to Romeo. I know for sure that he wouldn't be as nice. The image of Romeo taking Elena, hurting her as his reputation suggested, makes my stomach clench. There's no way I'm letting that fucker get his hands on her.

But she's not off the hook. She's the daughter of a Don. She should know how to behave. Then again, she betrayed her father by selling her virginity. But I'm not Giovanni. I'm the Soldier of Death. I've earned respect. It's time I demanded it from her.

I call to the house in the Hamptons to arrange for dinner tonight, including her attire and a note. It's time for her to learn how to behave like a proper Mafia mistress if she doesn't want to be sent away to less comfortable surroundings.

I'm angry that she's turning me into a putz, and so tonight, I'm set on teaching Elena a lesson in obedience.

15

ELENA

on't disappoint me again, cara mia. *You wear this, or nothing at all.*

Niko's words are a command. Except for a moment earlier, he usually exerts his control with subtlety. He's not loud or aggressive, but there's an undercurrent that says there's no room for disobedience. Of course, he doesn't need to be over the top in asserting his control. He's *Il Soldato Della Morte.* His name alone causes fear, encourages obedience. I'm no different.

I take a deep breath, trying to calm my nerves as I step into the barely-there red dress. It clings to my curves, making me feel both womanly and vulnerable. It reminds me of the dress I'd first looked at in Kate's closet when I needed something for the virginity auction. If she saw me in this now, she'd likely be shocked. Possibly horrified. Thinking of her saddens me. I miss her so much, but I know I'll likely never see her again. Not if I survive and not if I want to keep the horrors of my world away from hers.

My life isn't turning out like I'd hoped. I sold my virginity to get away, and now I fell deeper into the world I'd hoped to escape. I don't regret selling my virginity, although I'm disappointed I wasn't successful in my quest to build a new life. The thing that is the hardest to deal with is how easily I succumb to Niko's seduction. He's my kidnapper. I'm his pawn. So why does my body always heat up when he touches me?

At the same time, through his touch, I'm discovering that a woman's power can come from sex. I remember Lucia once saying that men are slaves to their dicks. I think that is true even for a man with such control as Niko. At first, I felt he was touching me to punish my father and the Abates and to remind me who was in charge. But there have been moments that I've felt that he was compelled to touch me. Not from power, but from a desire he doesn't control. Considering how new I am to all this, I could be completely wrong, but on the off chance I'm right, this could be something I can use to survive and protect my sister and Kate. Maybe with sex and telling Niko my Family's secrets, I can forge an alliance of my own with him.

But it's a dangerous game, and truth be told, I'm terrified. I don't know what he has planned for me tonight, but I doubt it will be pleasant.

I run my fingers through my hair, trying to tame my thick waves. The bathroom is fully stocked with creams and lotions, but no hair dryer. I wonder if that's on purpose and if so, how can a hair dryer be used as a weapon?

There is makeup, but I don't bother with much. Just a little rouge and mascara, finishing with a tinted gloss. For a moment, I study myself in the mirror. Will Niko like what he sees? Will he be pleased that I've obeyed and therefore not punish me?

A wave of despair slides through me. Is this how the rest of my life will be? Not knowing from one moment to the next what's happening, always walking on eggshells to avoid upsetting Niko?

I shake my head as if it will dislodge and get rid of the hopelessness of my life. As long as I have breath and my wits about me, there's hope for something better. At least that's how I plan to operate.

I leave the bathroom and exit the bedroom into the hall, trying to remember the instructions Rosa gave me for getting to the dining room. There's no guard outside my door, which surprises me. What does that mean?

I make my way downstairs and am surprised at how quiet and empty the home feels. As I reach the bottom of the steps, I'm not sure where to go. Did Rosa say to go left or right?

"Hello? Rosa?" I call out for anyone who might be around, but I'm utterly alone. The silence is deafening, and I can't shake the feeling that this is some sick game of Niko's... a game where I end up dead. Men like him like to toy with their prey, give them a sense of safety and calm right before they strike.

I turn right, going to the first double doors. My heart races as I reach for the door handle, my fingers trembling with fear. I take a deep breath to calm myself down. I still have value to Niko in his war against my father. I remind myself of my plan to tell Niko about my family in exchange for Lucia and Kate's safety. If necessary, I'll use my newfound sexuality as well.

As I turn the handle, the air around me supercharges with energy. He's there. Behind me. I can feel him.

I turn and am frozen for a moment as I take him in. Niko is wearing a tuxedo, his hands in his pockets as if he's relaxed but his expression contemplative. For a moment, I'm struck by how handsome and sexy he is... and lethal.

"What do you know of your betrothal to Romeo Abate?" Niko asks, his voice low and menacing.

I shake my head, trying to clear my thoughts. "My father wants an alliance with the Abates." I feel like I've told him that already.

Niko's eyes narrow, and he takes a step closer to me. "He told you that?"

The question takes me off guard. What else would it be? Mafia Families work like middle-aged royalty... kings marrying off daughters to form alliances.

But his question reminds me that I have more information I could tell him. "I'll tell you everything about my Family, but you have to promise you won't hurt my sister or Kate."

His smile is dark, like a cat toying with a mouse. "There's the woman I fucked at the club." His fingers reach out and toy with a strand of my hair. My breath stalls in my chest because I don't know whether it's a warning gesture or not.

"Your boldness was charming, but you ruined any leverage you might have had when you went behind my back. You have no power here, Elena."

I notice his use of my name instead of *cara mia*, and dread fills me. "I don't want power. I only want to protect my sister and my friend," I say, trying to convey my sincerity. "Please. I'll tell you whatever you want. I'll do whatever you want. Just spare my sister and friend."

He laughs, and it sends chills down my spine. "You'll do whatever I want you to do no matter what."

"Please," I beg.

He studies me and then reaches around me. A part of me thinks he plans to kiss me, but that's crazy. The door opens behind me and he smirks. He knows his effect on me, and I hate that. I thought I might be able to use my sex appeal, but I'm no match for him.

"What is the arrangement your father has with Tiberius Abate?" he asks again as he leads me to a long dining table in the room. He pulls my chair out and helps me sit, but there's nothing gentlemanly about it. I feel like a prisoner going to the gallows.

He sits at the head of the table and waits for me to answer.

"I don't know the details. You know I don't. I'm not privy to my father's business."

He cocks his head to the side. "So how can you offer to tell me what you know if you don't know anything?"

Ugh. He's right.

Another door opens, and a man enters carrying two plates, setting one in front of me and the other in front of Niko. He pours wine and then leaves us.

"The marriage is a merger. My father has no sons, and as you know, that leaves his organization's future uncertain. Lucia is older. She's also more beautiful and charming—"

"I doubt that," he quips as he sips his wine.

I don't know what he means so I keep going. "She fell in love with someone else and ruined her value to my father—"

"Like you did." His tone is even. I don't sense anger, but neither is he friendly.

"My father got angry and arranged for her to marry Don Conti, a really old—"

"I know who he is."

I nod. Of course he knows. "My father told her if she ever showed her face in New York and humiliated him again, he'd... well... you know." I can't bring myself to say the words. "So she won't come. It'll be too dangerous."

"Is she as loyal to you as you are to her? If so, she will come," Niko replies.

"She won't." God. I hope she won't or that her husband won't allow her to come. "After that, my father and mother devoted all their attention to making me a perfect Mafia wife—"

Niko lets out a laugh that is surprising. "You are so far from perfect, *cara mia*." His finger runs down the side of my face. In the movies, it's a caring gesture. Here and now, it feels like a threat.

"Perfect Mafia daughters don't sell their virginity."

Indignation gets the better of me. "No. Their fathers do."

His lips twitch up as if he's amused. I decide that's better than being offended.

"I don't want to be a perfect Mafia wife."

"Clearly," he quips. "You think you have more power than you do. You ask too many questions. You break the rules—"

"I'd be normal in the real world."

His eyes flash with heat. "This world, the greed and violence, is as real as it gets."

I shrug. "I don't want this life. I want to be able to make my own choices about how I live. I want to choose my mate—"

"And who would you choose? Some boring Wall Street stiff?" He leans closer to me.

"I'd choose someone who loves and respects me. Values me beyond sexual pleasures or a business deal."

He sits back. "Fairy tales aren't real."

I look down at my food, realizing I'm not eating. But since I'll likely throw it up, I don't even try.

"You say you want to be valued for you, and yet you considered yourself so worthless that you sold your body."

My gaze snaps to his in indignation. "You considered me so worthless as to buy me and then to kidnap me in your game."

"Worthless?" He scoffs. "I paid a lot of money for you."

Oh, yeah. He doesn't just control me because he took me from my father and Romeo. He owns me.

"I wanted to escape. I want my own life. I don't want to be in this game between you and my father."

He takes my hand, but it's not soft. It's a reminder that I'm powerless. Fear grips me until I can't breathe.

"This is no game, Elena." His eyes are dark and deadly. "This is justice. Revenge. Your father and his cronies took something from me, and now I have taken something from them."

16

NIKO

I've prepared myself to see her again. To not let her beauty and innocence mixed with fire affect me. But when I see her outside the dining room door, the red dress hugging every curve as if it had been painted on her, I know I'm in trouble. When she turns and I look into her dark eyes, my resolve slips. I'm finding it harder and harder to stop myself from wanting her in a way I shouldn't and it's driving me fucking nuts. The woman went behind my back, and yet all I want to do is to keep her. Protect her.

Taking her was supposed to be revenge against her father, nothing more. But something about Elena nags at me, causing me to think about her too much. Too often.

When she said she wanted a life outside the Mafia with another man, I saw red. If she succeeded in this new life, heaven help any man she wanted to be with because he'd be dead. I'd make sure of it. She's mine.

My Elena. Therein lies the problem. I'm thinking of her as my woman when she's nothing but a means to an end. The more time we spend together, the harder it is for me to remember that.

"That's what I mean," she says in response to my comment that

I've taken her in retaliation. "You don't see people... me... as a person. In this world, women are only to be pretty and obedient."

"Is that what you think I want from you?" I ask.

She arches a brow. "You have no power here, Elena." She tosses my words back into my face.

"And yet, here you are at my dining room table. Enjoying a gourmet meal." Except for the fact that she's not eating. She hasn't even tasted the wine. Does she think I poisoned it? "I've put you in a primary room in my home. I have guards ensuring that your father and Romeo, who is looking for you, won't get to you."

"Why?"

Why, indeed? I tell myself my feelings for her are simply desire, that she's a beautiful woman I intend to possess in every way. Her spirit only makes it more enticing to dominate her. There's also the added benefit that she's Fiori's daughter.

But even as I think these things, I know it's a lie. She's gotten to me in a way no woman ever has—beyond the physical. I want her fire, her passion, not just her body. I wonder if I could change her. Maybe I can make her see that she'll never be able to leave our world. Even if I let her walk out my door, her father or Romeo or Tiberius would take her and lock her away. Or another rival family would snatch her. None of them will treat her as well as I do.

Perhaps I can take her up on her offer to tell me all she knows about her family and in time, she'd see that only with me can she be safe. In time, she could come around to me... and... and what? Marry me?

I nearly choke on my wine as the thought hits me. Then again, Elena is the key to my revenge against Fiori and Abate. As my wife, I'd have inroads to take over her father's business. Our son could become more powerful than even I can imagine.

The image of Elena ripe and round with my child inside her makes me hard. I remember not using a condom when I fucked her the last time, so she could already be growing my son. The thought fills me with fierce power.

"Have you ever wanted anything else?"

Her words pull me from my reverie. The tough guy in me wants to lie and tell her no, I was born for this life. But I'm on a mission of revenge and seduction, so I opt for a version of the truth.

"My uncle was the Don. My father worked for him, so my being Don wasn't in the cards." Now I know differently. Now I understand that I was born to run this organization. To grow it. And to crush anyone who gets in my way.

"What were you going to do?" She seems to relax, but she still doesn't eat. Is she sick? I remember Maria telling me she was ill that morning. Perhaps this situation is getting to her. Maybe it's time to back off a bit, to give her some room to come around. To recognize just how much I can do for her.

"I considered either law enforcement or the military, but my uncle died... and even then, my plans didn't change until my cousin arranged for your Family or maybe Tiberius's to kill my father. So I had no choice but to kill my cousin and take over."

Wariness shines in her eyes. It annoys me. She acts like I'm a petulant teenager.

"You do see the irony, don't you? You wanted to go into law enforcement and now you're in organized crime."

I laugh as I cut my steak. "You know, don't you, that many cops and agents work for us?"

She sighs, letting me know she's suspected as much. "You still could have chosen something else. I envy you that."

Her words sting a little, strangely, and I don't know why. At the same time, I know she's right. I could have chosen a different path, one that didn't involve bloodshed and violence. But now that I'm here, there's no turning back.

"Do you really think you could have walked away?" I ask her. Very few leave the Family, at least alive.

She shrugs. "Maybe. I don't know. Maybe not. But whatever happened, it would be because I was exerting my own power, my own will."

"Is that what you want? Power?" I push my plate away, intrigued by her bravery to speak so candidly.

"Not power like you. I don't want to rule over people. I want personal power."

"To do what?" I pick up her fork and poke a cooked carrot.

"Be free."

"There's more than that." I hold the fork up to her lips, encouraging her to eat. She stares at the carrot with reluctance but finally bites into it. "What is freedom, really? Even in your so-called real world, people are ruled by others. Bosses in a job. Police. Rules of society."

"I could decide what my job would be."

"You have a passion?"

She looks down, and I see that she doesn't.

"So your goal then is just to escape your father? To avoid marrying Romeo, right?"

She shrugs again, and I feel like I'm losing her in this conversation.

"I can help you with that."

She purses her lips at me. "Your kidnapping me wasn't what I had in mind."

"No, but you proposed a solution. You tell me all you can about your father's business and anything you know about the Abates."

Her expression perks up. "And you won't hurt my sister or Kate?"

I stare at her, noncommittal. Her loyalty to them is my leverage, and while I'm not opposed to deception, I don't want to make a promise to her that I don't know I can keep.

"You said you'd do whatever I asked of you. I'm willing to agree to your terms. But you need to behave. You need to take whatever your parents taught you about being a good woman and use it with me."

Her eyes close for a second, as if she's repulsed by the idea. It pisses me off. I deserve more respect.

I toss her fork on the plate.

"Or, I can send you to spend your time locked in less comfortable accommodations. I'll find out what I need to know from your sister."

"No. Please. I'll do whatever you want."

She says the words I want to hear, but I hate that she doesn't mean them. She doesn't want me. How fucked up is it that I'm thinking that? That I care about how she thinks about me? I should send her away for how she's making me feel so pathetic.

But I remind myself that my goal is revenge against her father, including bringing her into my Family, making her the perfect companion for me, not Romeo Abate.

I sit back and study her. "Have I been unreasonable? I mean, for our world. Not your *real world*. Do you think Romeo would give a shit about your enjoying his touch? Worry about your health? Spare your life or at least not fuck you up for going behind his back? I'm not so bad, Elena."

She nods.

"I can make things nice for you." I can feel it already. The gloating I can do, telling Giovanni Fiori and Romeo Abate that Elena chooses me. She fucks me. She'll give me an heir to my family.

"What do you want to know?"

Her lack of affect is a problem, though, because I need her to truly want to stay with me. My victory will be all the sweeter when she's mine instead of theirs by her choice. My work is cut out for me.

"Why won't you eat?"

Her eyes widen. "I'm not hungry."

"Do you think wasting away will lead me to set you free?"

She shakes her head.

"Then eat. You won't leave this table until you do."

"I... ah..." She looks at the food like it's her enemy.

"Eat!"

She sucks in a breath and picks up her fork. She takes her time, fully chewing and swallowing before taking another bite. She barely eats a quarter of what's on her plate when she puts her fork down.

She looks at me, discomfort in her expression. "I'm finished. May I be excused?"

Matteo, one of my servers, enters to clear our plates. "Coffee, sir?"

"No. Thank you."

"Dessert?"

I look at Elena. "Would you like something sweet, *cara mia*?"

"No, thank you."

"We're done, Matteo."

"Yes, sir."

When he leaves, I rise from my chair and hold out my hand to Elena. "I'd like dessert."

Her expression is confused, and I find it charming that she doesn't realize the innuendo. I have much to teach her.

When she stands, I pin her to the table. "I'm going to eat your pussy for dessert. You're going to like it."

I pull the skirt of her dress up her soft legs and tug off her panties. I maneuver her onto the table.

"Does that excite you?" I ask her. I run my finger through her pussy lips, finding the answer to my question. She's already wet. I'm salivating to taste her. I sink down to my knees and open her legs. Running my tongue through her pussy, her taste is sweet with a hint of the exotic. She's delicious. I lick and suck, listening to her noises. She mewls and moans. Gasps and cries out. I have no doubt that she doesn't like me, and yet like this, she's completely open, giving over her body and her pleasure to me. I'm used to control. To taking it. But I don't remember anyone ever completely surrendering it to me like this.

Her hips rock and her body arches. Her essence coats my tongue as she comes in my mouth.

"Mmm," I murmur against her sweet pussy. I rise, undoing my pants. "You liked that, didn't you?"

She nods up at me, looking sated as she catches her breath. "I like the other better."

I arch a brow. "What other?"

"When you use... you know..." Her hand gestures to my dick that I've just released from the confines of my clothes.

"My cock?"

She nods. There's something adorable and sweet in her innocence.

"In your mouth? Or your pussy?"

"Here." She points to her pussy.

"If you can do the deed, *cara mia*, you can say the words. Tell me you like my cock in your pussy."

She bites her lower lip.

"Until you say it, you can't have it." I'm not sure that is a threat I can keep. My dick wants desperately to be inside her.

"I want your... cock... in my... in me."

Close enough. I thrust, filling her, feeling her tight pussy grip my cock. I close my eyes, savoring the sweet sensation coursing through my body. With it are other sensations. Unwelcome ones. Ones that suggest Elena may not be the key to my victory but instead, she might be my undoing.

17

ELENA

I t's surreal how much my body craves Niko's touch when I can hardly stand the guy. He tells me he's being nicer than anyone else would be, but so what? That's not saying much in my world.

But then he looks at me like he'll die if he can't touch me. He does things to my body that give pleasure beyond any I could have imagined. I'm helpless in these moments. Now is no different. His body is in mine, moving, the friction the sweetest torture. It's the same for him. I can see it on his face. It's the only time I feel equal to him. Yes, he's the one driving, thrusting, but the experience is the same for us both. Pleasure building and building. Us reaching higher for more... more sensation, more pressure, more everything.

I'm aware that at any moment, someone could walk in. Or maybe they know not to bother him. How many women has Niko taken on this table after dinner?

His hands cover my breasts, kneading and pinching, adding a whole new layer of feeling.

"Oh!" I cry out at the rush of it.

"You like me fucking you, don't you, *cara mia*?"

"Yes," I say on a hiss of breath. "You like it too, don't you?"

He chuckles, and I don't like that he finds amusement in my inno-cence. "I think it's obvious."

He grips my hips, his pace quickening, strengthening. "Touch yourself."

What? My hands are splayed on the table as I try to find purchase so I don't fly away.

"Elena. Touch yourself. Rub your clit. Make yourself come."

I'm uncertain as my hand slides down my belly. My finger brushes over a hard, sensitive nub and ratchets the pleasure up.

"That's right," he says encouragingly.

I rub again, and again, and next thing I know, I'm soaring. Liquid pleasure floods my body.

He yells and drives in hard. Warmth fills my womb. He collapses over me. I don't see the hardness in him. It's like he's relaxed for a single moment. A moment that causes me to want to kiss him again. But I don't. I know he doesn't like it. I wonder why?

Finally, he levers up and withdraws from me. The hard edges of his expression return. "That pretty much seals the deal."

Tears form in my eyes, and I chastise myself for being hurt by his reminding me that this is just a business deal. He never came out and said he'd leave Lucia and Kate alone, but I have little choice but to believe he'll meet his side of the bargain.

"Can you protect them?" I ask.

"Who?" He pulls his pants up and fastens them.

"My sister and Kate. From my father or the Abates?"

He arches a brow. "Are you changing the deal?"

"I've always wanted them safe." I manage to sit up and scoot off the table. I push the skirt of my dress down. "That hasn't changed."

"If you want them safe, do as you're told." He rolls his shoulders. "I can walk you up to your room."

I shake my head. "I know the way." I head toward the door to leave the dining room.

His hand takes my arm. "Don't think that because the house is quiet and you don't see staff that I won't know what you're doing. There's no escape."

I nod. "I know." I tug my arm free, feeling so low after such a lovely high.

"Elena."

I stop when I reach the door and look over my shoulder at him.

His expression is... well, I'm not sure. I get the feeling he wants to say something, but he doesn't.

I turn back to the door.

"Sleep well," he finally says.

THE NEXT MORNING, I wake to Rosa pulling out clothes from my drawer.

"What's happening?" I ask as I rub sleep from my eyes.

"Oh, good. You're awake. You're expected to be down in the garden in fifteen minutes."

"What?" Panic rises. Any change in my day makes me think the time has come and Niko is going to kill me.

"It's a lovely idea. A walk in the morning can do you good. Fresh air will strengthen you."

I dress in jeans and a T-shirt. Rosa hands me a zippered fleece jacket in case I get cold. When I reach the garden, Niko is already there sniffing a rose. He's also in jeans and a red-collared shirt. The dress is casual, belying the fierceness of his presence.

When he sees me, he waves me over. "These were my mother's."

I look at him and then the rose bush, wondering if I'm dreaming. Niko seems to be sentimental. He's sharing something personal. That's not the man I know.

"They're lovely."

He holds his hand out toward a path that weaves through the manicured yard. It makes me think of period movies set in England. "Let's walk."

We walk side by side in silence for several strides.

"Why do you think your father has such a hard-on for Tiberius Abate?" he finally asks.

I'm also relieved. This walk is part of the deal to share what I know, not a march to my death.

"I don't know for sure, except that my father feels he lost face when my sister tried to run off with her boyfriend. I wasn't kidding when I said her value to him—"

"What had been the plan for her before that? Not Romeo?"

"No. Not Romeo. I don't know who. He was relieved Don Conti would take her, but he didn't get what he wanted."

Niko was quiet for a moment. "What does that have to do with Tiberius?"

I shrugged. "I think he feels a partnership with him will strengthen the Family."

Again, he's quiet, as if he's assessing my statements. I'm worried I'm not sharing enough.

"If your father died right now, who would take over?"

My stomach clenches as I think about Niko gunning my father down. I don't want to go back to my family, but he is my father.

"I don't know who he's named. TJ would likely try—"

"TJ Rialto?"

I nod. "He's technically my father's oldest son. His mother was one of many mistresses. But I know my father worried about his impulsivity. Plus he's my age... a little young—"

"I was about your age when I took over." He slants a glance at me.

"Yeah, well, he's not you."

His lips twitch upward. "No. No one is like me."

It's conceited and yet, I'm beginning to realize it's true.

"My dad has a *capo*, Cal, who might make a move. I've heard him talking sometimes about how he thinks my father is weak. My father still has respect in the family, but if he died, I see him trying to take over."

"Cal isn't blood."

"He's like you were. My father's nephew. Well, my uncle's son by a mistress. My uncle is gone, so Cal is all that's left except for my mom and me and Lucia. But well, as you know, women don't generally become the heads of Families."

"Would you like to be the head of your Family?"

"No. I told you, I don't want this life."

We turn the corner of the path, and the angle gives us a view of the bay. I stop, taken by the beauty of it. The vastness of the water. My world has always been so small. Views like this remind me of how much there is. It makes me ache to know it.

IN THE NEXT FEW DAYS, a new routine forms. Each morning, I walk with Niko. Then the day is my own—well, as long as I stay at the house. Mostly, I read and nap.

In the evening, Rosa dresses me, and I have dinner with Niko and sex usually follows. On the second night, he took me to a room with a library, telling me I could read any book here, and then he stripped me and we had sex on the leather couch. The night after that, he took me back to the garden, where he had me suck his penis... or dick, as he told me to call it.

Last night, he escorted me to my room. He made himself comfortable on the window seat and told me to strip. Then he had me straddle him. It's always pleasant, but I have to admit, the position with me on top has been my favorite so far. Maybe because it puts me in charge.

Today, we're on our walk, but he isn't asking me about my father.

"What do you do for fun?"

"Here? Read—"

"No. In life. What do you enjoy?" he asks. He's walking closer to me than usual. Sometimes, our hands brush together, and I wonder if he wants to hold my hand. Maybe it's wishful thinking because I find myself wanting to hold his.

"I don't have hobbies, if that's what you're asking."

"You like computers, though, right?"

I glance up at him, realizing he knows about my studies. "It's okay. I wanted to learn something practical. Something I could use to support me when I left."

"Smart." He keeps his gaze ahead, so I don't know whether he's patronizing me or not. "Is there something you'd like to do? Learn about?"

"I don't know."

"Just reading, huh?"

"That's all there is to do around here."

"You seem to sleep a lot, according to Rosa."

I shrug. "It passes the time." I'm still getting sick too, mostly in the morning, but I try to hide it even though I know I'm running out of time.

Two days later, after our walk, Niko leads me to a section near the back of the house. The room appears to be a sunroom. One wall is mirrors with a dance bar attached. One area has an easel, with a table full of paints and arts supplies. Another table has a camera and stacks of puzzles. Near the French doors is a table with gardening tools.

"What is this?"

"This is for you, *cara mia*. To find your hobby. Right outside the doors is a plot of land you can garden in. My mother enjoyed that. Or paint. If you like to dance, you can do that. I can hire instructors, or there are books and videos."

I look at him, my mouth agape. "You set this up for me?"

He looks away, as if he's uncomfortable by my reaction. "There are sewing and other cloth crafts there. Rosa said she can teach you that, if you'd like. If you'd like to take up cooking or baking, the kitchen knows to make it available to you. Chef Brioni will teach you."

I'm touched by his thoughtfulness, and I can't help but wonder about the man behind the *Il Soldato Della Morte* persona. I've sometimes thought I saw a softer, gentler man, but the next moment, he'd become gruff. But I'm beginning to see he's not all evil, and I'm coming to realize that he's a man who loved his mother. I don't know for sure and I'm afraid to ask, but I worry that my father or Don Abate is behind Niko's loss. The idea of it breaks my heart for Niko.

. . .

OVER THE NEXT FEW DAYS, I add visits to the room to my daily routine. There, I spend time exploring the various activities he's arranged for me. When I'm with him, I'm enjoying his company, even when he's grilling me about my father.

As we settle into our routine, I find myself enjoying his company. Our conversations are no longer just about business but also about our lives and interests, to an extent. While he shares some personal details, it's nothing deep. Nothing about his mother and brother who died. Nothing about his sister, Aria, who is supposedly in Europe. But it's enough to see a different side from the Soldier of Death.

One afternoon, I realize that I'm so settled that I haven't thought about our deal or how I might escape. I chastise myself. I can't let my guard down. I can't forget why I'm here. I'm still his prisoner, a pawn in his game against my father.

I clean up my messy, drippy attempt at watercolor painting and return to my room. Rosa brings me lunch, which she sets on the table.

"Don Leone has returned to the city, so you'll be on your own for dinner. Would you like it in the dining room or here?"

I'm surprised at the disappointment that Niko didn't tell me he was leaving. It's a reminder that I mean nothing to him. I'm a means to an end.

"Here is fine."

She leaves me, and I sit to eat, hoping now that it's past morning, it will stay down. No such luck. Not long after, I'm in the bathroom, my head over the toilet bowl.

I'm just about to get off the floor when Rosa enters, looking at me in concern.

"I'm going to call the doctor. This can't continue," she insists as she helps me up and leads me to the sink where I can brush my teeth.

"No, please. It's—"

"I know very well what it is, Ms. Fiori. This isn't good. Not good at all." Rosa urges me back into the room and tucks me into bed. "Rest."

"Please don't call a doctor." I know I'm running out of time, but

I'm not sure what to do yet. What is Niko going to think? What will he do? This child is his, but also the grandchild of his enemy.

"How long do you intend to not say anything and suffer? You'll start to show, and then what?" Rosa's words tell me she knows exactly what my condition is. "Who is the father? Is that why you're worried?"

"Niko—Don Leone. He's the father."

She studies me like she's assessing the truth of my words. "If that is true, then telling him is the best option."

"He might kill me."

She purses her lips. "Oh, *Dio*, child. He isn't going to kill his child. However, when it gets out, there will be a target on you. There are countless people who'd love to take Don Leone's woman and his child."

"I'm not his wom—"

"You're going to need his protection." She pats me on the hand and smiles. "I'll bring you some tea to soothe your stomach."

"I just want to rest."

"Of course."

It takes a while, but soon, I'm asleep. Several hours later, I wake to someone coming into my room. For a moment, I'm worried it's Niko and he's going to be angry that I didn't tell him about the baby.

Instead, Rosa enters with a middle-aged woman. "This is Doctor Kaisen."

Dr. Kaisen extends her hand. "I'm an OBGYN. I understand you're pregnant."

God, no. I look at Rosa, feeling betrayed.

"Early pregnancy care is crucial to have a healthy baby. You want that, don't you?" Dr. Kaisen asks.

I nod and consent to her examining me. Once I pee on a stick, the pregnancy is confirmed, but she continues to ask questions and poke around. She exits the room for a minute and returns rolling in a machine.

"It sounds like you're close to twelve weeks, so let's do an ultrasound."

Giving in, I lie on the bed as she sets the machine up and runs the wand over my belly. She examines the screen and frowns, leaning closer to it as she focuses the wand on a section of my belly.

"Is something wrong?" Panic grows. For so long, I've been hiding this baby, trying not to think about it, but now, with the possibility of something wrong, I'm terrified to lose it. Until this moment, I didn't realize just how important the baby was to me.

The doctor turns her attention to me, her expression serious.

I press my hand over my belly. "What's wrong?"

18

NIKO

I hate having to leave the compound... to leave Elena. It's only been a few days, but I've come to look forward to our morning walks like a kid on Christmas morning. Her delight at the room I created for her makes me feel like a fucking superhero. Me! The man who killed his cousin and lives for revenge, a superhero. I find myself craving her more and more, not just her sublime body, but for this feeling. She makes something deep inside me ache, a yearning I can't afford. And for that, I resent her. I can't be distracted by her and by the emotions she evokes in me. They make me weak. Vulnerable. I can't afford that. Not now. Not ever.

The call from Liam telling me Lucia Fiori Conti is in New York is my excuse to leave. As much as I don't want to go, I'm relieved to leave to regain control of my life. I had Donovan find her and bring her to my office at the restaurant.

The drive from Long Island to Manhattan is a blur, as my mind is in a tug-of-war between concern for Elena and the anticipation of facing Lucia. I know I should focus on the latter. Emotions are liabilities, and Elena... she's becoming a liability.

"How is she?" I ask Donovan once I arrive. I meet him at the top of the stairs before heading down to meet Elena's older sister.

"She's like her sister on steroids." There's amusement in his voice, so I expect I'm going to be annoyed more than angry.

I head down with Donovan behind me. I enter a room off my office where I find a woman who has similar features as Elena tied to a chair, defiance etched into every line of her body. Her scowl could curdle milk, but it doesn't faze me.

"Lucia Fiori Conti, welcome back to New York. I'm sorry you won't be visiting your father—"

"My father can go to hell. Untie me and take me to my sister." Her words offer me some relief. Like Elena, Lucia doesn't seem to have any loyalty to her father.

I glance at Donovan who is leaning casually against the wall, his arms crossed, fighting to hide his amusement at the woman.

"Patience, Lucia. We have much to discuss before any family reunions can take place." I circle her like a predator. I like women with fire, but in this case, I need her to understand her situation. I have no qualms about disposing of her if she turns out to be a liability. Well... maybe a qualm about hurting Elena, but she'd never have to know.

"Talk, then. What do you want?" She is brazen.

I look over at Donovan again, noting the way his gaze lingers on her. Does he find her attractive? I study her, and she's definitely a Fiori, but Elena said she was more beautiful and charming than her. I don't see it. Lucia is pleasant to look at, but she's nothing like Elena.

"What are you looking at, toadie?" she sneers at Donovan who lets out a laugh.

"I can see why your father sent you away," I quip.

She rolls her eyes. "What is it about you men that keeps you stuck in the caveman era? Misogyny runs in your blood."

I arch a brow. "Those are big words for a woman tied up and wanting something from me."

She looks down, giving me the satisfaction of knowing she understands her situation. "I have no beef with you, *Il Soldato Della Morte*. All I want is my sister. In fact, I'm happy to thank you for saving her. I'll even pay for the trouble."

I grab an empty chair and sit in front of her. "Let's talk about your father, Giovanni Fiori." I note a subtle twitch in her jaw suggesting he brought as much pain to her as he had to me. Well, not as much, but suffering, nonetheless.

"Let's not," she snaps. "I'm here for Elena, not to discuss that man."

"You will not see Elena until you answer my questions." While I can see her contempt for her father, I can't dismiss that this is a ruse. Perhaps she's helping Giovanni. Maybe he'll bring her back into the fold if she helps him get to me. I can't rule anything out.

"Fine. What do you want to know? That he's an asshole? He's weak-minded?"

"Does he know you've come to New York?"

She purses her lips at me like I'm an idiot. "No. Surely, you know my situation. You're a fucking Don against my family."

I hear a snicker from Donovan. It has the effect of my wanting to slap Lucia for her disrespect but also for Donovan's finding humor in it.

I lean closer to her, making sure she understands the situation she's in. "I am more than a Don, Lucia. I'm *Il Soldato Della Morte*. I could end this all for you right here, right now, and no one would know. Elena will believe you're living in quiet solitude in Italy. Conti is so old, his dementia probably means he doesn't know you anyway. He won't miss you." I glance at Donovan, whose jaw tightens. He doesn't like me threatening her like that. Interesting.

"I was wrong. It's not caveman DNA, it's asshole DNA." She talks a big talk, but I see the fear in her eyes. "What do you want to know?"

"Does he know you're here?"

"No. Telling my dear old dad I was in New York would be my death sentence."

I sit back. "And yet, you're here."

"I told you. I've come for my sister." Her eyes soften slightly. "Please, Don Leone. Let me take her to Italy and keep her safe from my father and the Abates."

"Your father is a pussy, yet he's raised two women with grit and a little too much mouth."

She smirks.

"It must scare the shit out of him." I lean forward again. "I bet you could run the family better than him."

Her eyes flicker with surprise. "Whatever he feels, he has power. Power to get even."

"Is that why he sent you away? Was he getting even with you or someone else?"

She looks down again, and this time I see sadness. "What does this matter now?"

"Why did he try to give Elena to Romeo Abate?"

She shrugs. "Business, I imagine."

"He sells his daughter to keep his empire afloat?"

"Empire," she scoffs. "That's generous."

I glance at Donovan who, like me, is intrigued by her response. I know something is up with the Fiori Family, but not quite sure what. "Not an empire, then?"

"My father likes money and power and giving pain, but he sucks at managing it." She looks pointedly at me. "I have no qualms about your killing him. All I want is my sister. She's not made for this world. She's made for better."

My heart twists in my chest at her words. She's right. Elena is too good, too pure for the darkness of this world, and yet, I hate hearing that. Hearing that I'm not good enough for her. That my world, my life, what I can give her isn't enough. I can see that this life has made Lucia smarter, harder, and the same could happen to Elena. That would be a fucking shame.

"Please." Her voice shows the reverence and desperation that I usually demand. "Give her to me. Let me take Elena back to Italy."

I sit back and cross my arms, pretending to think about it. Would Elena rather go with Lucia? Of course. Would Elena be better off with Lucia? Probably. Would Elena be safer? That's debatable and the reason I decide to keep her with me.

"How much do you want for her?" She turns to Donovan. "Give me my purse, toadie."

Donovan's chuckle reverberates off the walls, the sound rich with mockery. "Sure thing, Princess."

I ignore him, my attention fixed on Lucia. "What price do you put on your sister's safety? How much is she worth to you?"

"More than anything you could comprehend," she retorts, her gaze challenging mine. "Tell me, Niko Leone, what's your price?"

Elena's face flashes in my mind—her soft laughter, the way morning light dances in her hair during our walks. Priceless is the answer.

Fucking hell. She shouldn't be mucking up my mind at a time like this. Why can't I focus on her real value as a pawn as a means to exact revenge? She is priceless, yes, but acknowledging that fact is dangerous.

"Then name it," Lucia presses, mistaking my silence for hesitation.

Refocused on the ultimate goal of revenge, I answer her. "The return of my dead mother and brother."

Understanding dawns on Lucia's face with a flicker of empathy. "Look, I'm sorry if my father took them from you, but that's not Elena's fault. Kill my father, if you have to—"

"Oh, I will. You can count on that."

"Elena shouldn't have to be a part of your plan. You don't need her. Let her go."

She's right, of course. While Elena could be a coup for me, the fact that she's fucking with my head and my heart is all the more reason to hand her over to Lucia and get her away from me so I can focus.

"She's mine." In this moment, I realize I've cast my die, and that's to keep Elena even as she could be my Achilles' heel, the distraction that ultimately causes my downfall.

Lucia rolls her eyes, I'm sure at my chauvinist comment. "She's not safe with you."

A cold, mirthless laugh escapes my lips. "You think you can protect her better than me, *Il Soldato Della Morte*?"

"Better than anyone here. She'll never be safe in New York." Her chin lifts, an act of sheer bravado.

I let out a breath to release the growing tension that has me wanting to shut Lucia up. "You're formidable, Mrs. Conti, but you have no power here."

"No, but I do... or my husband's family does... in Italy. My father wouldn't dare try for her there, and I can't imagine the Abates would bother. She should come home with me."

Finally, I lean forward, my elbows resting on my knees as I feign deep consideration. "She can't travel. She's ill." That's not a lie, necessarily. Elena continues to look tired and fragile, even after all I've tried to do. The morning walks. The room full of activities to find her passion. They should have chased away the demons eating away at her health.

Rosa's words echo in my head, a litany of concerns. "She's still not eating much, Don Leone. And the nausea..."

"Unwell?" Concern fills Lucia's tone, but then it turns cold, condescending "Is this how you protect what belongs to you? By letting her wither away under your watch?"

My hand reaches out and grips her chin. "Watch yourself." My anger at her isn't so much at her disrespect as at the accuracy of her words. I'm the one making Elena sick, stealing her vitality, her spirit. I'm the poison, and the antidote is to send her to Italy with her sister. The problem is, Elena is the antidote to the hole in my soul. How can I send that away?

I release her, gathering my composure. "Being here is suicide for you, Lucia. You think you can just waltz into New York and outsmart death?"

"Death has been breathing down my neck since the day I was born. I'm used to it. But Elena isn't. I won't let my parents win. You send her with me and you win too. You humiliate them—"

"I've already humiliated them."

She leans toward me. "I'm going to get her back. It's a promise. There's not a damned thing you or your toadie can do about it."

I glance at Donovan, who is still amused by this woman, but when he catches me looking at him, he schools his expression.

"Let's not pretend you'd fare any better in Italy," I counter. "Your power is limited to what your husband will allow and can provide. Giuseppe isn't well."

"But Luca is, and he'll protect her."

A picture starts to form. "So, you and Luca..."

She jerks. "No. God, is that all you think about, fucking and murder? Luca is his father's son. He'll protect me and Elena." She watches me for a moment and smirks. "Maybe Luca can marry her."

"Over my dead body." I don't realize how lethal my voice is until I hear Donovan clear his throat. When I look over at him, he's staring at me like I've grown a horn on my head.

"Nothing will stop me from trying."

As I stare at her, bound and yet unbroken, I feel a grudging respect for this woman who dares challenge me on my own turf.

"If you want to know about my father, I'll tell you everything. He's bad at business and Don Abate is propping him up. Is that what you want to know?"

The tension lessens slightly. "Explain. What do you mean by 'propping up'?"

She purses her lips, her gaze unwavering. "I'm not saying anything more unless you agree to give me Elena. At least take me to her. Let me see her."

I know why Elena was given to Romeo, but not the details. I consider that I can make a deal similar to the one I have with Elena. I can take Lucia into my fold and in return, get what I need to exact my revenge.

"Take you to her. Not give her to you."

She stares at me with hate. If she could fire lasers from her eyes, I'd be a pile of ash. "Fine."

I rise from the chair. "Untie her." I instruct Donovan without taking my eyes off Lucia.

Donovan moves behind her, flipping open his knife to cut the zip-ties. "I'm not sure it's a good idea to let her roam free." He leans forward, his lips close to her ear. "She's a wild one. Maybe we should keep her on a leash."

She jerks, giving him a hateful glare over her shoulder. "Toadie."

He laughs, unbothered by the disrespectful nickname. "I like her. She's got spunk."

I'm annoyed by whatever is going on. "If she wants to see Elena, she'll behave."

She stands, rubbing her wrists.

"Let's go. I'll take you to Elena, and on the way, you can tell me what you know."

"Fine."

"Keep an eye on her," I tell Donovan, though I know he needs no such instruction even on usual days, but especially now that he's taken with the mouthy woman.

"Always do." A smirk plays on his lips, but beneath the humor, I detect a desire for her to try something so he can enjoy the thrill of the chase. "Come on, Princess." Donovan escorts her out.

We ascend the steps and into the alley to my waiting SUV. Donovan drives while I sit in the front passenger seat and Lucia is in back. As we make our way through the city, my phone rings. Liam's name flashes on the caller ID.

"Liam." I answer.

"You told me to keep tabs on Kate Emerson."

"Yeah." God, another woman in Elena's life is causing me trouble. "Yes."

"She's been taken."

"Christ. Any idea who?" My mind races, flipping through the list of enemies, each capable of such a move. Or maybe it has nothing to do with my world and instead is related to her father or her being in a dangerous situation on her own. Hell, maybe she just went on vacation.

"Too early to say. But it's not random—has Fiori written all over it."

"Get your people on it. Meet me at the compound. We're on our way." I end the call, trying to decide what this means and if I can keep the news from Elena. No doubt, she'll blame me.

"Problem?" Donovan asks.

"Kate Emerson. Kidnapped. Probably by Fiori."

"My father doesn't traffic—"

"Kate is a friend of your sister. She was involved in your sister's plot to escape."

"God. Heaven help her." Lucia shakes her head, her expression sad. "Can you save her? Elena will crumble under guilt if she thinks her friend was hurt because of her."

"It will be taken care of." I turn to Donovan. "Liam will meet us at the compound, hopefully, with more information."

"If it is Fiori, he might call, use her as an exchange," Donovan says.

"That's not happening," Lucia quips. "If he won't give her to me, he's not going to give her to my father. She's dead for sure."

19

ELENA

The news from Doctor Kaisen shocks me. My mind is in a whirl as she explains and gives instructions. I'm told to lie down and rest as the doctor packs her things and leaves.

Rosa returns to check on me once the doctor is gone. The news is sinking in, and so are the ramifications.

"Rosa. You are not to speak of this to anyone. Especially not to Niko."

Her eyes widen, probably at the command in my tone.

"Don Leone—"

I straighten, lift my chin. "I said no one." I know that she'll need to choose Niko over me since Niko can fire her or worse, kill her. But I'm still exerting whatever control I have. Power rushes through me as I stare into her eyes, telling her that in no uncertain terms should she say anything. "It's not for you to speak of."

"Of course." Rosa bows her head, acquiescence mixed with resignation. "You should rest—"

"No. I'm going to my hobby room." I rise and head out of the room. I'm feeling surprisingly strong, confident. Once in my room, I lose myself in painting. I'm terrible at it, as I am at most things I've tried, but I enjoy it. The mix of colors. The control. I spend hours painting flowers, the scene outside, and I even make an attempt to paint Niko.

Hours later, as I'm cleaning my brushes, I hear staff running around. That can only mean one thing. Niko has returned. A thrill runs through me. It's strange since I wouldn't have seen him until dinner anyway, but knowing he'd been gone, I'd missed him. I wonder what he'd think of my painting of him. He'd probably offer to hire an instructor.

I leave the room, making my way to the foyer to greet him wondering how I'm going to tell him the news. A part of me still wonders if I should. I smooth my hand over my stomach, willing my nerves to settle.

The door opens and Niko, along with Donovan and another man, strides in, making a beeline to Niko's office.

"Niko," I say.

He doesn't look my way. He keeps walking, past the staff and me, disappearing with his men into his office. Resentment sparks inside me. Where is the man who took me on a walk this morning? Who generously created a room where I can indulge my interests? Not a single hello? Not even a glance my way. Were the last few days just a way to keep me compliant? A manipulation so I don't get in the way of his plans?

I step back, feeling rejected and stupid. But at least I know now that my news wouldn't mean anything to him. At least not anything good.

"Elena?"

I startle at the sound of my name, a familiar voice cutting through the fog of my indignation. Whirling around, my eyes meet my sister Lucia's.

"Luce!" I throw myself into her arms without a second thought, the relief flooding through me. "You're here? How?" She isn't restrained or being locked up. Does that mean Niko brought her for me?

"You've gotten so thin, Elena." Concern laces her words. "Are you sick?"

"I'm so happy to see you." I ignore her question. "Is he going to let me go with you?" I'd determined that fleeing to Lucia's side was a fantasy that would never come true, and yet here she is. I have bittersweet feelings about it now. To go with her means leaving Niko.

Lucia's hands find my shoulders. "We need to talk. Alone."

The gravity and urgency of her tone worry me. "We can go to my room." I lead her upstairs to my bedroom. We settle into the window seat. The scene looks perfect, two sisters confiding together in the brilliant sunlight filtering into the room. But in our world, there's no giggling and gossiping. Just comforting.

"What's wrong?"

"First, are you okay? Is he treating you well?"

I nod.

She cocks her head to the side. "Has he... you know—"

"Will he let me leave with you?" I ask, not wanting to discuss the physical relationship I have with Niko. She'd understand but likely not approve of how much I enjoy it. Crave it. How sometimes, I think about staying.

"Not yet."

I should feel disappointment, and maybe there is a little bit. If Niko's behavior the last few days was fake, just to keep me compliant, then I don't want to stay.

"I can be here for now, but of course, I have a home in Italy. I can't stay too long. He seems adamant that you're to stay with him." She studies me. "He says you're his. I'm sure it's just that fucked up male-dominance thing, but..."

"But what?"

"I don't know." She looks around the room. "Maybe he likes you."

I smile and her expression turns horrified. "Oh, no, Elena. You're not falling for him, are you? Even if he likes you, you're still not equal or respected. You're like a pet."

My smile falters. My instinct is to defend him, to tell her about the lovely walks each morning. The room he made for me. The way he touches me like I'm treasured. But she's right. It's all fake. He doesn't even kiss me. If he liked me, he'd kiss me, wouldn't he?

"It's good that he's treating you okay, but you're not out of danger. He's playing a very serious game, and I'm afraid you've been put into the middle of it. We need to be careful, act smart."

The nausea that had become my constant companion threatens to rise again, but I swallow it. Lucia is right. Caution is paramount. If only my heart would listen. If only it didn't yearn for the impossible, a life of my choosing with Niko and a family made of love.

The light outside has begun to fade, the warmth of the sun cooling. A metaphor for my life at the moment.

"At the same time, Elena... and I hate to say this, but I think right now, being here with Niko is your safest bet."

"I don't understand." Confusion fills me.

"Things have escalated is this idiotic feud."

"What are you talking about? What happened?" My mind is filled with questions. Possibilities of what could have led Niko to go to the city today. Had he killed my father? Romeo? Tiberius? Or had he simply humiliated them again?

Her gaze holds, and the intensity scares me. "Your friend Kate has been taken. They think it's Dad."

"Kate?" My voice cracks. "No. She's not a part of any of this."

"I'm sorry." Lucia puts her arm around me, holding me close. "Why would Dad do that? There's nothing she can give him."

"I don't know. I don't think Niko and his goons know, either. But for now, you need to stay put. Niko has the power to protect you."

"Protect me?" I scoffed as anger grew. "Or keep me his prisoner?"

"Sometimes, a cage can be a sanctuary."

"He promised me." Now I'm seething.

"Promised? Promised what?"

I shoot up from the window seat and rush out the door, down the stairs and to Niko's office. It's a fool's errand. It will quite possibly result in punishment, but I don't care.

I reach his office, the towering dark wood of the door cautioning me that I shouldn't try to penetrate his inner sanctum. But I'm too angry to heed the warning.

I knock. "Niko!"

I can hear the talking stop.

"Let me in." I pound again.

I hear laughter that I suspect is Donovan.

"Open up!" I yell out.

"Enough!" Niko's voice thunders, his displeasure laced with a threat.

Like an idiot, I don't heed it. "Open this door, Niko!"

There's a moment's hesitation before the door swings inward, revealing his form. His menacing stare tells me I'm walking on a fine edge.

"This had better be a matter of life and death."

"Yes, it is. Kate's life. You promised me—"

"Stop. I don't have time for this now." His words are a dismissal, but I don't accept it.

I push my way in. "Too bad. I'm not leaving until you hear what I have to say."

His men watch, and only then do I recognize that my actions are even more dangerous than I anticipated. I am disrespecting him in front of his men.

I turn to him, wondering if he's about to order Donovan to get rid of me. His expression is dark and yet also, there's a sense of surprise.

I decide to take advantage of the moment by pleading my case. "We made a deal. You promised to keep Lucia and Kate safe, and you've failed."

"Maybe I was wrong about her. She's got more spitfire—"

"Quiet," Niko cuts off Donovan.

"You're the Soldier of Death and yet you let someone slip by you and take Kate. Are you a liar or just inept?"

Donovan and the other man exchange a look of shock, their bodies rigid with discomfort. Niko's eyes narrow to a dangerous glint targeting me with fury.

"Are you done throwing your tantrum?" Niko's voice is deceptively calm, but I know better. I'm about to die.

My voice softens as I try to show more reverence. "I asked for one thing, Niko. I know you don't care about me, but at least I held up my part—"

"You don't know shit." He turns away, running his hands through his hair. When he turns back, he notices Donovan and the other man. "Leave us."

It seems to me the men practically run from the room in relief.

When the door closes, Niko's voice is low and calm, but the tension radiating off him is lethal. "As far as your friend, Liam is looking for her. He's FBI and working with her father."

Niko has a federal agent in his family?

"Second, I never promised I'd protect them."

"You did."

He shakes his head. "You asked me not to hurt them, and I haven't."

Was that right? I knew my first request was for him to not hurt them, but I thought I'd asked him to look out for them too.

"If you want to blame someone, blame your father. Or maybe it's the Abates. They're using your friend to bring you out of hiding, *cara mia*."

"I'm not hiding," I say, hating how he's trying to use his pet name for me. It makes me think of what Lucia said. I'm a pet to him. "I'm a prisoner."

He flinches as if I slapped him. Then he sneers. "Do you know the real reason you were to marry Romeo? You're payment for a debt. There's no business agreement. Your father handed you over to save his own skin. Better you to be tortured and killed than him."

This time, I'm the one who flinches. But then it occurs to me that there's no difference really between my being a deal in a partnership or a debt repayment.

"I took you, and now your father is back under Tiberius's thumb."

"I'm just a commodity to all of you."

He leans in closer to me, and I should be afraid, but mostly, I'm tired and defeated. I'm back to feeling like nothing.

"I have two bosses wanting to get their hands on you. Do you know what sort of torture that would be for me?"

"Yeah, right. Your little prize stolen from you. You'd just go kidnap the next—"

"Wrong!"

His voice is so loud, so booming, I take a step back.

He advances on me. "Believe what you want. But know this—I'll burn down the world before I let anything happen to you."

My heart pounds, heavy and erratic, as I try to make sense of his words. It sounds like I'm important to him. But I'm reminded that it's not about me. It's about how I can be used to humiliate his enemies.

"All in the name of getting your revenge."

His eyes flash with what I first take to be pain but quickly morphs into emptiness. A deadness. "Get out."

"Niko." I reach out for him, not understanding the guilt I feel.

"Don't." He pushes past me, exiting his office. "Donovan!"

I take a breath, working to figure out what just happened. Then I follow him out. He's heading to the front door.

"Niko."

He ignores me.

"Where are you going?"

"Elena." Lucia calls my name as she descends the last steps of the stairs. "Let him go. He can't save your friend unless you let him go."

I watch Niko exit the house, and something inside me shifts. Despite everything, part of me longs for him. Not his protection, but his love. Is he capable of that?

Lucia's arm comes around me. "He'll take care of it all. And when the dust settles, you can come with me to Italy."

I should be relieved by her assurance, but the turmoil inside me only intensifies.

I'll burn down the world before I let anything happen to you.

Does he feel something for me, or were those just the musings of a man possessed by power? I wonder if I've somehow just ruined something that could be real.

"Are you okay?" Lucia watches me.

My hands tremble as they slide over the growing swell of my abdomen.

Her brows lift. "Oh, God, Elena. Are you...?" Her question hangs in the air, as if she's too afraid to know the truth.

I nod. "With twins. He doesn't know."

20

NIKO

My chest burns with rage as I leave my office. Elena's defiance, her brazen challenge in front of my men, is enough to make me see red. In this life, such insolence is a death sentence, yet here I am, walking away. My men will question my authority. They'll think I'm weak. God damn her!

The memory of her standing there, chin lifted, eyes blazing with a fire that should have been extinguished by fear, replays in my mind. The worst part isn't just that she embarrassed me in front of my men. It's that I found it sexy. That is, until I revealed a part of myself and my feelings for her and she dismissed it like it was trash.

Her voice trails after me, but I don't look back. I can't afford to. If I catch sight of her again, I might do something foolish. Whether that's kill her or kiss her, I can't be sure.

I shove through the front door, hating what a pussy I'm becoming. I shouldn't want her—not like this, not when she challenges the very authority I've bled to establish. Yet, the infuriating woman rouses a part of me that craves her flame, even as it threatens to burn it all down.

God, why had I shown my hand? It was true that I'd destroy

anything and everything that tried to hurt her, but exposing that reality is a risk I can't afford.

My blood is simmering as I make my way to Liam who is leaning against his car, his attention on his phone.

He looks up, his eyes watching me carefully. "Hope you're not waiting on me to haul out a body." His voice is light, but there's an edge to it, as if he wouldn't be surprised if I'd killed Elena and needed him to deal with it.

"Fuck you."

Liam straightens. "Donovan handling the disposal?"

"I didn't kill her. I didn't even touch her." The memory of wanting to kiss those lips spewing fire my way flashes again. "Fucking hell."

"Oh. Well, good for you for showing restraint and recognizing that she's more valuable to you alive."

He holds the same opinion of me that Elena does. She's just a commodity. It hurts, and yet I know I need them to think that. It's better that I'm a fucking heartless, lethal asshole than a man in love.

The silence stretches between us. His gaze probes, looking for answers.

I fear he's going to see the truth so I say, "Have you found anything out yet?"

"I've got men going through surveillance cams." He cocks his head. "You sure you're alright?"

"Fine," I bite out.

The door to the house opens, and Donovan trots out with half a cookie in his hand and the other crumbling around his mouth.

"So, where's the body?" he asks as he shoves the last bit of cookie in his mouth. "Do I deliver the body to Fiori or Romeo? Or maybe Tiberius?"

The remark slices through me. They're right. The Soldier of Death would have snuffed her out without blinking, a swift retribution for the disrespect she showed me. I wonder how long before they realize why. How long can I hide it? The answer is to send her to Italy with her sister. Get her away from me. It's the only chance I have to save myself.

Liam gives a quick shake of his head as I narrow my eyes at Donovan.

"What?" he asks, looking between the two of us.

"Elena is alive and well," Liam reports.

"Oh... well... good. We can still use her to get those assholes."

I have an urge to grab Donovan and shove him against the car with my gun butted to his temple for suggesting that I use Elena. It's ridiculous, of course, because I am using her.

"Any news on the friend?" Donovan says, oblivious to my murderous thoughts.

"Nothing specific."

"You'd have thought I'd have had a call from Giovanni by now that he took her." That thought is gnawing at me. What is the point of taking Kate? Yes, it would cause Elena to do anything to help her friend, but he knows Elena has no power here. And I don't give a shit about her friend. There's no one Giovanni could take who would have me giving Elena back to him. Well, maybe my sister Aria, but I'd just find a way to kill Giovanni and save my sister.

"Could've been Romeo. Or Tiberius," Donovan suggests.

"Even then, they'd call, right? Why the silence?" I shake my head. "Any chance this has nothing to do with us? Maybe it's something against her dad."

"No. The chief hasn't gotten a call, either." Liam gives me a pointed look. "There are rumors about his being in Giovanni's pocket."

"Really?" both Donovan and I say in surprise.

"So maybe it's that," Donovan says. "He wants something from the chief."

"Keep working on it. In the meantime, let's return to the city."

"Little lady chasing you out of your own home?" Donovan is joking, but his words cut too close to the truth. I can't be around Elena. Not right now.

"Careful, Niko has his want-to-kill-somebody expression," Liam warns.

Donovan's brow furrows. He looks like he's going to ask something, but then he apparently thinks better of it. Good, because Liam is right and I don't want to kill Donovan.

He shrugs. "Want me to stay behind? Make sure they don't do anything stupid?"

It's an odd question since I have plenty of men here to make sure Elena and her sister stay put. And if Lucia were smart, she'd convinced Elena that their safety right now is in my hands.

But then I think back to Donovan's behavior around Lucia. "She's married to a Don, you know."

Donovan gives me an expression of confusion, like he doesn't know what I'm insinuating.

Liam laughs. "Even you're smart enough not to turn a Don's wife into one of your whores."

He frowns. "Fuck off."

In the end, I decide maybe I will leave Donovan behind. Not because he has a strange attraction to Elena's sister, but because they both know where Donovan sits in my Family. It's possible the two women would attempt to get around my other men, but they won't fuck with Donovan.

"Fine. Stay. Keep them out of trouble."

"Absolutely. I'm getting more cookies." He heads back to the house.

"What's that about?" Liam asks as we watch Donovan disappear through the door.

"Not sure. I'm going to the penthouse. Let me know if you discover anything."

"Will do." Liam gets in his car and leaves.

I stand feeling torn. I should go in and let Elena know I'm leaving, right? But I push away the feeling of obligation or good manners. She's my prize, not my wife. Considering the disrespect she showed me moments ago, she doesn't deserve my consideration.

Since Donovan is staying, I drive myself, deciding the solitude in the SUV will be nice. The drive is uneventful for driving from Long Island to Manhattan. For a moment, I consider going down to New Jersey to check on business there. Hell, maybe I'll be lucky and walk in on another virgin auction. It would be nice to clip the tether Elena has on me in the pussy of another woman. If only that would work. Fucking hell.

Instead, I go to my office in the basement of the pizzeria. It's time to stop fucking around and decide my next move. The sooner things end for Giovanni and Tiberius, the sooner I can send Elena on her way. She'll be happy to go to Italy, and while I'm not sure Giuseppe Conti can keep her safe, I feel fairly certain that his son, Luca, can.

Maybe Luca can marry her. Lucia's words come back to me. My fingers grip the steering wheel as I imagine Luca Conti fucking Elena as his wife. I can't stand the idea even as I know it's a good solution to my problem. How do I excise Elena from my soul?

I spend the evening buried in business. It almost works. I almost forget about Elena.

As I head to my penthouse, I call Liam. "Any updates on Emerson?"

"Not where Fiori is concerned."

"What about the Abates? I can't help but think this move is something Romeo would do, although how did he know about Kate?"

"Already working on that."

"Keep me posted." When I hang up, Elena's tirade comes back to me. It was the first time I'd seen that much life and fire in her. It made me hard just thinking of it, even as it pissed me off. She should know better than to be so insolent. At the same time, it showed her capability for loyalty. What would it be like if she showed that level of care toward me?

I shake my head. *Don't go there, Leone.*

When I get to my place, Maria greets me. I haven't let her know I was returning, but my staff knows to be ready for anything.

"I'm going up to my room."

"Do you need dinner?"

"I ate at the restaurant." I go upstairs. Once in my room, I shed my clothes and hop in the shower to wash away the day. With my head under the spray, I hope to clear out the tangled mess Elena has made of my mind. It's time to get back to my mission. I need to stop fucking around.

I grab the soap and wash, and the memory of Elena stepping out of the shower... this shower... returns. Her skin is wet and soft and warm. My cock immediately responds. Fucking hell.

I continue to clean up, hoping that by ignoring my dick, he'll settle down. But of course, he doesn't. Pissed off, I grip him hard, nearly painfully. I imagine Elena in my office at the compound. She's accusing me of being inept, but this time, I don't stand there and take it. This time, I teach her a lesson.

I strip her bare and bend her over my desk, her sexy heart-shaped ass exposed. I spank her hard. She lets out a sound that's between a yelp and mewl. My handprint is red against her ass. My cock hardens even more.

"You think you can disrespect me and not pay?" I hiss in her ear.

"No."

"Damn right." I drive my dick into her from behind with such force my desk shifts. She cries out. "Don't think that because I've been nice that I'll put up with your mouth."

At the thought of her mouth, I withdraw and push her to her knees. "Here's your penance." I thrust forward, my cock disappearing into her mouth. She looks up at me with those large, dark eyes of hers. She's taking her punishment, and yet I still see a fire of defiance. It makes me hotter, harder, and soon, I'm stroking my dick like a teenage boy who is discovering masturbation for the first time. The tension in my balls coils, and with another stroke, I coat the shower tiles with my cum.

I press both my hands against the stall wall, catching my breath. As my world rights again, I realize I don't feel better. I don't feel vindicated. I feel empty and like a fucking fool. It's at that moment that I realize Elena is going to be my undoing.

21

ELENA

"Let's go back upstairs." Lucia leads me up to my room.

I'm feeling a little numb. I know Niko is angry at me. To be honest, I don't know what came over me. I know better than to talk to him like that. I should be grateful he hasn't sent Donovan in to kill me. Doing so could easily fit into his need for revenge. Not that my father or Romeo would care if I were dead.

"Is everything okay?" Rosa asks as we enter my room. "Can I get you anything?"

"No. Thank you."

When she leaves, I flop back on the bed.

Lucia sits next to me. "I don't even know where to start."

"About what?" God, I'm so tired.

"You're pregnant. God, Elena." She looks at me. "Are you okay? What are you planning?"

I let out a nervous laugh. "I don't know."

"Is it Niko's?"

I frown. Why does everyone ask that? Who else would I have been with? "Yes."

"Fucking bastard. I wonder if Luca would kill him—"

"It's not like that."

She stares at me like she's trying to read my mind. "What is going on with you two?"

I suppose now is the time to come clean and tell her everything. "I sold myself to him."

Her brows shoot up. "What?"

I explain the auction and how I planned to use the money to escape but how our father had found it.

She gapes. "I don't even know what to say."

Is she judging me? Feeling like she is, I rise from the bed and move to the window seat. "It seemed like a small price to pay for freedom."

Her expression softens. "I suppose you're right when you are staring at a lifetime with Romeo Abate, but God." Her brow furrows. "So, wait... how did you end up here?"

"Niko crashed the wedding. I think he was planning on killing Dad and Tiberius, but in the end, he kidnapped me. I don't think he knew it was me until he put me in the trunk of his car."

"Why didn't he kill them?" The venom in her voice tells me she wishes he had.

"You know how it is. He wants his revenge, and a big part of that is humiliation." I think of Kate. "I shouldn't have tried to escape. I should have just done my duty and not gone to school. It didn't matter, but now Kate is missing."

"Don't say that." Lucia sits next to me. "It's not wrong to want to be able to live your own life. And you couldn't have known all this would happen."

"Couldn't I? I know how the men in this world think. Eye for an eye. Women are possessions." My stomach turns over, but it has nothing to do with the pregnancy. "Oh, God, do you think whoever took her touched her?"

Lucia puts her arm around me. "You can't think about that. Let's hope that Niko and his men can find her."

"One of his men is in the FBI."

"Really? Well, that's good. He can help too." For a moment, we sit in silence. "What are you planning about the babies?"

I sigh. "I don't know. I was planning to tell him tonight, but now... I don't know."

"You're going to have a hard time keeping it a secret unless he lets you go."

"I know."

She studies me. "What is the deal with you two?"

"Just like I told you. I sold my virginity to him and later, he kidnapped me. I made a deal with him to keep you and Kate safe." I think of our walks and the room he made for me. What does it all mean? Was it just a way to placate me, or did it mean something?

There's a knock on the door and Rosa enters. "Dinner is ready."

"Can we eat up here?" I ask.

"You're expected downstairs."

"Tell Don—"

I pat my sister's hand to stop her from going off on Rosa. "Let's go eat downstairs."

She purses her lips at me.

"I need to show respect."

"Idiotic world." She stands, and we go downstairs together.

When we enter the dining room, Donovan is sitting at the table, cutting a steak.

"Don Leone lets his dog eat at the table?" Lucia says.

"Luce!" It's bad enough what I did earlier in Niko's office. Lucia doesn't have to anger his enforcer. Then it hits me, Niko isn't here. Donovan is. Is this my last meal?

He smirks at Lucia. "Can you eat with that mouth or just spew garbage?"

"Surely, we can eat in your room," she says to me.

He shakes his head. "Have a seat, Ladies."

We sit as far away from him as possible. His smug smile tells me he knows I'm afraid.

"I have to tell you, Princess, I'm surprised I'm not out back digging a hole in Niko's mother's garden."

"What's wrong with you?" Lucia snaps.

He arches a brow at her. My impression is he's more amused than offended.

"I swear, you goons are the most insecure men on the earth."

I place my hand on Lucia's. "Maybe let's not upset him."

"Insecure? Do tell me more."

"Why else would you live your life picking on people smaller than you? You feel small, and threatening us makes you feel big. It's disgusting."

"What's disgusting is how Elena spoke to Niko. Do you have a death wish, Princess? You must. Why else would you call him inept?"

Lucia's head snaps to me, her mouth gaping again. "You did what?"

I shrug. "He said he'd protect you and Kate. I thought he failed. My anger got the best of me."

Donovan sips his wine. "Niko showed more restraint than I've ever seen." He studies me. "He must like you." The waggle of his brow tells me he means Niko must like me in bed.

"You're crass," Lucia says.

He shrugs. A servant enters carrying two plates, giving one to me and the other to Lucia.

"Where is Niko?" I ask, picking up my fork in an attempt to eat. My stomach is in knots, but for once, it isn't about the pregnancy.

"He went back to the city."

"Without telling me?"

Donovan's head cocks to the side, his expression one of curiosity. "You're not his wife, Princess. He doesn't have to report to you."

I nod quickly. "Yes, of course, it's just that—"

"You should be glad he left. He could change his mind about you."

Fear trickles down my spine. Have I signed my death warrant?

"Asshole." Lucia shakes her head. "Do you have anything useful to say? What about her friend? Any word on that?"

Donovan shakes his head. "Nope. Now eat up, Princess. Rumor has it you don't eat enough."

. . .

LATER THAT NIGHT, I lay in bed. Lucia is sleeping next to me, but I'm wide awake. I'm thinking about Niko. How mad is he? Is he so mad that he won't help Kate as payback to me? Will he return here for me? When he does, will it be to kill me?

I quietly get up and head downstairs in search of Donovan. I find him in the kitchen eating pie.

"If you're thinking of escaping—"

"Can I call Niko?"

His head jerks back as if he didn't expect that. "Why?"

"To apologize."

He smirks. "You can grovel and beg for your life when—"

"Please, Donovan." I hope that using his name will bring some humanity to this exchange.

"What's in it for me?" He puts his plate in the sink, then leans against the counter.

"What do you want?"

"What's the deal with your sister?"

"Lucia?"

He nods.

"Ah... she's married to a Don in Italy."

"Sold, right?"

I frown. "I guess you could put it like that. Why?"

He shrugs. "Just curious."

"Can I call Niko?"

He sighs. "You know, I shouldn't call him for something so frivolous."

"I'm not frivolous." I'm tired of being made to feel small.

"But I'll make an exception this time. But if he's pissed about it..." He doesn't finish the sentence. He doesn't have to. I know what can happen after making a powerful man angry.

He pulls out his phone and pokes the screen. "Hey, Boss... Yeah, all is quiet except someone here wants to talk to you." There is quiet for a moment, and Donovan smirks. "Yeah, she's here."

He hands the phone to me, covering the receiver with his hand. "You must have my boss by the balls."

I take the phone and watch as Donovan leaves the kitchen. I bring the phone to my ear. "Niko?"

"Is something wrong?" His voice is cool, distant.

"No. I just wanted to apologize for the way I acted this afternoon. I was upset and scared for Kate, but I should have acted better."

"Fire burns, *cara mia*."

I'm not sure what he means. Is it a threat?

"You need to learn to control yours."

I sit in the chair at the table. "I know." Admitting that kills something inside me. I don't want to control who I am. "I'm sorry."

"Are you and your sister planning your escape?"

I don't know why, but his question makes me laugh. "No. I know that for now, I'm safest with you. Luce thinks so too." I pause, realizing just how ungrateful he must think I am. "Thank you for bringing her to me. I've really missed her."

The line is quiet for a moment. "Do you miss me?"

I'm surprised by his question. "Yes." I want to ask him the same, but I don't. Niko doesn't miss me.

"Do you miss me or my touch, *cara mia*?"

My cheeks heat. "Can it be both?"

"Yes."

"Will you be coming back?"

"Soon. In the meantime, you'll have to fantasize about me. I have yet to teach you how to touch yourself."

I bite my lip as everything else in my body heats up. "I imagine it still won't be as good."

"No. It won't. I know firsthand as I jacked off to you when I arrived home."

I gasp, the titillation growing as I imagine him stroking himself.

"You like that, don't you?"

"Yes. I wish I could watch."

There is a pause on his end. "Do you, now?"

Something is shifting here. The question hints at a change. Now, versus before. Willing partner versus captive. I feel it deep inside me, but I'm probably reading it wrong. After all, we're talking about sex, not love or commitment.

There is a sound like someone has joined Niko wherever he is.

"I have to go. Dream of me, won't you?"

I smile. "Good night." I hang up the phone and go looking for Donovan. He's in Niko's office. "Thank you." I set his phone on the desk.

"All made up?" He looks at it. "Just making sure you didn't make any other calls."

"No. I only did that once."

Donovan laughs. "I swear, Princess, you have nine lives." He studies me. "Makes me think there's more going on between you and Niko."

I can't speak for Niko, but I doubt there's more going on with him. "I'm just a valuable pawn." Saying it out loud is a reminder of my reality, forcing me to dismiss the warm feelings I had earlier. I'm a means to an end. Niko is being nice as captors go, but it doesn't mean anything. Eventually, he'll be done with me. I can only hope and pray that when he is, I'll be able to go to Italy with Lucia and not end up in a hole dug by Donovan in Niko's mother's garden.

22

NIKO

Surprise doesn't begin to express my feelings about Elena's call. Did I think she'd understand the potential ramifications of her actions? Yes. Did I believe she could regret them? Sure, insofar that she didn't want to die. But in the call, I heard authenticity in her apology. She showed the respect I required. So why the fuck did it bother me when it sounded like all life had gone out from her voice when I told her she needed to control her fire?

As the call continued, the connection felt different, almost as if she were giving herself to me. Not just sexually, but emotionally. I wasn't her captor and she wasn't a woman holding up her end of a deal. We were two people connected by something else. I thought back to my efforts to encourage her to stay. How her choosing me would be the ultimate revenge against her father. My plan could be working... too well, maybe, because I thought less and less about her being my source of revenge and more and more about keeping her with me because I wanted her. It scared the shit out of me.

But I didn't become as powerful as I am by being stupid. I had to consider that Elena had other motives for calling me. When I hang up with her, I wait several minutes and call Donovan.

"Hey, Boss. Nice chat with the princess?"

"Did you leave her alone like I asked?"

"Yeah. I don't want to listen to your phone sex—"

"Did you check the call log?"

He sighs, probably because I'm not joining in on his joke. "Yeah, yeah. She didn't make any other calls. No texts. No emails. No morse code. Nothing."

A wave of relief and emotion fills my chest. She really did just want to talk to me. "Okay. Thanks."

"Sure thing. Anything new on the friend?"

"No. But I want you with me tomorrow. It's time to end this thing."

"I'll leave first thing. I can leave Mikey here. I think he has a crush on the princess."

"Tell him hands off."

"He knows. We all know. She's yours." He's quiet for a moment. "Is it something more than just her being Fiori's daughter?"

The question I've been dreading is here. "Meet me at the restaurant. Early."

"Will do."

The next morning, I stride into my basement office and Donovan is already there.

"Picked up coffee and bagels." He nods to my desk.

"Thanks. Everything is quiet at the compound?"

"Yep. The two princesses were sleeping."

"Good. I went through reports last night looking at Fiori. He has shit for successors."

"His girls could do it," Donovan quips. "Luce could make any of them shit their pants."

"What is your fascination... never mind. That's not an option. Abate will feel entitled to it and take it from Fiori's bastard or whoever tries to take over."

"Unless you take it."

I nod.

"But you'll be fighting Tiberius on two fronts since he's trying to encroach on you."

"But if we have Fiori's daughters, we can get his family on board with us, don't you think?"

Donovan shrugs. "Depends. If they're on our side, maybe. I'm not sure how loyal they'll be." He laughs. "God, if Luce were here she'd be screaming about misogyny."

I frown. "Focus. We need a plan to go into Fiori's area. Do we have any other allies in there besides Elena and maybe Lucia?"

"Yeah. Maybe."

"Work on it."

I spend the morning working and the afternoon visiting a few of my establishments in the city. One of the clubs has had a big write-up in the paper, so patronage and profits are up. Good. It's always easier to launder through a business that is doing well on its own.

I'm heading back to meet with Donovan when my phone rings with a call from him.

"I just got word that Romeo's circling like a shark that's scented blood."

"Where?"

Donovan names one of the clubs in Atlantic City.

"I'll meet you there."

"Already on my way."

I poke the button to call Liam. "Any word on the girl?"

"She's not at any of Abate's usual holding spots. None of the warehouses."

I think about that. Is it possible she's just lying low? "Romeo's sniffing around. I'm heading down to Jersey to head him off."

"Think Romeo's looking for a sit-down?" Liam asks the question I'm wondering about.

"Maybe. If he has the girl."

There's a pause. "I've still got a few ideas. I'll be in touch."

"If you find her, let me know ASAP."

"Will do."

I'm pulling in back of the club when Liam calls. "I think I've found her. That stupid ass has her at his place."

"What?" That makes no sense. "Do you suppose he's operating on his own? Without Tiberius's knowledge?"

"Who knows? That guy is several cards short of a deck."

"Extract her. Put her somewhere safe. Where's her father in this?"

"I haven't updated him."

"Don't. Keep as much of this to yourself as you can. Perhaps let her know that it's in her best interest to forget who took her and why."

"I can try."

"Call me when it's done." The line goes dead. I sit for a moment, gathering my thoughts. I need to be hyper alert if Romeo is lurking. If this is about Elena's friend, I hope to have the upper hand at any time.

I step out of my SUV, looking around. A few of my men nod to me and I nod back.

Donovan opens the back door and steps out to me. "That motherfucker is in the club. He's got mush for brains but balls the size of Everest."

"That's not a good combo."

"He'll eventually end up dead, for sure." Donovan holds the door as I walk into the club. The baseline of music thumps hard, reverberating through my chest. I don't like loud. It's too hard to hear danger. But it's a club. Its patrons expect deafening music.

"He's in VIP. He's been searched. He didn't try to bring anything in," Donovan says loudly to be heard over the pounding music.

I search the club as I make my way to the VIP area. Just because Romeo isn't packing a weapon, doesn't mean someone else who works for him isn't.

In the VIP area, I find Romeo with a woman in his lap. When he sees me, he sneers and pushes her away.

"I hope you bought her drink. It's the least she deserves for having you paw at her." I take a seat across from him while Donovan lingers back. I know he's watching for trouble.

"Mr. Leone, your usual?" a server asks.

"Yes. One for my guest too. You're alright with scotch, aren't you?"

When the server leaves, I say, "Are you looking to change sides, or do you have a death wish?"

"You took something that's mine. I want it back."

I feign thinking about it even though I know he's talking about Elena. "Is that so?" I lean back, crossing one leg over the other. "I can't imagine what that is."

The server brings two scotches and sets them in front of us.

"Cut the bullshit. You stole my wife."

I laugh. "Your fiancée, and I have to say, Romeo, she didn't fight me very hard when I took her. I get the feeling she wasn't looking forward to wedded bliss with you."

"Fuck off, Leone."

"This is my club." I sip my drink and then lean forward, getting annoyed by the situation. "You'd be wise to respect me in my own establishment."

He sneers. "Until my father takes it from you."

I sit back. "He can try."

Romeo watches me for a moment. His sneer relaxes, and I know he's about to change tactics. "I'm feeling generous. I'm proposing an exchange."

I laugh. "I can't imagine what you have that I'd want."

"Elena's friend."

I shrug. "Don't know her."

"She's Doug Emerson's daughter."

I whistle. "Kidnapped the police chief's daughter. You do have balls, Abate. Why not keep her? Use her to your advantage."

"Because she's not what I want." His eyes narrow, a hint of impatience coloring his tone. "I want what's mine, Leone."

"Ah." I let out a low chuckle, stalling as I wait for Liam's call and thinking what to do if the call doesn't come in time. "Why? What's so special about her?" I glance at Donovan, making sure there's nothing going on I need to be concerned about. I'm not sure this isn't some sort of trick on Romeo's part. I can see his father sending him to the lion's den as part of a plan to take me out.

"She's mine."

I give him a sympathetic look. "Let's not pretend Elena is the same innocent flower who stood at the altar, shall we?" I smile full of smugness. "She's changed."

Romeo's jaw tightens, his eyes flaring with the kind of anger that speaks more of wounded pride than concern for the woman he claims is his.

"Since when do you care about her, anyway? There has to be other ways for Fiori to settle his debts with your father."

Romeo's eyes flash with surprise before he schools his expression back to a sneer. "No one walks into my place and takes what's mine."

"Your 'place' seems to be a matter of perspective." I tap a finger against the glass, willing Liam to call me. "And possessions... well, they have a way of slipping through the fingers if you don't adequately protect them."

"You think you're fucking invincible, but you're not, Leone."

His comment has me on edge thinking there's something else going on here. But I don't want him to know his words impact me, so I shrug. "If you're looking for love ever after, perhaps your daddy can find you another one. Or perhaps consider not brutalizing or killing the women in your life. That can put a damper on a relationship."

"What do you know about women?"

"I know they're more enjoyable to fuck when they're alive."

"I should kill you."

"Funny. I was thinking the same about you." My gaze doesn't waver from his, daring him to make a move. We sit silent, tense, as the dance of wills goes on.

My phone shatters the silence. Without breaking eye contact, I bring my phone to my ear. "Yes."

"Good news." Liam's voice sends relief through me. "He really was dumb enough to keep the girl at his own place. The one in his daddy's building. We faked a fire emergency, and she's out. Safe and sound."

I'm an expert at poker faces, but I can't stop the smirk that slides across my face. "Excellent. Thank you." I end the call and rise from my chair, ready to end this meeting. "Seems your grip isn't as tight as you thought, Romeo." I down the last of my drink and button my coat. "No deal."

His face contorts. "I'll get her back, Leone, and when I do, I'll rip her to shreds."

A red haze consumes me. In an instant, I've grabbed him, hauled him from his chair, and pinned him to the wall. In the dim, loud club, no one notices.

"You touch her, and I'll cut your dick off one inch at a time and make you eat it."

I've caught him off guard, but his composure returns when I release him.

"Get the fuck out of my club."

"This isn't over." He points a finger at me until his phone rings.

"Does he know we could pop him now and get rid of him, never to be found?" Donovan asks in the corner.

"If he did, he wouldn't be in here." I watch him, on his call. He glances at me, and I know that the caller has just told him that another woman has been snatched from his grip.

"Son of a—" He hurls his phone toward the wall.

"Once again, Romeo, I've taken something from you."

"You think you've won?"

"Think?" I laugh. "I know, but this doesn't have to be a complete humiliation for you. You're not getting Elena. But I'm a reasonable guy. I'm willing to give you something else. What would you like?"

"You're delusional."

"Maybe. But you give me Giovanni Fiori, and I'll give you whatever you want, except for Elena."

The hate in his eyes is lethal. "You think you can buy me?"

"Everyone has a price. Even you."

"Go to hell, Leone."

"Eventually, I'm sure. But I'll see your father and Fiori there first."

His hands fist at his sides. Behind me, Donovan steps forward in case Romeo decides to try something. "I tried to handle this like a gentleman, but you're making it impossible."

"You're a comedian. Can I hire you?" I laugh again. "Civil? You wouldn't know civility if it kissed you on the mouth."

Romeo's jaw clenches. "It's war, then. I'll ruin you, and then I'll kill you."

"Get in line. There's nothing left to take, Abate. All I care about is watching your father and Giovanni Fiori crumble to dust." The lie rolls off my tongue, smooth as silk. But deep down, where no one can see, I know the truth. Despite my best effort to never care about anyone, Elena has wormed her way into my soul.

"Then what do you care about the woman?"

"I only care because you do. And Fiori does. She's just a pawn I'm going to use to bring you all down." The words taste like ash in my mouth. How is it that a man with no morals can feel like a fucking asshole for suggesting a woman is nothing more than a means to an end? Yet here I am, feeling like an asshole. If someone said to me about Elena what I just said, I'd shoot him. Or at least put him in a whole lot of hurt.

"It's not over." He pushes past me.

Donovan starts to move, but I nod for him to let Romeo go.

"That was fun," Donovan says.

I nod, but I'm still feeling unsettled. Is it because my feelings for Elena are fucking me up, or am I missing something about this visit?

A scream tears through the club. Donovan turns to leave the area. "Get to the car, Boss."

It's his job to watch my back, but I'm not one to run. With adrenaline flooding my system, I follow him to the main area of the club. Several bangs ring out. Shots. Some motherfucker is shooting in my club. How did they get a gun in?

The dance floor erupts into a mass of hysteria, bodies colliding and stumbling to reach the door. Goddammit. Someone is going to get trampled and killed.

"Lock it down!" My voice cuts through the panic. My men spring into organized action amid the disorder. I don't want to scare my customers, but there's no way I'm going to let Romeo and his men out of my club alive. My hand instinctively goes to my side, gripping the cold steel, ready to take Romeo out and send him in a body bag to his father.

I push through the throng of people, my senses heightened, every sound and movement amplified. I exit the club through a side door, hurrying to catch up to Romeo and his goons. A sharp pain pierces my shoulder blade. I turn, my hand shooting out to grip the neck of the person behind me.

His eyes widen like he didn't expect me to respond. I look down to see the knife in his. I grab it with my tree hand, and my gaze holds his as I squeeze his larynx. He's clearly new at this, and I sort of feel sorry for him, but not enough to let him go. I thrust the knife in and upward into his gut. Then I let him drop as I race to the front of the club. Headlights flash as two cars peel out of the parking lot.

"Boss!" Donovan rushes up beside me. "You're hit."

"The guy there tried to stab me." I'm pissed. "Follow them."

Donovan nods and rushes off. I don't expect to hear from him until he's killed them.

I stand alone for a moment, the aftermath vibrating through me. It was a trap. It's bad enough that Romeo got through me, but now I have serious cleanup and coverup to do. Fortunately, shootings in clubs occur often enough these days that cops don't automatically think organized crime. Still, it's no secret who I am.

I enter the club, thankful that my men are already soothing the crowd with free booze and cleaning up the mess. I let one of them know about the guy outside, and then I go to the back of the club, grabbing a drink on the way and calling Liam.

"Jesus. Is he dead?" Liam asks of Romeo.

"Donovan is after them. I need cleanup."

"Yeah, yeah. I'll take care of it."

My shoulder hurts like hell. "I'm going to see Doc."

"What? Did you get hit?"

"Knife to the back... or shoulder. It's nothing."

He's quiet. "That's a little too close for comfort."

He's telling me. "I'm fine. I'm going to head to the compound tonight. I don't want to be around when the police arrive." I need to get going as there is no doubt that their arrival is imminent.

When the call ends, I leave and head to Doc's, a retired doctor my father had brought into the business. He stitched and patched my wound without a word. I left a large wad of money and made my way back to Long Island. My foot pressed harder on the pedal than usual, eager to return home.

Home. Since when have I thought about any of my places as home?

I scrape my hand over my face knowing the answer. Hating the answer. How had this heartless man grown a heart that could feel something beyond hate? That could long for something beyond revenge?

Agitation courses through me. Abate got to me. Elena got to me. Both are leading me around by my fucking dick. I'm distracted. Reactive. It has to stop. I need to take control.

By the time I arrive back at the compound, my mind is clear. My intention set. Fiori and Tiberius's time on this earth is coming to a close. But first, I'm claiming Elena. There will be no going to live with her sister. No wandering around the world looking for herself. She is mine. She can try to fight me on it, but she'll lose. Her place is with me. When this is said and done, she'll be by my side, the queen of my empire.

23

ELENA

I 'm in bed but again unable to sleep when the door to my room bursts open.

"Get up."

I sit up, startled.

Lucia, sleeping next to me, does too. "What are you doing?" She moves to block me.

"I said get up." Niko looks like the devil himself in the dark, silhouetted by the moon's glow around him. His expression is fierce, and I feel like I should be afraid, but I'm not.

I move to get out of bed.

Lucia grips my arm. "No. She stays with me. That's our deal."

He scowls. "The Fiori women are either liars or have terrible memories." His attention turns to me. "Get up, or I'll drag you from the bed myself."

I move again, but Lucia holds me firmly in place. "You can't. Whatever she did, she was naïve."

"I don't think he's going to kill me," I say to her as I extricate my arm. "Are you?"

His eyes are hard. "No."

I get out of bed and walk toward him.

"Elena." Lucia's voice is filled with desperation and worry.

"I'll be fine." I reach him and look up into stormy eyes.

His hand cups my cheek. "You shouldn't be so trusting of me, *cara mia*."

A sliver of fear slides down my spine, but I try to hide it. For some reason, I feel like if I show fear, it will upset him. Like he needs my trust.

"You won't hurt me." I tilt my head and kiss his palm. He jerks it away like I'd burned him.

"Come with me." He strides out of the room, and I go to follow.

Lucia scrambles from the bed to follow me, but as we exit, another man steps into the doorway.

"Three's company," he says to her. He pushes her into the room and shuts the door.

"Let me out. Elena!" She pounds on the door.

"It's okay," I call back. Then I hope she stops because while I don't believe Niko plans to hurt me physically, I can't be sure he won't hurt her.

He leads me to the next room, the one I remember Rosa telling me was his room. He tugs me through the door and slams it.

"Strip."

I sigh. It's not that I don't want to have sex, but I hoped for something more. I hoped he might have missed me. Maybe we'd have a sweet moment, and I could tell him about the babies. But looking at him, I see no tenderness. No sweetness. Just tortured need.

He goes to a closet. Opening it, he comes out with a bottle of something potent.

"You have a bar in your room?" I ask as I pull my night shirt off.

"Saves me time going downstairs." He takes a swig and then sets the bottle down and unbuttons his shirt. As he takes it off, he turns his back and I see a bandage.

"Niko? What happened?" I rush over to him, but he moves away.

"Your fiancé tried to set me up."

"Fiancé? Romeo? Really?" Was Romeo that stupid? "Why?" I wonder if this is about Kate.

"He wanted to exchange your friend for you." His eyes bore down on me. "That would never happen, Elena."

My heart drops. "So... you just left her with him?" I move away from him, reminded of the monster he can be.

His hand grabs my wrist and pulls me toward him. "Don't ever shirk away from me. There's something that you need to hear. You're mine now."

My eyes close, realizing that I'm still just a commodity. I tug my hand away. "I understand that."

He lets me go as he takes another drink from his bottle. "She's safe. Liam was able to find her."

"He's the FBI man?"

He nods.

Relief floods me. I wish I could go to her, at the very least call her and apologize, make sure she's okay, but I know that's impossible.

"Get in bed," he commands as he undoes his belt.

Dutifully, I pull the sheets down and get into bed. He doesn't waste any time. He's over me, his large body pressing me into the bed. There's a part of me that wants to resist. Another is fascinated by the way he seems possessed by his desire for me.

"This is your room from now on, do you understand?"

"With you?"

"Yes. You're mine." As if to highlight the point, he thrusts inside me, the power of it causing me to cry out and gasp. "Elena." His voice is tortured as he pulls my hands over my head, his fingers entwining with mine. "*Mine.*" Then his lips are on mine, and sensations and emotions sweep through me. I've never kissed a man before, so I don't know what I should have expected, but this isn't it. His kiss is hard, rough, demanding. Not soft and sweet like I see on TV. Not that it's bad, it's just not what I'd expected.

He starts moving, his lips drawing down my neck, sucking my nipple. All thought leaves, replaced by sensation over sensation. My body feels like it's lighting up from the inside out. Warmth. Electricity. Pleasure. All swirling together, coalescing in my center.

He pushes back to his knees, his large hands gripping my hips, lifting them as he drives into me, again and again. My fingers grip the sheets, holding on tightly as I near destruction.

"Say it," he demands.

I can't think, much less understand what he means.

"Say it, dammit, Elena. Tell me you're mine." He releases me, lies over me again, his face just inches from mine as he continues to move in and out of me. "Say it."

"I'm yours."

His head rears back, and he thrusts hard, grinding against me. The movement shoots me to the stars. The most delicious flood of pleasure slides through me. He continues to move, drawing out the pleasure. Finally, he stops, rolling off me.

We lie side by side, our breaths coming in heaving gasps. When his breath has turned to normal, he turns toward me.

"From now on, you stay here. With me, do you understand? I'll provide for all your needs. All your enjoyments. You'll be happy here, *cara mia*."

I finally understand what he's saying. He's claiming me. At first, I want to grab on to him and tell him that I'm his. The problem is that he's taking me whether I want him to or not. It's still not my choice.

"What if I don't want that?"

His eyes darken, and he jerks away, leaving the bed. Naked, he stalks over to the bottle, taking another long drink.

"You'd rather have Romeo? Used as a debt payment by your father."

"You know I don't. I want freedom to make my own decisions."

"Freedom," he sneers. "You know what freedom will get you, Elena? A grave. Do you really think you could walk out of here and live without a care in the world? There is no place, not even with your sister, that you'll be safe. Not without my protection. I've given you more than any man would, and you toss it away. I'm not good enough for you, is that it?"

"No. It's not about you—"

"No. I guess not."

"Niko." I get out of bed, wrapping the sheet around me. "Do you really just want to take me, not caring what I want? Against my will? Wouldn't you rather be with someone who chooses you?"

His jaw tightens. "You won't choose me. You don't want this life."

He's right. All the moments I've been vacillating, considering changing my mind, have been because I do care for him, but I could never give myself over as his property. I'd lose respect for myself.

"I want to make my own choices."

"What will it take for you to choose me?"

His words make my heart ache. He turns away, and I'm sure he's wishing he didn't reveal so much.

"I don't know," I say.

He goes to the bathroom. I consider following him but then decide he needs time. When he returns, he gets dressed.

"What are you doing?"

He says nothing, so I wait. When he's finally dressed, he looks at me sitting on the bed. "Fine. You're free. For right now, of course, you need to stay here. If you leave here, your father or the Abates or some other family will take you, and I promise you, Elena, they won't be as good to you as I've been. But when this is done, your father and Tiberius are dead, and Romeo too, then you can go to Italy with your sister. I'll offer whatever support the Contis need to keep you safe."

My heart is thundering in my chest. I want to leap into his arms. Again, I want to tell him I'm going to stay, but I can't.

"Just know that even there, you'll be guarded. You won't be able to move about the real people as you hope. The truth is, you can't live without the threat of other Families."

"I could if I changed my name."

His eyes close, and I get the feeling he was hoping I'd choose his protection over the Contis'. When he opens them, the emotion I thought I saw before is gone. His expression is empty.

"I'll ask Liam about that." He rolls his shoulders. "Until then, you stay here." He goes to the door.

"Where are you going?"

"I have work to do. I'll be going back to New York tomorrow, and I'll stay there."

I move to him, wanting to touch him. He tenses, so I keep my hands to myself.

"Can I come to see you?"

He shakes his head. "Not unless you change your mind." His gaze rakes over my body as if he's taking one last look at me. He turns, leaving the room.

I should go after him. But no, I'm on the verge of having what I want. But the babies...

God. I sink down on the bed, paralyzed with doubt and confusion. I don't want to live in the world Niko lives in. But I'm pretty sure I don't want to live in a world without him.

24

ELENA

Freedom.

It's right there for the taking. Sitting on Niko's bed, I catch my reflection in the mirror across the room, the curve of my belly barely visible beneath the loose fabric of my night shirt. If I take him up on the offer, he won't know about the twins. The twins won't know about him. The idea of my babies growing up in the violent, suffocating world Niko lives in should make this decision a no-brainer, and yet, my heart breaks.

Niko wants me to stay in his room, but I'm compelled to let Lucia know that I'm okay. Besides, the room feels lonely, sad without him. I step into the hallway, noting that the guard who was there earlier is gone. I guess Niko only wanted him there to prevent Lucia from disturbing us.

I make my way to the room.

Lucia rushes to me when I enter. "Oh, my God, Elena. Are you okay?"

"I'm fine. Really."

"What did he do to you?" Her gaze scans me as if she's looking for signs of trauma. "Did he touch you?"

I sigh and sit on the window seat. "Yes, but not in the way you think. Or at least, not in a way that I didn't want."

Her brow arches. "You like it when he touches you?"

I guess sex with her husband isn't as nice as it is for me with Niko. "I do." Maybe I shouldn't admit that. The truth is, there is much I like about being here with Niko, including the sex. I like his company on our walks. I like how he worries about my health. I appreciate that he wants me to find my interests.

I look over at her as she sits on the window seat with me. "He said he'd let me go."

She blinks. "What's the catch?"

"Only that I have to wait until it's safe."

She rolls her eyes. "You'll never be safe—"

"When this thing with Romeo and his family is done. He said I could go with you. He'd make sure it was all clear with the Contis."

Lucia's hand takes mine as her eyes light up. "We'll be together."

I nod, smiling back but not feeling it deep in my heart.

"Oh, it will be so wonderful. You'll love it there. The countryside is so beautiful. The area is walled, so there is a place to walk. The babies will have room to run and play." She stops and looks at me. "Does that mean you're not telling him about the twins?"

I shift uncomfortably. "I don't know how I can and still be let go." The words feel so wrong.

She squeezes my hand in reassurance. "I'm sure it will be fine. Niko Leone doesn't want kids. They'll just be a liability to him."

If it gets back to him that I've had twins, he'll suspect they're his, but I can't worry about that right now.

"Imagine it, Elena." Lucia looks wistful. "We can spend our days together raising the twins. We'll be safe. Giuseppe already agreed to accept you into the family, and I know Luca will take you under his protection as well. Maybe you and he could marry. He could be the father of your children. It would keep them safe from anything Dad or the Abates might try. Or Niko."

My stomach recoils. A fortified villa in Italy. A Don accepting me into the family. Under their protection. A marriage for family stability and safety, not love. Having someone other than Niko by my side, raising our children. It feels so wrong. It also feels too familiar. Going to Italy with Lucia means moving from one gilded cage to another.

"Is something wrong?"

I stare at her. "It's not freedom. It's the same prison, just a new location."

She frowns. "It's not like that. I mean, yes, we have to be careful. It's the world we live in. But Giuseppe is kind—"

"I'm sure he is. But it doesn't change the fact that we're commodities. Pawns."

"There's nothing we can do to change that. That is the curse of being born to the parents we have. But at least we'll be pawns together."

I should be happy about that. I've missed my sister so much. But it doesn't feel like enough. Guilt grips me because I know it will hurt her.

"Niko told me he'd give me a chance at a new life. A new identity, if I preferred."

Lucia stills. "New identity?"

"It would mean complete freedom." I let the words hang between us, heavy with the weight of their implications.

"From everything?"

I nod.

"Even from me?" The vulnerability in her question undoes me. "Because if you do that, you'll have to cut us all out of your life. You know that, right?"

"Lucia, I—" My throat tightens. "I don't want to lose you."

"Then don't. How would you survive, anyway? What job could you get that will support two children? How will you live? You'll be completely alone. Is that what freedom means to you? Being alone?"

Her words plant seeds of doubt in my dream. I'd been trying to learn a skill but never finished my studies. I don't know the first thing about finding a place to live or even paying bills. Kate was helping me figure that out. But she couldn't help me anymore if I decided on total freedom. Neither could Lucia. My world feels very small to me, but having to leave the few people I love behind makes it seem like the world would be even smaller. Darker. Lonelier.

"Freedom isn't just about being untethered, Elena. It's also about choosing who you'll have in your life." Her gaze holds mine.

Choosing. The power in that word roots me to the spot. That's what I want. Choice. The ability to make my own decisions.

What will it take for you to choose me?

Niko's words reverberate through my mind. I've been offered what I want, but instead of elation, I'm feeling confused and guilty.

THAT NIGHT, sleep doesn't come easily. I toss and turn in the bed next to my sister. If Niko realizes I'm not in his room, he might get upset. But I can't bring myself to sleep in his bed with him not there.

My thoughts are a jumbled mess. Freedom. Family. Twins. Niko. Choice. If I stay with Lucia or Niko, my kids are condemned to the same life I want to escape. But to leave means losing Lucia and Niko. It means being alone in a world that I know I don't yet have the skills to master.

In the morning, I wake, feeling as lost as the night before. I rise and dress while Lucia still sleeps. I make my way downstairs. Niko said he didn't want to see me unless I chose him, and while I can't do that, I'm compelled to see him.

I reach his office, but it's empty.

"He left."

I turn to see a young man walking through the foyer. I remember seeing him the day Niko had Donovan bring me to his office to confront me over calling Lucia.

He's eating a Danish with a cup of coffee. "Back to New York."

I nod. "Thank you."

"I'm Mikey." He gives me a lopsided smile. I get the impression he's new to Niko's family. He can't be older than me, but he has an enthusiasm, a friendliness that hasn't yet been squashed by hate or violence.

"Elena."

"I know."

"It's good to meet you. I... ah... I'm going for a walk." I wonder if he'll let me. Niko promised me freedom when the danger left, but that didn't mean I was free within the confines of his protection.

"Sure thing. It's nice out this morning."

I weave through the gardens, the dew-kissed petals of Niko's mother's roses looking like they're from a garden magazine. My fingers brush against the velvet texture of a bloom, careful to avoid the thorns. Beauty and danger mixed together, much like life with Niko.

I continue on the path, the gravel crunching underfoot. An ache has settled in my chest. I yearn for something more than the confines of Mafia life. For being more than a means to an end in a war. But leaving all this? Leaving Niko? For the first time, I feel connected to something. Like there's a tether linking me to him. Is it just the babies or something more? And if I break that tether, then what?

You'll be completely alone. Is that what freedom means to you? Being alone?

Lucia's words echo in my mind as they had all night long. Alone. I don't want to be alone, either.

I wrap my arms around myself, trying to comfort my babies, myself, from the world's cold truths. Niko's world is steeped in shadows, but within those shadows, he's offered me slivers of light. His tenderness, a contrast to his reputation, nurtures parts of me that have never been cared for before.

I pause on the path, looking out over the bay as the water glistens under the morning sun. Niko might be the Don of a ruthless empire, but he's also the man who listened to my dreams, who promised a life beyond comfort, to include caring and respect. Would that be enough for me? Could I stay in this cage and find fulfillment in Niko's kindness and support?

I glance around the garden, imagining two children running and laughing, being chased by Niko. I see them indulging in their passions and interests, supported by their father. And I know without a doubt that while they could be a target, no one else would be able to offer the protection and love that Niko and I could give them together.

My chest fills with emotion, a yearning for the image to be real. Like that, the choice is made. For better or worse, I choose this life with Niko. He's given me what I've wanted. Caring. Support. Respect. Family in the true sense of the word. And the freedom to make a choice.

I hurry back to the house, finding Mikey back in the kitchen chatting with the cook. "Can you take me to Niko?"

He arches a brow.

"I need to see him. Can you drive me to the city?"

"Does he know you're coming? He didn't say anything about bringing you—"

"I want to surprise him."

He grins. "I thought there was something going on between you two. Some guys think it's just Niko getting his rocks off, but I knew it had to be more."

"Can you take me?"

"Yeah, sure. I just need—"

"As soon as possible. I just need to get a few things." I didn't have any clothes at Niko's in Manhattan, so I'd need to pack ones he'd arranged for me to have here.

"Twenty minutes?"

I nodded. "Thank you, Mikey." My heart races with urgency to be near Niko, the excitement building. It is a similar feeling I had when I got my passport. It represented freedom. But now, I understand that it represented life. That's what I found with Niko. Life.

I rush up to my room. Rosa is already there with breakfast.

"Can you pack me a bag, Rosa? I'm going to the city."

"What? Now?" Lucia asks from where she's having coffee at the table.

I nod. "Yes. I need to see Niko."

Her brow arches. "Why?" Her expression is tense, worried.

I go to her, taking her hand. "I'm not asking for a new identity. I'm going to stay here with him."

"What? Why? You said you wanted freedom."

I nod. "I want to be happy and be me, and he gives me that."

"He kidnapped—"

"You're fond of Giuseppe, aren't you? Even though you were essentially sold to him."

She purses her lips at me. "Yes, but—"

"Don Leone is fond of Ms. Fiori," Rosa states as she gathers clothes.

"He told you that?" I ask.

"No. But I know him. He's a good person. Yes, he can be hard, but he knows love. His mother lavished him with it. Ah, how he adored her. It was her death that killed something inside him. Something that has bloomed again with you here."

I look at Lucia. "Dad killed his mother."

Lucia let out a breath. "I know."

"His brother too," Rosa said. "Niko had plans in life, but sometimes, life puts you on a new path. His has been revenge for so long. Now, with you, maybe he can find peace and love."

I smile, hoping she's right.

"I'm coming with you," Lucia says. "Where you go, I go. That's the deal I made with him."

We pack and meet Mikey in the foyer. He helps us with our bags and then we're off. The drive toward Manhattan is lovely. The sky is blue. The sun is shining. It's like a sign from God that I'm doing the right thing.

Mikey keeps his eyes fixed ahead, hands steady on the wheel. Lucia hums a song in Italian, and it reminds me that she must speak Italian all the time when she's home. While we have Italian heritage, the language wasn't spoken in our home. I wonder if it was hard for her to learn.

I lean my head back, closing my eyes as I sort through my head what to say to Niko and hoping he's happy about my choice. A smile teases my lips. Yes, I've made the right choice. Everything is going to be fine. Perfect.

My body is jerked to the side as a loud crashing sound fills the vehicle. My world spins. Glass shatters. Screams escape my mouth. The car finally comes to a stop against a roadside barrier.

"Oh, my God. Are you okay?" I reach over to Lucia, who is slumped in the seat next to me. "Mikey."

A man approaches the driver's side door, and I'm relieved that help is on the way. The man opens the driver's side door and, lifting a gun, shoots Mikey in the head.

I scream until he turns the gun on me. "Quiet."

Two other men appear. "Let's go. Now!"

The three men pull me and Lucia, now awake but groggy, from the vehicle and put us into another car pulled up behind where we crashed.

"Put these on." One of the men puts a cloth sack over my head. Another zip-ties my hands and ankles.

I reach out next to me, hoping to find Lucia. Her shoulder bumps into mine, and we lean into each other.

What is happening? Who is doing this to us? Is it our father? Or is it Romeo? Didn't Niko tell me he had a run-in with him yesterday?

"Let us go," Lucia yells, apparently coming fully out of the stupor she'd been in. "Do you know who we are? You're so fucked—"

"Shut up or I'll shut you up."

"You know you're dead, right? You—" Lucia goes silent.

"God, shut the fuck up."

"Lucia?"

"You too, bitch."

A burst of pain echoes through my head, and then darkness.

When the light comes back, I'm in a room. The silence is deafening and scary. I take in the room. I'm still bound, but this time to a bed. It feels like an altar of sacrifice.

The door creaks open, and my fear ratchets up as I wait to see who has me. A figure enters, and while on one hand I'm not surprised, on the other, I'm disappointed. He grabs a chair and sits next to the bed.

He runs a finger down my cheek as if to comfort me, but instead it sends a chill down my spine. I stare at my father, wondering how he can be so cruel to his own daughter.

"Has Leone made you his whore, Elena?"

My eyes narrow into slits, the only weapons I have left.

A part of me wants to tell him everything. How I sold my virginity so that even if I had married Romeo, he wasn't getting a virgin. I want to tell him how Niko touched me and how much I liked it. Instead, I simply narrow my eyes at my father. I'm so filled with hate at this man. Not just for what he has done to me, but to Niko as well.

A slap comes swiftly, stinging my flesh. It makes me wonder if he read my mind. "You will never see the light of day again," he hisses, each word laced with venom.

"You've cost me money, power." He leans back, studying the impact of his words. "You were meant to settle a debt, but Leone ruined you, and now you're worthless."

I am not worthless. I run it like a mantra. I know I have value. Niko helped me see that.

"Lucky for us, Romeo still wants you. Not as his wife, of course. You're too tainted for that. He's coming to collect what's rightfully his."

My father rises from the chair. "He promised me that he'd be easy on you when you married, but now that you're ruined, well... he has free rein. I suspect Tiberius will want some of you too."

Bile rises at the thought of those men touching me.

"Give him what they want and you should be okay."

Should be okay? Romeo's reputation comes to me, and I know that I'm likely dead.

My father's footsteps retreat, leaving me alone. How much time do I have? Despair fills me. And guilt that I'd never told Niko how I felt about him. How he'll never know about the twins. I pull on my restraints. I rack my brain for a path of escape. The room is empty of solutions.

All I can do is wait.

25

NIKO

I sit in my office, staring at my computer but not seeing the numbers that tell me how my business is doing.

What the fuck did I do?

I offered Elena her freedom. I gave her permission to leave me. It's a mistake. I know it by the way my chest aches. How I can't seem to breathe. She is mine. She belongs to me.

Elena has ruined me, turned me inside out. Before her, I took what I wanted without question, ruled my kingdom with an iron fist. What other people wanted didn't matter. Now look at me. Pathetic. Weak. All because of one woman. A woman I couldn't stand to see unhappy. In a moment of weakness, I gave her what she wanted. Deep down, I think I hoped she'd turn it down. That old adage about if you love something, set it free and if it comes back it's yours or is meant to be, or something. But she didn't come back. She is choosing to go free.

I open the drawer in my desk and pull out a bottle of scotch, pouring several fingers, and down it, hoping it will burn away the emptiness and pain. But of course, it doesn't. Elena has become more than my prize, a pawn in a sick game of revenge. I want her by my side, and I know I can make that happen. I can prevent her from leaving. I can force her to stay with me. But like a sucker, what I want is for her to choose to stay. For her to look at me as hers, not just as her captor.

"Fucking hell." The words come out in a growl, a release of frustration that echoes through the room.

There's nothing I can do, so I make an effort to shift my mind to the darker path in front of me. Revenge. Giovanni Fiori's name burns my thoughts, Tiberius Abate's along with him. And now, Romeo, a name added to the list after his botched attempt on my life last night at my own club. They will pay for their transgressions with their lives.

Once they're gone, Elena will have no reason to stay, no looming danger to bind her to my side. I laugh bitterly. Doing nothing, I keep her with me for her safety. But succeeding, I lose her.

My phone buzzes, and I glance at the screen. Liam. "Talk," I bark into the receiver.

"We've got a problem. One of your cars was in an accident just outside of Queens. Witnesses said three men killed the driver and took two women."

My heart stops in my chest. "Who was driving? Who did they take?" Why the hell was one of my cars in Queens?

"Mikey was driving. And..." Liam hesitates. "The descriptions sound like Elena and Lucia."

The world goes black at the edges of my vision. Elena. Taken from me. Rage boils in my veins, white-hot and venomous. I will slaughter them. I will rip their hearts from their chests and crush them in my fist. They have no idea what's coming for them.

"Tell me you know who these fucking bastards are? Fiori men? Romeo?"

"Still working on that."

"We need to find them. I'll burn this city down if I have to."

"Let me see what more I can find out. I'll be in touch." The phone goes dead.

Elena. Lucia. They were supposed to be safe at the compound. Why had they left it? Why had Mikey taken them? Was he part of this? I shake my head. Liam said he was shot. I feel bad about that. Mikey was a good kid. I had high hopes for him.

I call the compound and demand to know what is going on.

"Elena wanted to see you." Rosa's voice quavers. She knows I can be lethal, even to those who work for me. I hadn't had to be like that in some time. Once everyone realized my cousin was gone and anyone who supported him was dead, they all came around. I'm a benevolent boss when I have the loyalty and respect I deserve, so no one has tested me in years. So what the fuck went wrong?

"Why? She could have called? Why didn't anyone check with me?"

"Elena... she... she left no room for question. She's the mistress of the house."

I close my eyes. My staff could see too that Elena was a part of my world. Not the greater Mafia world, but mine. With me.

"Where were they going?"

"I... I think the penthouse. I don't know. I'm sorry—"

"I've got to go." I hang up wondering what was so important that Elena had to come to the city to tell me. Was she planning on staying? Or did she intend to take me up on my offer to set her free?

Next, I dial Donovan's number. I don't wait for a hello. "Elena and Lucia have been taken. Mikey is dead."

"What the fuck? How?"

"Apparently, they were coming to the city. I don't know the details. Liam is seeing what he can find, but I need to know, Donovan, who is behind this."

"Romeo? It has to be after last night. I'll see what I can learn."

"I'm going to pay Tiberius a visit. Make him give up Romeo or Giovanni."

"Alone? Are you out of your mind? You can't get them back if you're dead."

"I'll kill him before he kills me." I hang up and storm out of my office. I oust my driver from the car, opting to drive myself. I don't know where Tiberius is for sure, but I know he has a titty bar he likes to do business in.

I arrive, and the extra security outside tells me he's here. I leave my gun in the car knowing I won't be able to gain entry with it. Two of his goons near Tiberius's table still try to stop me, but one loses several teeth before hitting the ground, and the other probably won't walk right ever again.

"Enough," Tiberius booms as other men step in to help. "Let the Boy King through."

I sit across from him, the stench of his cigar and arrogance grating on my nerves, "Where's Elena?"

He laughs. "I've always liked that about you. No pretense. No small talk. Just to the point. Why is the girl so important?"

I wonder if he can tell too that Elena is more than a pawn in our game. That she means something to me. If so, she's in greater danger.

I go with my original intent when I took her. "Her father took something from me once. You know how it is. An eye for an eye."

He smirks around his cigar. "Yes, I do know. Eye for eye. You took what belonged to my son."

"There are plenty of other women for him. You and I both know that Romeo doesn't give a fuck about her specifically. Let me keep her and you can have Giovanni repay his debt some other way."

He snorts. "Giovanni has nothing else."

"Then join me and we can take him down. Split his territory. But the woman stays with me."

He sighs and flicks his cigar. "There's no splitting—"

"Fine. Take it. Just tell me where Elena is, and I'll help you bring him down."

"I don't need your help. And what makes you think I know where she is?"

"Because you have Giovanni's thumb up your ass, and if it isn't him, it's Romeo, who does all his thinking with his dick." I narrow my eyes at him. "Did you know he came into my club? Tried to have me killed." I shake my head. "I doubt it. It was such a dumb plan. I know you're smarter than that."

Tiberius has a look of distaste that I know is for his son. "Romeo."

He exhales the smoke from the cigar. "The boy has never been anything but a disappointment."

"Then it should be no loss when I put a bullet between his eyes." The words hang in the room, a promise I intend to keep.

"Ah, but what kind of father would I be then?" His chuckle is dry, hollow.

"Romeo's a liability to your business, and you know it." I lean forward, feeling like I'm making headway. I have no intention of working with the man, but if I can have him on my side for a moment, I'll get Elena back and then kill them all. "He's reckless, weak. And his next mistake could be your downfall."

"Perhaps," he concedes. A smirk curls his lips. "Little King, you have some nerve coming into my house and demanding things, threatening my son."

"Your goons took something of mine and I want it back. That's all. We can do this easy. Civilized."

His smile turns sinister. "Romeo has plans for her, and so do I. Our desires differ... but they will both be sated."

A primal growl rumbles in my chest, my vision tinting red with deadly fury. For a moment, I consider beating him to a bloody pulp right here and now. I could probably kill him before his men killed me. But no. I can't die before finding Elena. Tiberius's suffering can wait. Right now, she's all that matters.

"You've just signed your death warrant. Romeo and Giovanni's too."

He surveys me with a predator's gaze, assessing whether to strike or to bide his time. "Your threats are wind, Niko." He puffs on his cigar and then blows the smoke at me. Then he laughs. "Giovanni should have killed you too."

"I know you were a part of my brother and mother's deaths. Giovanni couldn't do it on his own."

He shrugs. "Only your brother. I always liked your mom. But Giovanni... well... I don't think he ever got over her choosing your father over him."

I scoff, hiding the sickness I feel at the idea of Giovanni ever touching my mother. "We know it wasn't her choice."

"Your mother was a sweet woman. The type who knew her place and made those around her to want to make her happy. Your grandfather gave her the choice. Admittedly, he was disappointed as your father was just a *capo*. I think in the end, he wished he'd forced her to marry Giovanni as Giovanni took everything from him. Your mother's family is now all dead because of him."

I wasn't aware of all this, but now isn't the time to process it. "You were still a part of it. I'm going to make you pay, but first, you will talk."

He laughs. "I'm getting bored, Boy King."

I know I'm not going to get anything from him. Staying here and arguing only makes him feel more powerful over me.

"Enjoy that cigar and have a lap dance, Tiberius," I say, standing up. "Enjoy it now because soon, you'll be dead."

I stride out of the bar. I'm just out the door when my phone rings. Donovan.

"Any news?"

"Yeah, Boss. I've found Lucia, but Elena isn't here."

"Fuck. Bring her to me. At the office."

I RUSH BACK to the office. As I step through the doorway, I see Lucia, her normally fierce demeanor replaced by agitation as Donovan hovers over her like an overprotective hawk.

"Drink this. It will soothe your nerves."

"You're the one on my nerves." But she takes the drink that I suspect is from my scotch bottle.

I don't have time to make sure she's okay. My focus, my priority, is Elena. "What happened?"

She glances up at me. "Elena wanted to come to the city. She said she had to see you."

I remember Rosa saying that Elena was clear on what she wanted, and the staff indulged her. I thought of my mother and what Tiberius had said about her being sweet in a way that had people enamored. That was my Elena.

"Then what happened?"

"It's all a blur. We were in the car and... someone hit us, I think. I don't know. All of a sudden, we were out of control. I think I was knocked out, but when I came to, three men showed up. One killed our driver, and then they took us. I tried to fight—"

"I bet you fought like hell." Donovan's voice holds pride.

"They'd covered our heads, but I guess they didn't like me yelling and hit me. When I came to, I was restrained and duct taped on my mouth. The hood was off so I could see, but Elena wasn't there."

"I figured this could be Giovanni wanting her back. The accident was near Queens, so I asked my informants about places Giovanni has in Queens. We found her in one of his safe houses there."

"Good work," I acknowledge, though my mind races ahead, plotting our next move. "Was he there?"

"No. No one is there now that we've taken care of the goons who were guarding Luce."

Luce? I realized it must be his nickname for her. "Arrange to have her taken to the penthouse. She'll be safe there, but let's double security just in case. Maybe pass a little extra to officers Dobbins and Gray to patrol."

"Maybe I should take her," Donovan says, glancing at Lucia. "She could still be a target."

Donovan put his hand on Lucia's shoulder, and I'm not sure if he's trying to comfort her or claim her. I've got that feeling again like Donovan likes this woman. This is why love is bad.

"I need you with me. Your men are capable." My voice is a low growl, brooking no argument. I need him to help me get Elena back, not to babysit her sister.

He nods, but he's not happy. Sorry, buddy, but I don't give a fuck. He can be with Lucia later once Elena is safe.

"Luce." He says her name as he helps her up.

"You will find Elena, right?"

I nod.

"And you'll make those assholes pay?" Her voice quavers with fear for her sister, but also with the rage of vengeance that I also feel.

"I promise."

I watch the door swing shut behind them and pick up my phone to call Liam.

"I've checked on the friend, Kate, just to make sure she hasn't been tangled in all this again."

"Need you here, Liam. We need to end this damn war." A part of me thinks I should have gone with my original plan and killed Tiberius and Giovanni in the church. If I had, my vengeance would be complete and I wouldn't be feeling like my world was going to end with Elena not in it.

"Give me twenty." The phone call ends, and I sit at my desk, scraping my hands over my face. I'm so fucking tired.

Donovan returns. "She's on her way." He leans against the door frame, arms crossed over his chest. He's not happy with me, but he's a good soldier. He'll do what I ask. Besides, I imagine Lucia would rather he be with me to get his sister back.

"Liam is on his way. We need to figure out where Giovanni would have taken her. He separated them for a reason."

"Do you think he's trying to pay the debt again? Maybe he's taken her to Romeo."

God, I can't even think about that. About what Romeo would do to her.

"All ideas on the table. Call everyone in. I want someone raiding each and every property Giovanni owns or visits. Romeo too."

Donovan and I are making a list when Liam strides in. "Anything new?"

"We've got Lucia. She was at a Fiori safehouse, but Elena wasn't with her," I inform him. "We need people in every location Giovanni even passes. All of them. Romeo too in case Giovanni is trying to pay the debt." I look pointedly at Liam. "People are dying tonight, Liam. You have to decide which side you're going to be on tonight. Mine or the FBI's?"

He smirks. "Aren't I always on your side?" He looks at our list. "Giovanni will likely keep her close."

"Until the exchange, if that's what he's doing," Donovan says.

The image of Elena frightened, perhaps hurt, sears on my brain. I can't let that happen.

"It's what he's doing. Tiberius was adamant that Elena was his and Romeo's."

Liam and Donovan look at me in surprise.

Donovan shakes his head. "Tiberius too? Father and son sharing a fuck—"

I grip Donovan's shirt. "Careful."

He nods his understanding and glances at Liam. They have to know that there's more to this than getting back a prize, a pawn. But I can't think about that now.

"If Giovanni is giving her to Romeo, where would he take her?" Liam asks.

"He won't be dumb enough to take her to his place like he did with the friend."

"Kate. Her name is Kate."

Donovan and I look at Liam, wondering why that's important.

"He's right. It's too obvious, even for Romeo," I say.

"Rumor is that he has a hideaway where he does all his kink. Upper West Side."

Kink. Jesus. How am I going to survive this? "Would he really take her there? That's a nice residential area. People will notice. Hear screams." Liam winces, knowing that I don't need to hear about the torture Romeo likely has in store for Elena.

"Again, rumor says that's where those two missing women were right before they went missing," Donovan says.

Kink. I think of the word again. "He'll take her there. He'll want to degrade her to get back at me."

"Alright. How do you want to do this?" Donovan asks.

"What if we're wrong?" Liam adds.

"Donovan, organize all the men among the locations on this list.

All of them are to be scouted, invaded if necessary. I'm taking Romeo's hideaway of hell."

"Let me get this organized and I'll go with you," Donovan says, not waiting for me to answer before he leaves to talk to my men.

"I'm with you too. You never know, an FBI agent could be helpful."

"Thank you." My gratitude for him grows.

"Look, it's none of my business, but this thing with Elena—"

"You're right, it's not your business. But if we fail..." Pain lances through me, nearly bringing me to my knees.

Liam puts his hand on my shoulder. "We won't fail."

God, I hope he's right.

26

ELENA

Terror paralyzes me. I sit on the bed, leaning against an ornate headboard with depictions of sexual acts carved into it. My legs and wrists are zip-tied. My mouth is covered with duct tape. I could possibly get up and break the ties. I could search the room for a weapon, but I'm frozen in place. I don't even dare remove the tape over my mouth.

I take in the room. Din of sin is what comes to mind. The bed is dripped in red satin sheets. The walls are adorned with paintings that blur the line between eroticism and violence. In one spot, there are chains with manacles like in a medieval dungeon. On a table, I see items that I suspect are for sex and torture. This is what is waiting for me when Romeo arrives.

I listen but hear nothing. There's no sunlight. No sound. Is that on purpose? Is this room designed to not be detected? Fear weaves through me again. I have to find a way to survive this. Not just for me but for the babies inside me. By now, Niko must know I'm missing. He'll search for me, I know. Even if he doesn't care for me anymore after my rejection of him last night, he won't tolerate anyone taking something from him. For the first time, I'm glad to be a pawn.

The door opens, and I realize how heavy and thick it is. I can scream and yell, and no one will hear. Romeo enters the room, his smile as sinister as the devil's own. He strides toward me, his every step oozing the confidence of a predator who has cornered its prey.

"Finally, you're mine, Elena," he purrs. I recoil from the sound of him. The sight of him. "You know, had you married me like you should have, you wouldn't know about this place. About the things I do here. I'd have been nicer to you, treated you like a wife, not a whore."

I want to say something, but the tape on my mouth prevents me from speaking coherently. But what can I say? Men like Romeo don't care about how I feel. Quite the opposite. He'd get joy from my fear.

"Ah, but I must admit, I am disappointed." His tongue clicks against his teeth, disapproval dripping from his tone. "To think someone else claimed your virginity before me... Niko Leone has tainted you. But no matter, I'll show you what real pleasure is."

HE STANDS at the end of the bed, looking at me. His eyes are black, soulless. He undoes his pants and pulls his erection out without dropping his pants. A gun is holstered at his side, attached to his belt. For a moment, I wonder if I can somehow grab it.

"You like my cock, don't you?"

I realize he thinks I'm looking at him. When I finally look at his dick, I can't bear it. I turn away, not wanting to see it.

"Look at me!" His voice reverberates around the room.

I do as he says, telling myself I have to survive. Just go along and I'll be okay.

He strokes his dick, and he makes a satisfied sound. "I bet Niko's wasn't as large. As long."

I don't respond.

"You know, someday, I might let you suck it. Make you drink it all. But not until you understand your place." He kneels on the bed, his dick protruding through the opening of his slacks. If he did try to put it in my mouth, I hope I'd have the strength to bite it off. I fight that survival voice. I remind myself to just go along.

He grips my ankles and jerks me down until I'm lying on the bed. "Your innocence might be gone," he sneers, "but I'll take everything else. You'll beg for me before the night is over."

My mind races, fear mingling with disgust as I imagine being just another conquest to him.

I whimper and pray for strength to endure. The panic makes it hard to breathe. My survival instinct kicks in, and I squirm, trying to get away from his touch as his hands slide up my body and undo my pants.

The zip-ties bite into my wrists. My gaze goes to his gun again. Can I get it before he does? I know trying for it will be my death sentence if I fail.

My muscles tense, and I wriggle, eager for escape. But Romeo straddles me, opening my pants and pushing up my shirt.

He holds his dick as he strokes it. "You're going to like it, Elena. I'm going to fuck you until you can't walk." He rubs his dick over my skin, and I whimper at the disgust I feel.

I try to wriggle away again.

He laughs. "You think you can get away? Or maybe you think Niko will show up like some fucking knight in shining armor? He won't, you know. He doesn't give a shit about you. He told me so. Besides, he doesn't know about this place."

His hands work at my pants again. "You're better off relaxing because we're going to be here a long time. Who knows? Maybe you'll end up liking it."

My heart hammers against my ribs as he gives up on my pants and slides his hands under my shirt and grabs my breasts, squeezing them hard. I arch and cry out in pain.

"See, I told you you'd like it." His sinister smile is on me again. "First, I'll have you spread out, helpless. When I fuck you, you'll feel every second, every inch."

I twist under his grasp. The room seems to shrink, walls closing in.

"Your cries, they'll be music," he continues, the words spilling from his mouth like toxins. "Oh, how I love the cries of pleasure and pain." He tugs on my pants but can't get them over my hips.

A grunt escapes him. His patience unravels. "Fucking ties." He gets up and goes to the table and picks up a knife.

I thought I was afraid before, but seeing the glint of metal as he walks toward me sends a whole new level of fear through me.

He laughs. "No worries, Elena. I won't use this on you. Not yet, anyway." He kneels on the bed, his hands reaching to the ties binding my legs. "I'm going to rip you open." He laughs. "Not with the knife. With my cock. You'll be mine then."

He slices through the ties with the knife. "Time to show you ecstasy you've never known."

My instincts scream, a primal, urgent call to protect not only myself but the lives I carry inside me. The resolve to go along with him is blown apart by the instinct to stop him. My mind, my body isn't my own as my leg draws in, and then I kick out, my foot connecting with his face. The crack of bone is audible.

"Fuck!" He tumbles diagonally, landing on his hip and then rolling to the floor.

I'm dead. That's my first thought. Then I see it. The gun is sitting on the bed. I glance at Romeo, on his knees, cupping his nose.

I scramble to the edge of the bed and reach for the gun. My hands are still tied, but I manage to get a grip on it.

"Stupid cunt. You're dead now." He rises from the floor, glaring down on me, death shining in his eyes.

My hands shake as I hold the gun up, pointing it at him.

His laugh is as menacing as it is mocking. "Put that down. You won't use it."

I level the barrel at his face, hands awkwardly clasped around the grip. I've been around guns all my life but never held one. I've been around people who kill all my life but have never killed. I want to pull the trigger because I'm so scared, and yet, can I take a life? Can I become the type of person I for so long wanted to escape?

He stares at me, so sure of himself. So sure I'm not brave enough to shoot him. "Well? You'd better kill me because if you don't, I'm going to kill you. I'm going to fuck you first, of course, because it would be a shame to miss out on some fine Fiori pussy, but then I'm going to choke the life out of you. I'm going to watch as the life drains from your eyes."

He reaches down and rubs his dick again. I can't believe it. It turns him on to think about choking me to death.

"We both know you don't have it in you," he says.

Do I? I think of my unborn children. Wouldn't it be better to murder and save their lives than not to kill Romeo and let him kill me and the babies?

He laughs again and moves toward me, reaching for the gun.

The room shrinks and the air thickens as the distance between us narrows. I am a mother, a protector, but at what cost? I could walk out of here now that my legs aren't restrained.

But what are the odds that he has men in this place? Could I get away from all of them?

Time slows down as he draws closer. My finger trembles on the trigger, every moral I've held dear balancing precariously against the instinct to survive.

I hear a sound, almost like an alarm. It must be buzzing in my ears.

His fingers wrap around the barrel.

I close my eyes.

A gunshot shatters the silence.

27

NIKO

Donovan drives while I ride in the passenger seat. Liam is following in another car. My blood is agitated. It's taking too fucking long to get to the Upper West Side of the city. Needing something to do, I pull my gun out, making sure it's ready to end the life of Romeo Abate. God, please let me find her before he does something to her.

I shouldn't have left the compound. She's in trouble because I left and she tried to come to me. If I'd stayed, she'd be safe. If she dies… If she's hurt… I'll never be able to live with myself. All the guilt and failure at not being able to protect my mother comes back to me. This is why love is bad. Death is the end. But the loss of love is worse than death. It means living with a hole in your soul.

"Park here." I point to a spot a few blocks from the address we have for Romeo's house of hell.

Donovan pulls over, parking. Then he pulls out his gun, checking it. He looks at me. "Ready?"

"Past ready." I can't stop thinking about everything I've done wrong, starting with not protecting my mother. Not killing Giovanni and Tiberius sooner. Not staying with Elena.

We wait in the shadows until Liam joins us. Silently, we approach the house. It's quaint. Unassuming. Perfect for a lair.

"Alarms." Liam nods to evidence of security. He pulls out something from his pocket. It's not his phone but about the same size. A few moments later, he says. "All good."

I nod to a shadow in the house. "There's one near the door. Probably more inside," I say in a low voice.

"Keep sharp," I caution, though it's unnecessary. It's not like we haven't been in this situation before. Only before, I didn't feel like my entire life rode on the outcome.

We slide through the door like smoke. Donovan takes the man at the front. With a quick torque, he's broken the man's neck. Donovan gently lowers him to the floor, and we move on silently.

We move deeper into the house, each corner we round a potential ambush. My blood thrums in my ears. I focus on my breath to keep me calm, alert. I can't let my fear or rage distract me from my goal.

"Clear," hisses Donovan from a side room. His silhouette cuts through the gloom as he moves on.

A creak sounds above. Donovan, a man the size of a linebacker, is sprinting up the stairs as if he weighs nothing, like his feet aren't touching the steps. Whoever is up there will be dead before they realize Donovan is there.

From the back, a silhouette appears. He's carrying a sandwich, clearly not anticipating my visit. Not wanting to make a sound that could warn Romeo of our arrival, I rush him, punching him in the neck, breaking his larynx. He's stunned, and I use the moment to wrap my arm around him and strangle the life from him.

Donovan appears from the stairs. "Clear up there. No sign of Romeo."

Liam jerks a thumb over his shoulder. "Got one back there. No sign of Romeo either."

Fucking hell. Where is he? I enter the kitchen and look around. I note a door. "Basement?"

Both men nod. I open it and look down the stairs. The stairs to hell, I imagine. The silence shatters as an electronic wail fills the air.

"Fuck!"

"We should go. If it's not Abate's men, it will be cops," Liam states.

"I'm going down there with or without you."

Their hesitance hangs heavy.

I take the first step but then stop. "Listen, if I don't get out of here, promise me you'll find Elena. Protect her. When she's safe, set her free." I look at Liam. "You can do that, right? Give her a new identity."

Liam and Donovan look at each other in surprise and then back at me.

"Yes. I can do that," Liam agrees.

"And then kill Giovanni and Tiberius."

They nod. Then Donovan smirks. "You know you're too damn stubborn to die before you've had your revenge, Niko."

I give them one last look just in case it's the last time. Then I move down the stairs, descending into uncertainty. My hand tightens on the grip of my gun. I'm doubting myself. There's an alarm going off. If someone is down here, wouldn't they be coming up to find out why? Is there another exit? Dammit, I should have had Donovan and Liam check.

But I keep making my way down. In my mind, dread coils, making it hard to breathe. Will I find salvation or sorrow? Will I pull Elena back from the brink, or will I arrive only to mourn her? Fucking hell, is she even here? What if I'm wrong?

I reach the bottom. There's a single door that has some heft to it. Taking a breath, I slowly turn the knob hoping I'm not heard. I crack the door. My heart is hammering.

A gunshot pierces the quiet.

I barge into the room, my eyes scanning to take in the situation. I see Elena kneeling on a bed, her arms in front of her. A gun shaking in her hand. Her head and arms swivel toward me. I see it in her eyes. She's panicked and trying to protect herself.

Instinct has me dropping and rolling toward the bed as another shot rings out. I drop my own gun as I lever up, grabbing her wrists and taking the gun from her.

"No!" She screams and flails. I want to pull her close, help her see that it's me, but I have to figure out where Romeo is.

I hold her tight as she hits me. "It's Niko," I say as I glance around the room. I see Romeo on the floor, his dick hanging out of his pants, his face covered in blood. I think he's dead, but just to be sure, I point the gun I just took from her and shoot him in the chest. Then put it in the back waist of my pants and give one hundred percent of my attention to her.

She's crying, weeping and thrashing.

"It's me, *cara mia*." I cradle her cheeks in my palms. "Look at me. It's Niko."

It takes a moment for her eyes to clear. But then I see it. The relief. She sags against me.

"You're here."

"I'm here. Did he hurt you?" I'm trying to inventory her body to find wounds, but I can't let her go enough to be thorough. I can see that her pants are undone and I fear the worst. Well, not the worst. The worst would be if she were dead. But he took her... God, I'd want to revive him just to kill him again.

"I'm okay." Her fingers grip my shirt. "He was going to... but I kicked him and he fell. And then his gun... It was on the bed. I shot him. I killed him. I'm a murderer."

"Oh, baby. No, you're not. You're a hero. You've saved countless women from him."

She sniffs and looks up at me. "You think so?"

I smile. My chest has inflated. Never has so much happiness filled it. "I know so."

"I shot at you too."

"I know. Try not to do it again."

"I didn't know it was you."

"I know." I look around and see a knife on the floor. I pick it up and cut the ties on her wrists. "We need to go."

Her arms come around me, holding me tightly, and I've never felt so full and warm and complete as I do at this moment. Even not knowing whether she's going to stay or leave, in this moment, she's mine because she wants me, not because I've taken her.

"There's an alarm going off. We need to get you out of here." I reach down to get my gun.

"Lucia? What about her?" Elena grips my arm.

"She's fine. Worried about you. I can tell you all about it, but we need to get moving. Can you walk?" I really want to carry her out of here, but I need to be able to protect us.

She nods. I take her hand and lead her out of the room and up the stairs. At the top, I peer into the kitchen before entering. Then I look down the hall.

"Car's out front." Liam is at the door. "The alarm is next door, but we should go."

We leave the house by the front door, moving steadily but not rushing so much as to draw attention. Liam gets into the front passenger seat as I help Elena into the back and climb in next to her.

"I see all went well."

"I shot him," Elena says. I take her hand because I can tell she's going into shock as the endorphins crash.

Donovan laughs. "Fucking hell, I would have loved to have seen that." He steps on the gas pedal, taking us away from the horror.

We pull into the garage of my building, silently taking the elevator up to the penthouse. The minute we step in, Lucia is there, pulling Elena into her embrace.

"Are you okay?" She's crying, as is Elena.

Elena nods.

"She shot him." Donovan grins.

Lucia laughs. "Good for you, baby sister. Oh, my God." She tugs Elena back in for another hug.

"Donovan, can you call Doc? I'd like him to check Elena."

"Yes, she needs to be checked—"

Elena reaches out and grips Lucia's hand, giving her a hard stare. I wonder what it means, and yet, it doesn't matter. All that matters is that she's alive.

"Sure thing." Donovan takes out his phone. "Do you know how to use a gun?" he asks Lucia as he drapes an arm around her as he makes a call.

"I'm about to learn by shooting you," she quips.

I pick Elena up. "You need to rest." As I carry her to the stairs, I call for Maria. "Can you make a tray for her? Soup, maybe."

"Yes, of course."

I reach my room, carrying her in and laying her on the bed. She looks exhausted. I sit next to her. There's so much I want to say, words I've never said before. But I'm a coward. Oh, I'm brave enough to face gunfire and violence, but to hand my heart over...

Her eyelids droop. "Will you stay with me?"

"Always." I lean over and kiss her temple. I watch her sleep, keeping my promise. But already, I'm planning her father's execution. Tiberius's demise. I will clean the earth of the men who hurt her even if it means dying myself.

28

ELENA

My eyelids flutter open, and for a moment, I'm not sure where I am. Then the memories crash into me—the squeal of tires, the sickening crunch of metal, the world spinning. The car accident. Except, it hadn't been an accident at all. It was an elaborate plan orchestrated by my father to take me and my sister.

I squeeze my eyes shut, trying to block out the images that follow, but they're seared into my mind. Romeo looming over me, his hands eager to claim what he believed was his. My survival instinct took over. I kicked him and seized his gun. My fingers had trembled around the cool metal as I pulled the trigger.

"Easy, Elena." Niko's voice cuts through the fog in my head, gentle yet firm. "You're safe."

My memory flicks to him. He'd entered the room and I'd nearly shot him too. God, what if I had? Tears sting my eyes.

"You're safe," he says again.

I curl into him beside me. "You stayed."

"Of course, I stayed." His lips curve up in a half-smile, though shadows linger in his eyes. "The doctor is on his way up."

My hand goes to my belly. Are the twins okay? They've been in a car accident and were subjected to my father and Romeo's manhandling. I realize I haven't told Niko my plans or about the babies.

"I need to talk to you."

"Later," he says, a subtle furrow etching his brow. "You need to be checked over, and I have business to take care of."

I know business actually means violent vengeance. Maybe it's wrong, but I'm glad. I know Romeo won't hurt me anymore, but my father or Romeo's father still can. Niko can stop them, but I know only their deaths will achieve that. In killing Romeo, have I become more comfortable with murder?

A knock at the door slices through our bubble. Niko rises from the bed, and I immediately miss his warmth, his comfort. "I've got a surprise."

"Oh?" I sit up, and my body reminds me of all I've been through with aches and pains.

He opens the door and two familiar faces appear, Lucia, rushing in worried sick, and Kate, looking uncertain.

"Lucia, Kate!" Their presence is a balm to all the painful ugliness of the day.

Lucia steps forward, sitting on the bed and taking my hand, while Kate hangs back, her own fears shadowed in her expression.

"This is Doc," Niko says of a middle-aged man who enters behind the woman. "Make sure she's okay. Whatever she needs, give it to her."

Doc nods and approaches me. Lucia moves out of the way to give him room.

Niko looks at me, and I see a torrent in his eyes. "I'll check on you later."

I nod, wanting to tell him to be careful, but I know he's going to do whatever he feels needs to be done.

The doctor approaches. He smiles reassuringly. "Let's see how you're doing." His hands are steady, but I can't help flinching as he reaches for me—the involuntary reaction of flesh that remembers pain all too well.

"Sorry," I whisper.

"No apologies needed," he replies with practiced kindness as he uses his instruments to assess my health. "Your heart rate is a bit elevated, but that's to be expected. You've had multiple scares and traumas. You've been through a lot."

"That's the understatement of the year," quips Lucia.

"You have contusions and some scrapes but those will heal. You don't seem to be showing signs of a head injury—"

"We were knocked out," Lucia states.

His eyes narrow as he studies my head. "Does it hurt?"

I have to think about it. So much of me is sore. "I suppose when you touch it here." I press my hand to the side of my head.

He runs a few other tests I suspect are to assess brain function. "Do you have a headache or any vision problems?"

I shake my head.

"What about the twins?" Lucia asks.

I tense. I know the babies need to be checked, but I still haven't told Niko.

Doc arches his brow at me. "I don't have an ultrasound with me. But I do have a fetal doppler." He smiles. "You'd think with my clientele, I wouldn't need one. The men in your world are quite fertile."

"More like horny," Lucia says.

Doc laughs. "That too." He presses the wand of the small device on my belly, and soon, the room is filled with the rhythmic beat of my babies' hearts.

"Oh!" Tears fill my eyes as I look at Lucia. She's smiling, her arm looped through Kate's, who has a tentative smile.

"Two..." Doc moves the wand around. "The heartbeats sound strong. I would recommend that you get into your OB/GYN for further evaluation. This isn't my specialty, but I don't see any cause for concern at this time."

"Thank you."

Doc packs up his things. "Take it easy. Rest. A warm bath or compresses might help ease the aches and pains. If you're in a great deal of pain, you can have pain reliever, but take as directed. One or two tablets."

"So everything is okay?" I need to be sure.

"Like I said, there's nothing I see that indicates something's wrong, but see your regular doctor when you can." He stands. "I'll see myself out." He nods to Lucia and Kate. "Ladies."

When he leaves, Lucia sits on the edge of the bed. I study her, noting that she looks sad. There's a lot going on, but I'm fine and the babies are fine. I wonder if there's something else going on that I don't know of.

Kate moves closer to the bed but stays standing. She looks lost.

"I'm so glad to see you both, but Kate... did something happen?"

"My father's gone missing."

My gaze goes to Lucia, wondering if she knows what's going on and whether our father or Niko is involved.

"No one is sure who is involved," Lucia says as if she can read my mind. "Liam grew concerned, though, considering what happened to Kate."

Guilt fills me. "I'm so sorry, Kate."

"I knew your family was strict, but I didn't realize—"

"I should have never befriended you. This is my fault."

Lucia squeezes my hand. "It's not your fault that your father and mother are terrible people."

"But I knew what they were capable of... I..." Sorry didn't seem to be enough. I hate that this woman who was nothing but kind to me is caught up in my family.

"I thought you'd gotten away," Kate says.

I shake my head. "My father found the money. I still have my passport, though." I remember it now and how I've hidden it in the mattress back at the compound. I wonder if anyone has found it. I doubt it. I can't imagine Niko wouldn't have confronted me about it.

"So... you had to get married?" Kate asks.

"Girl, you're in for a story." Lucia tugs Kate's hand to have her join us on the bed. It makes me think of scenes on TV when teenage girls have a sleepover, something Lucia and I never had.

I explain how Niko took me during the wedding. Then I tell Kate he's the one who paid for me at the club and the father of the babies.

Kate shakes her head. "God... this is crazy."

I take her hand. "I know, and I'm so sorry that you've been brought into it. I never wanted that."

"I can't deny that I'm scared."

"Liam is putting her into Witness Protection," Lucia explains.

"I won't see you again?"

Kate shakes her head. "Not my father, either, assuming he's okay."

Lucia surreptitiously touches the side of her nose twice, telling me that there is something off about Kate's father. Is he in with one of the Families?

"I'm sorry."

Kate shrugs. "It will be an adventure, right? Agent Rostova is nice."

I look at Lucia. "That's Liam," she says.

"Is it odd that Niko's men have Irish first names but Italian or, in Liam's case, Russian last names?"

"Not in America." Lucia smiles, but her eyes are still shadowed in pain.

"Is there something else going on that you haven't told me?"

Lucia looks down. "You've been through a lot—"

"So have you. You were in the accident. Dad took you, too."

She nods. "I got a call today that Giuseppe died." She sniffs, and tears drip down her face. It's the first time I realize that she really cared for her husband despite the fact that she was essentially sold to him.

I sit up and put my arms around her. "God... and you've had to be here. You—"

"It's not a surprise. He was frail, sick for a long time. Since I married him, actually."

"Lucia, I'm so sorry." The words feel inadequate for the gravity of her loss.

"Thank you." She sniffs again. "It's strange. Ours wasn't a marriage of love—not at first. And not a traditional marriage, but..."

"You cared for him."

"More than I thought I would. When Dad sold me—"

"Sold?" Kate looks horrified.

"Our dad doesn't see us as daughters. We're things he owns that can bring him value. But I defied him by daring to fall in love with someone not of his choosing. He believed I was ruined, and to punish me, he killed my boyfriend in front of me."

I wince, thinking Kate doesn't need to know the heinous details.

"And then sold me to Giuseppe. I imagined an old, perverted Don," Lucia says. "But he was gentle and sweet. And Luca, his son, was kind too. Not like any family I've ever known."

"I'm so glad. God, if Dad knew he gave you safety and salvation, he'd have a stroke," I joke.

There's a light knock on the door, and Liam steps in. "Kate, it's time."

"Already?" Her voice breaks.

I feel it too. "Kate."

"It's okay, Elena. You're safe and seem happy. To be honest, I was thinking it might be fun to have a change in life. I just hope I don't end up in Podunk or something."

"Kate is family," Lucia tells Liam. "Make sure she doesn't end up in Podunk." Lucia looks at Kate. "Where is that?"

"It's anywhere boring."

"I don't think it's Podunk."

I rise from bed, feeling the protest of every bruise, every scrape on my body. Kate stands too, and suddenly, we're in each other's arms, clutching onto the moment, onto each other.

"Thank you for your friendship, Kate. It meant the world to me. I know it has cost you everything, and I'm so sorry for that."

"Promise me something?" she says. "Keep fighting, Elena. For yourself, for those babies. You can still have what you want."

"I promise. Take care of yourself, Kate. Find happiness, wherever it hides."

She pulls back and nods, her eyes reflecting the pain we both feel. "You too, Elena. Be happy. You deserve it."

"Take care of her, Liam" I say, the command leaving no room for argument.

"Of course." Liam smiles at Kate as he holds his arm out for her to leave with him.

The door closes behind them. I sag back onto the bed, feeling emotionally and physically exhausted.

"Kate's strong," Lucia says. "Like someone else I know."

I give her a wan smile. "Takes one to know one." But I realize she's right in some ways. I am strong. Maybe I don't have power, but I have strength.

She sits on the bed with me, taking my hand. "I never asked. Was this trip back to New York because you'd decided to stay with Niko?"

"Yes."

"Even after everything?" Doubt laces her tone, but it's not judgment I hear—it's concern.

"Even after everything. I know how Niko seems—"

"He's *Il Soldato Della Morte*," she reminds me.

"At one point, you said I should stay."

"I said for now since he didn't seem to want to kill you. He can protect you from Dad and the Abates. I didn't mean forever."

I sigh. "Back at the compound, Rosa said that Niko can be hard, but he knows love. I believe that too. I see it—"

"You think he loves you?" She arches a brow.

"I don't know if he loves me, but I believe I'm more than just a pawn."

"Do you love him?" Lucia's voice is softer.

I nod. "I think I do." For the first time, I feel solid in my decision. I'm ready to face whatever comes, with Niko, with our children, in a world filled with danger and uncertainty.

29

NIKO

The weight of urgency presses down on my chest as I sit in my office preparing to take my revenge, not just for my mother and brother, but for Elena as well. Donovan stands across from me, his eyes hard as flint, absorbing my vengeance as his own.

"Timing's everything," he murmurs. "That and hoping Tiberius's mistress doesn't double-cross us."

"She's smart enough to take the money and run," I say. There's no doubt in my mind that she knows the world Tiberius lives in and she wants out. I think of Elena. She wants out too. And I promised it to her. It's a promise I'm more inclined to keep after what happened today. But God, do I want her to stay. The way she clung to me, I never want her to let go. I'm a selfish man. Selfish enough to force her to stay. But if something happened to her, I wouldn't be able to live with myself. Freeing her is the only way to ensure her safety.

"Liam will meet us after he delivers Kate to the wit-pro guys," Donovan says regarding Kate's entry into Witness Protection. I feel sorry for her as she was completely clueless to our world. I imagine Elena is going to feel guilt at having involved her friend. However, I'm not convinced that her father, Chief Emerson, doesn't have ties to a Family.

"She'll be safe now," he finished.

"None of us are safe until those bastards are dead." I glance down at the plans for tonight's mission. "So, we're set."

He nods.

"What about Giovanni? Any clue where he's hiding?" When I've killed Tiberius, I'll move on to Giovanni, although he's proving more elusive to find. I imagine him in some sewer, hiding after Romeo's death and my taking Elena back from them again.

"No, but we've got eyes and ears everywhere."

A knock at the door interrupts our focus. "Come in."

Doc enters, and immediately, my plans vanish, replaced with concerns for Elena. "Is she okay?" I rise and go to him, thinking Donovan doesn't need to hear the details of Elena's condition or the depth of my concern.

He nods as we step just outside my office door. "Ms. Fiori is stable. Her injuries are mostly superficial and will heal with time and rest. I don't see any sign of concussion. The fetuses have strong heartbeats. I recommended that she see her OB/GYN."

For a moment, I stare at him wondering who we're talking about. Fetuses? A baby? No. Fetuses is plural.

"Thank you, Doctor." My voice doesn't betray my complete shock at the news.

"Of course. I'll find my way out."

I stand outside my office, paralyzed. Elena is pregnant? Did she know before now? Is this why she wants to leave? To protect them from this life? From me?

I remember fantasizing about filling her belly with my child. Even now, I can see it. Her and me, and a child... no... more than one. But she didn't tell me.

Anger simmers, but it's doused by the cold realization of Tiberius's threat. Our children would be targets from their first breath. Maybe Elena's silence was from that knowledge.

"Boss?" Donovan's voice slices through my reverie. "You good?"

I pull it together. "Better than ever. Let's get going. We end this tonight."

"We should go."

"HATE TO KEEP DEATH WAITING," I quip as I grab my coat and gun.

I want to run upstairs and confront Elena. I'm not sure whether I want to hold her to keep her and our children close or rage at her for her keeping the news from me. For planning to leave without telling me. I'd go my entire life never knowing I was a father.

We leave the penthouse. I sit in the passenger seat as Donovan drives. I should be focused on our plan, but all I can think about are Elena and her pregnancy. My mind is going round and round and round, trying to make sense of her decision not to tell me.

"You sure you're okay?" Donovan gives me a concerned glance.

"Yep."

"It's been a big day. The scare with Elena. Dealing with Romeo—"

"I'm fine. I just want to be done with this."

We park down the street from Tiberius's mistress's place. We've already handed her a duffle bag full of cash, a fake ID that includes a passport, and a ticket to some Caribbean island where she can live in bliss. Once she made a call to Tiberius telling him she wanted him to come over and fuck her tonight, we got her to the airport. I imagine she's paying some cabana boy for a fruity drink as Donovan and I ascend the staircase toward her apartment.

When we reach it, Liam is already there, lurking in the shadows. When he sees us, he straightens from the wall he was leaning against. "Any last words you want him to hear?"

I've been thinking of a few things to say. "*Enjoy hell*, I suppose."

Donovan uses the key the mistress handed over to open the door. Inside the apartment, we fan out, taking positions, waiting for Tiberius to arrive. I decide that Tiberius should die like Romeo... at the foot of the bed with his dick hanging out. Well, maybe not that. I don't want to see Tiberius's dick.

I sit on the edge of the bed imagining Tiberius's surprise when he realizes he's about to be fucked a whole different way. With my gun in hand, my mind is a whirlwind of thoughts and memories. I can almost hear my mother's laughter, see my brother's impish grin—both stolen with the help of Tiberius's hand. I roll my shoulders as the anticipation of my promise to my mother and brother is about to be fulfilled.

I hear a slight knock on the wall outside the room. Donovan's signal that someone is entering the apartment. I rise and wait, running the words I want him to hear before he dies through my mind.

"Where are you? I need a good, hard cock sucking." Tiberius Abate enters the room.

The dim light from the moon filters through sheer curtains. I tighten my grip on the gun as I lift it toward the man unzipping his pants. The speech I've been planning evaporates. All I need to see is the knowledge in Tiberius's eyes that he's about to die by my hand.

He stops short. His eyes widen in surprise. Then I see it. He knows he's dead, but I also see he's going to try and run. I squeeze the trigger. The shot rings out. Blood and bone paint the wall behind him. Revenge is sweet, and at the same time, not. He's dead. He's paid the price for what he helped take from me. But my mother and brother are still gone.

Donovan and Liam appear in the doorway.

"You didn't give him a chance to beg," Donovan says. "I really wanted to hear him beg."

Liam snorts. "I'll get this—"

"Leave him," I command. I reach down and pick up Tiberius's phone. "Maybe there's something here that can tell us where Giovanni is." I scroll through it.

"Anything?" Donovan asks.

"Nothing." Frustration seeps into bones. "Motherfucker."

The image of Elena, looking terrified as I entered the room where Romeo kept her, flashes in my mind. With Giovanni on the loose, she's in danger. She and the babies. My babies. If Giovanni knew that, he'd kill her for sure.

"Let's go." I step over Tiberius. At some point, his men will come looking for him here and find him. Hopefully, they'll get the message. I need to start thinking about what to do about Tiberius's business, but first, Giovanni needs to go.

"What's next?" Donovan asks as he drives me back to the penthouse. Liam has gone home but is on call should something come up on Giovanni.

"We call it a night." It's nearly ten at night. The close of a day that's been filled with anger and vengeance. Two of my enemies are dead. Giovanni is in hiding. I figure let him hide. Give him one more night to live. Tomorrow, he'll pay with his life.

"When we get back, I'll check in to see if there's any news. They'd call, but you never know," Donovan says.

I nod. When we arrive back at the penthouse, Donovan heads to my office. I grab a drink and descend into the thoughts about Elena and her not telling me about the pregnancy. As the booze burns its way down my gut, anger and a feeling of betrayal grow. From the time I took over the Leone Family business, I've never allowed betrayal to go unpunished. I set my glass aside and head upstairs because I'm not going to let it go this time, either.

30

ELENA

Steam swirls around me, the hot water carrying away the horror of the day. My fingers trace the bruises on my arms, a stark reminder of the crash and Romeo's grasp. I should be resting, but I'm aware that Niko is gone and I'm worried. Lucia had to take a call from Italy in regard to Giuseppe. Feeling tainted by the events of the day, I climbed into the shower to cleanse it away.

I rub soap over my belly, thankful that the babies are alive and well. I hope Niko comes home safe so I can finally tell him of my decision to stay and about the babies. My heart flutters with hope that he's happy.

I turn off the water, stepping out into the cool air. I wrap myself in a plush robe and open the door to enter the bedroom. My heart stops as I see Niko, alive and well, sitting on the edge of the bed. Relief floods me. I want to rush to him, give myself over to him.

He lifts his head, and his eyes, dark and fathomless, steal away the happiness inside me. My breath catches, and for a moment, I'm a deer caught in the headlights. I have twin urges to flee and stand my ground, but from what?

"Why did you leave Long Island today?" His voice rumbles low. "Were you planning to escape?"

"What? No." Is that what he thinks? "I was coming to see you. I, ah... I..." His dark gaze is menacing, making it difficult for me to think. What happened between this afternoon when he was so gentle and caring to now, where he looks like wants to throttle me? Fear seeps in, and I press my hand over my belly.

"What is it, Elena?"

"I..." My mind is tripping over all the words I want to say but can't seem to get out. "I needed to... I came to tell you... I decided to stay."

"Stay?" His voice remains cool, nearly soulless.

I nod, my heart beating frantically. "And to tell you..." The rest of the sentence withers under his gaze. I wasn't sure what he'd think about the babies, but I hadn't considered that he'd hate the idea. But now I'm forced to consider that he'd find them to be a liability. Maybe he'd be a danger to them.

My stammering lingers in the air. His silence fills the room.

"About what?"

"About everything... about us." I swallow hard. "I wanted—no, needed—you to know."

"Know what?" He rises from the edge of the bed and takes a step toward me.

I'm shaking in fear. Had I been wrong to think there was goodness in him?

"Tell me, *cara mia*, how long have you known you were pregnant?"

My breath hitches. He knows. How? Then again, how doesn't he? Rosa could have said something. The doctor today? Even Lucia could have let it slip. Or Kate.

"I... I was going to tell you—"

"How long!" His voice bellows through the room.

I flinch and instinctively step back. "Since just before I was supposed to marry Romeo."

His brow furrows in confusion. "Are they even mine?"

Despite my fear, a flash of anger surges through me at his insinuation. "Who else's would they be? I sold my virginity to you!"

He shakes his head in disbelief. "I pulled out."

"Apparently, not soon enough." The words tumble from my lips, bitter and tinged with a sadness that he's not happy about the babies.

Silence stretches between us, and I know now that I was a fool to think I could have a happily ever after with him. Those don't happen in our world.

"Were you with someone else after that? Did Romeo—"

"No!" I want to slap him. I want to cry. I want to shake him. "You're the only one, Niko. And I plan to keep them."

His nod is slow, deliberate. "But you don't want this world. You especially don't want to raise children in this world." He steps back. "That's why you wanted your freedom, isn't it?"

I nod because initially, that was part of it. Before I'd considered a life with him. Before I started to love him.

"Fine. But you're not going with your sister. You and those babies will always be a target. I'll get in touch with Liam and get you new identities, protection..." He trails off, but the implication is as clear as day. He doesn't want me or the babies.

I'm not sure what to say, but it wouldn't matter as a knock on the door interrupts us.

"Come in." Niko's gaze stays on me as Donovan enters the room.

"Sorry to interrupt, but we've got a possible lead on Giovanni."

Niko holds my gaze a moment longer and then turns to Donovan. "Where?"

"One of his men was caught around one of the clubs in Jersey."

"Get the men—"

"Already on it."

"Let's go. I need to call Liam." Niko heads to the door behind Donovan.

"Wait. Please, Niko."

He turns, eyes piercing through me.

"I know you need to do this... to kill my father, but surely, this" —I press my hands over my belly— "is more important right now. We need to talk."

He shakes his head, each move breaking my heart a little bit more. "I'm not putting off what I should have finished a long time ago. Besides, the decision is made. And with him gone, you'll be able to live free." He doesn't wait for my response. He leaves the room. He leaves me and his children.

31

NIKO

In my office, I listen as Donovan tells me what's going on.

"I've got Lou at the club holding the guy," he says.

I'm trying to focus because the idea of eliminating my biggest enemies in one night would be a coup. If people feared me, imagine how'd they feel after learning I took out two Dons in a single evening. Instead, I've got Elena and fatherhood on an endless loop in my head. Elena. She's been fire to my ice since the night I met her. The challenge to my control. And now, the mother of my child... no, children.

Frustration coils in my gut. I should have known, and yet, how can I blame her when in a single day, she's been attacked, forced to kill, and I'm on my way to eliminate her father? I feel torn between *Il Soldato Della Morte* and being a man. A man who wants to love and be loved.

"Boss?" Donovan's voice slices through my introspection.

"Yeah."

"Do you want to get him at the club or have him brought to you?"

"Let's get him. I want to control this the whole way."

"Alright. We've got men on standby."

"I need to call Liam. I'll meet you in the garage."

Donovan studies me, and I can't imagine he can't tell something is up, but I arch a brow at him. He shrugs and heads out.

I call Liam and ask him to arrange a new identity for Elena and plan to send her somewhere safe.

"Is something up?" he asks.

"I am on my way to kill Giovanni, but Elena doesn't want this life. I promised her I'd get her out. I need it done ASAP. Tonight."

He sighs, and I suspect I'm interrupting a night with a woman or perhaps he's just watching sports recaps. But he agrees.

Moments later, I'm in the car heading to New Jersey with Donovan. The ride is quiet, at least in the car. In my head, Elena is on constant replay.

"You okay, Boss?"

"Yep."

I have a profound sense of déja vu. We've had this exchange before.

"We can grab this guy and hold him until tomorrow."

"Why would I want to do that?" My life since my mother and brother died has been planning to kill Giovanni Fiore.

"Your head doesn't seem to be in the game. Did something happen with Elena?"

I glare at him. "Why would you say that?"

He glances at me, then turns back to the road with a shrug. "We've already determined that it's none of my business, but it seems like she's more than just a way to fuck with Fiori."

I turn to look out the window. I'm not a man who shares his feelings. Feelings are a sign of weakness. They give people power over you. But Donovan is right, my head is cluttered, fogged up by Elena.

"Tonight, we kill Giovanni and Liam gets her set up to go free."

He glances at me again, his brows raised. "You said that earlier at Romeo's."

I nod. "I promised her."

He considers that and nods, and I think he's accepted my answer. "You want her to stay, though, don't you?"

Fucking hell. "What makes you say that?"

"Look, I'm no expert on love, but—"

"You think I love her?"

His fingers grip the steering wheel, and I imagine he's filtering his brain for what he wants to say next. I'm not likely to kill Donovan for anything he says, but then again, he may not know that for sure.

"Yeah, I do." He looks at me pointedly.

I look out the window again because he's right. "What's that saying? If you love someone, set them free?"

He lets out a sigh of relief, which tells me he wasn't sure how I'd respond. "Yeah, but doesn't it end about their coming back?"

"She can't stay. She's pregnant."

His jaw drops. "Ah... congratulations?"

"You and I both know that any of my kids would have targets on them. Everyone around me does. I can't put her—them—through that." As the words drip from my mouth, I realize that I was an asshole to her. She was protecting herself and the babies from my life, just as I want to do for them.

"It's too bad. I like her. She's got spunk. I like how you are around her."

I don't even want to know what that means, so I don't ask.

We reach the club and enter from the back. I find three of my men, including Lou, watching over a hulk of a man with a scar down his cheek and a murderous scowl on his face.

"Meet Ugly Eddie," Lou says.

"Who is he?" I ask.

"Works with Fiori. Low level, but enough that he likely knows where Fiori is. Isn't that right, Eddie?" Lou bends over him. "You are one ugly sonofabitch."

Eddie sneers. "Fuck you."

Lou laughs. I can see why he and Donovan are friends. "Load him up. Donovan, with me." I let the others know what I want from them.

With Ugly Eddie tied in the back, we head back over to Manhattan to a warehouse once owned by my uncle. It's owned by me, but I don't use it. I lease it out as part of my legit business. We take a roundabout way, making sure Ugly Eddie doesn't have friends who are following him.

We pull into the warehouse, and Donovan gets Eddie out and restrained in a chair.

"This can be easy or hard, Eddie," Donovan says.

"Fuck you."

"Hard it is." Donovan punches Eddie in the jaw.

"Where's Giovanni?" I ask.

"You think you can intimidate me?" He spits out blood onto the concrete floor.

I laugh, and the menace in it has Eddie's eyes flashing with fear. "Intimidation is a tool for those who lack conviction. This night doesn't end until Giovanni is dead. How's that for conviction?"

Eddie pulls himself together. "You're going to kill me anyway."

I nod. "Yes, but I can do it quickly, painlessly, or I can do it inch by inch."

Donovan leans next to him. "Starting with your cock."

Eddie turns to Donovan, horror shining in his eyes. "You're sick."

"You're the one who wants to do this the hard way."

"I ain't telling you nothing," he sneers, but I can see his bravado cracking.

"Wrong answer," Donovan chimes in, punching Eddie again. "I can do this all night."

I lean in, letting him see the coldness in my eyes up close. "Why did Giovanni send you?"

"He must not like you," Donovan says. "He had to know we'd get you and kill you."

I nod. "How does it feel to be expendable by your boss?"

Eddie's eyes dart between us, a flicker of fear finally breaking through as Donovan picks up a crowbar, letting it catch the light menacingly.

"I don't know."

"Ah... I see."

Donovan takes a practice swing.

"I swear," Eddie says, his gaze not leaving the crowbar. The next minute, there's a hole in Eddie's head, but neither Donovan nor I put it there.

"Down!" I yell out.

Gunfire shatters the stillness. Bullets spit around the area, lodging into concrete and wooden crates, and Eddie as well.

Instinct kicks in. I'm moving before I think, reaching for the gun strapped to my side. Donovan and I rush for protection behind some crates.

"It's a fucking trap," Donovan calls out. He pulls out his phone, and I know he's calling men in. I know they're not far, but at this point, they may not be close enough for me and Donovan. It's a reminder of the violent world I live in and how fucked-up I am to have been upset that Elena didn't want her or our kids to live in it.

"Where are those fuckers?" I need to look around but don't want to get my head blown off.

One crate over, Donovan peers from around it. Shots ring out, and he recoils back.

"What are the odds they've got men coming from behind?" he says.

"That's what I'd do."

Sparks dance as rounds ricochet around us. Wood splinters. My breath comes fast, my heart thundering even as I seek calm. Panic only leads to death.

"To the left!" Donovan points with his gun barrel, teeth bared in a grimace.

"Cover me." I don't wait for a response, already moving, trusting Donovan to watch my back. I weave between crates and machinery. A bullet whizzes by my shoulder, making me flinch.

"Got one!"

I don't celebrate his success. There's no triumph until they're all dead. Or we are.

Someone pops up in front of me. I fire and duck. I peer from behind the crate to see that I hit my mark. He's dead.

Another appears. "Keep countin'!" I fire back, squeezing the trigger and watching him crumble. One less threat.

"Two!"

I fire again. "Three!" I'm not sure whether it's vindication or desperation that fuels the tally. How many of these fuckers are there? And where are my men?

Then everything goes quiet. For a moment, I stay in my crouched position and listen. The silence is more chilling than the gunfire.

"Is that all of them?" Donovan's voice holds doubt. Like he too thinks something isn't right.

"I don't know?" Scanning the area, I make my way back to him.

"That felt a little too easy."

"How'd they know we were here?" Then it comes to me. "Fucking hell, did they search Eddie at the club? Does he have a tracker?"

"That would mean this is a trap."

Instinctively, I look around again, waiting for the trap to be sprung because surely, this isn't it. And where are my men?

"I think it's safe to say that Eddie isn't going to give up Giovanni. We should go," I say.

"Right behind you." Donovan and I tentatively make our way through the warehouse. "I'll have Lou arrange clean-up when we can be sure it's clear."

My nerves tingle as I anticipate another round of attack. "Stay sharp."

The silence stretches like a taut string as we move toward the exit. As we round a corner, something shifts—the air seems to charge, electrify. I pause, instincts screaming that something's off.

"Ah, Niko. Always so predictable." Giovanni's voice slices through the tension. He holds a gun, as do the men around him.

Even so, the man who needs to die is standing in front of me. This is my chance. But I really need my men here if I plan to walk out alive. "You flatter me, Giovanni."

"Now I'm going to kill you."

A loud crash sounds, distracting me.

"Fuck!" Donovan yells as he steps in front of me. Then he's propelled back, knocking me onto the ground. My head hits the concrete, and stars swim in my eyes as darkness descends.

"Kill them both."

32

ELENA

It's late. Past midnight. But I can't sleep. I sit in the dark of the penthouse living room with Lucia, who's just gotten off the phone to someone in Italy.

"You really should rest," she says.

"I can't." I can't get the image of Niko out of my head. The way he looked at me and talked to me. There'd been a moment when I thought he was disappointed and hurt that I hadn't told him about the pregnancy. But his reaction changed my mind. He didn't want me or the babies. He wouldn't even talk to me about it. Killing my father was more important than anything else. I should have known that. How had I talked myself into thinking he could be more than the Soldier of Death?

"If he succeeds, maybe he'll change his mind." Lucia holds my hand, trying to comfort me, which is idiotic since she's the one who just lost her husband.

"I don't want to talk about it." I lean my head over on her shoulder. "I should be asking about you. How are you holding up?"

She sighs. "I'm okay. I mean, I'm sad. I'll miss him. But I know now that one of the reasons he let me come here, insisted I come when you didn't show up like you said you would, was that he knew his time was coming. He didn't want me to see him like that. He'd want me to remember the good times."

"Good times? I was so worried when Dad sent you away. I was afraid he'd be mean to you. I'm so glad it turned out to be the opposite."

"I was lucky. Giuseppe never asked for more than my company. He's definitely a rarity in our world."

For a moment, I thought Niko might be a rarity. "When do you have to go back to Italy?"

She turns within my embrace, facing me, her eyes rimmed red but fierce. "Luca wants me to stay here in New York. It's... unsettled times when a Don dies."

"Luca? That's Giuseppe's son, right? Is he kicking you out of the Family?" I figured if Giuseppe was a rarity, his son could be like the rest.

"He says I'm still Family, that I can return if I choose to." Her hand squeezes mine gently. "He said I could bring you with me. He'll protect us. I think he's grateful for all I did for his father."

I think about Niko saying I would be free. Funny how just a few weeks ago, I'd have been elated at the prospect. "Does he know about the babies? About them being Niko's?"

"Yes. He has no problem with that."

"Niko wants me to get a new identity."

"What Niko wants doesn't matter once he decides he doesn't want you or the babies." Her voice is gentle, but it still hurts.

We sit in silence. Decisions need to be made, but not at this moment. I figure I have until tomorrow to decide what I want to do.

A commotion sounds near the door.

"In here!"

Lucia and I startle, jumping up from the couch.

Three of Niko's men storm in, their faces etched with lines of urgency.

"What's wrong?" All I can think of is that Niko is dead.

"We need to go. You have five minutes to pack. Both of you," one says. I remember him from the office Niko has at the pizzeria.

"Where?" Lucia demands.

"Why? What happened?" I ask.

"Giovanni set a trap. We need to take you to the compound. Now."

My heart leaps into my throat. Lucia's grip on my hand tightens.

"Where is Niko—"

"We don't have time for this. Pack so we can go!"

"No." I step forward with bravado I don't really feel. "I demand to know what's going on."

"If they're moving us, Niko is probably fine." Lucia puts her hand on my shoulder.

I swing around. "But you don't know that, do you?" I whirl back toward the men. "Tell me everything."

The man looks to the other three as if he isn't sure how to proceed. Technically, he could haul me out of here under Niko's rules. The fact that they're not sure what to do suggests that I may have more sway than I realized.

"We have orders to take you both to the compound in Long Island immediately."

"Who ordered? Niko? Where is he?" I search their faces for any hint, any clue, to Niko's condition but find only the hardened masks of soldiers in service.

"It's protocol," one of the other men says. "Your safety is our priority." I'm sure he's trying to reassure me, but it's nothing but cold comfort.

"Is he hurt?" I push. "I'm not stepping one foot outside this place until I know exactly what's happened to him!"

"We really must insist—" The third man, younger, with unease clouding his eyes, makes a move as if to usher us out.

"Insist all you want, but I'm not moving!" My feet root to the spot, and I hope they don't carry me out.

"Boss would want you safe—"

"Then he can come and tell me himself!" Defiance surges, fierce and powerful within me.

Next to me, Lucia stands tall and firm. She arches a brow at them, expecting them, like I do, to follow my orders.

"Please," the first man implores again like I need good manners to persuade me to leave.

"Tell me where he is. Now. Is he hurt?"

The first man sighs. "It's complicated."

"Just because I'm a woman, doesn't mean I'm stupid or ignorant. I'm the daughter of a Don. Do you think I don't know what goes on?"

"We're not at liberty—"

"And I say you are. Niko isn't here, and that means I'm in charge."

The three men glance at each other, clearly uncertain of the truth of that.

"The woman of a Don is to be held up, respected," Lucia informs them.

"They're not married—"

"That's inconsequential. Do you think Don Leone would want to see you bullying the woman he sleeps next to?" Lucia continued.

"We're not bullying. We have orders to keep you safe."

"I'm safe here. Now, tell me where Niko is?"

Movement across the room has us all looking, tensing as if my father's men had breached Niko's sanctuary.

Liam strides in. "Aren't you supposed to be taking her to the compound?"

"You weren't with them?" I ask him.

"No. I was preparing your documents and travel plans." He turns to the men. "Why aren't they on the way to the compound?"

"Because I'm not leaving without answers," I say firmly. I'm not sure I can stand up to Liam. I recognize that he's important to Niko. "Answers you're going to help me get."

Liam's gaze sharpens as he looks at me.

I arch a brow, challenging him.

He sinks his teeth into his lower lip as he turns to the men. "Well? What's the hold-up?"

"Orders are to take them to the safehouse," the younger man says, almost apologetically.

"The mistress of the house has other plans." Liam's words are clipped, authoritative. "Elena, what do you need?"

"Information. Confirmation. Assurance that Niko is not on death's doorstep." I'm working to ward off panic, but it's getting harder the longer I go without answers.

"We don't know where he is or how he is," one man finally says. "All we know is that Giovanni ambushed him."

Liam turns to me. "That's all I've heard too. But" —he puts his hand on my arm— "there is a protocol. We'll know soon. In the meantime—"

"In the meantime, we secure this place. If he is okay, he'll come back here, right? This is his most secure location in the city."

Liam nods. "Right."

I turn to the three men. "Station men outside the garage and at the elevator. At least two men should be in the hall, and one at the stairwell outside the penthouse. No one, except Niko or his known men, goes in or out without my say-so. And you." I turn to Liam. "Get on the phone. Find out everything you can about Niko's location and condition."

"What about Donovan?" Lucia asks. "Niko doesn't seem to go anywhere without him."

Liam nods. "I'll get on it." He turns to the other men. "You have your orders."

"Are you sure that's wise?" the man challenges, more out of worry than defiance.

"You are asking Elena, right?" Liam says.

At that moment, I realize what he's doing, and I could kiss him for it. Especially since Niko might not like it.

The men spring into motion, a testament to Liam's influence, or maybe just the realization that my determination is unbreakable. I watch them, my chest tight as I worry about Niko.

"If Dad killed him..."

"Don't think of that." Lucia rubs my back.

One of the men approaches. "We're following your orders, but the compound is truly the safest place."

"The last time I was on the road between the compound and here,

I was driven off the road and kidnapped by the very man you say has ambushed Niko. I'm staying here."

As if summoned by our urgency, the door crashes open and Niko strides in. My knees go weak from the relief. Except for the blood.

I start toward him, but he looks at me with the same darkness as he had earlier. "Why are they still here?" His words are a snarl to the men.

Liam steps up to him. "They've been taking charge."

"Taking charge? What the fuck, Liam?" Niko stabs him with his forefinger. "You're in charge in situations like this."

He shrugs. "Elena had it under control. She's the mistress—"

"She's leaving, remember? I gave you an order—"

"Yeah well, that was before you walked into Giovanni's ambush."

"Where's Donovan?" Lucia asks. I look among the men and don't see him.

"I want them gone," Niko says, ignoring Lucia. "Now."

"I'm not going." I straighten, lifting my chin even though I know I shouldn't defy him.

His jaw clenches, a muscle ticking in his cheek. He moves closer, and I feel the heat of his anger, the cold of his doubt. But I don't back down. "What do you hope to gain by staying?"

I honestly don't know.

"Whatever." He turns away. "I'm going upstairs to clean up. We meet in my office in fifteen, then we go end that motherfucker and burn his business down."

Niko turns to leave, and as he does, the door opens and two men enter, dragging a moaning Donovan inside. Blood seeps through his shirt over his chest. Oh, God.

"Get him to a room now. Where's Doc?" Niko's command slices through the tension, and yet, I can hear the crack of fear in his voice. His friend, his brother in arms, is injured.

Lucia gasps and rushes to him.

"Hey!" One of the men carrying Donovan grabs her and pushes her back.

Donovan grips the man's arm. "If you ever put your hands on her again, I'll rip your throat out!" Then he passes out.

I don't have time to process the moment as Niko again tells them to minister to Donovan while he goes upstairs.

My feet move before I even decide to follow him. Up the stairs, his stride is long and determined, his shoulders bearing the weight of impending war.

"Niko." My voice is steady, stronger than I feel.

He pauses at the top of the staircase, his hand on the rail, turning his head slightly. "Didn't Liam give you what you need?" His words cut, an insinuation that I should be ready to disappear.

"I'm not leaving until we talk because you clearly weren't listening to me earlier."

"You seem to be under the impression that you have any sort of power here."

I stand up to him. "I do. You gave it to me when you gave me a choice to stay or go."

His jaw tightens.

"I get that you don't want me or the babies, but I won't leave until you hear what I have to say."

"I never said I didn't—"

"No. It's my turn to talk."

He jerks back in surprise. His eyes narrow again. "Fine." But there's no sign of concession. He turns and retreats to his room. "Talk, then."

"I was coming to the city because I chose this—I chose you. I was under the mistaken impression that you wanted me to stay. Now that I know differently, I'll go."

He stares at me like he's trying to process what I'm saying. I give him a minute just in case he changes his mind and wants us to stay. But he's still staring at me with those intense, dark eyes.

"I've said what I needed to say. Now I'll go." I turn to leave. I see the door, and through it is freedom. No more gilded cage. I should be excited, but I'm angry and sad. Because when I look into Niko's eyes, past his anger and vengeance, I see the man Rosa was talking about. The one capable of love.

But his need for revenge is too entrenched. His hate for my father is more powerful than any caring he might have for me and the babies.

33

NIKO

Her words ricochet around my brain, not making sense. The foremost thoughts in my mind are how twice tonight, I've been ambushed. Once by Giovanni and now by Elena.

Maybe it's the bump on my head from falling tonight that is keeping me from making sense of my world at the moment. Maybe it's the anger. Anger at myself for not seeing sooner that tonight was a setup. For all intents and purposes, I should be dead. Giovanni pulled the trigger, and Donovan put himself between me and that bullet, knocking me down. I hit my head, and for a few minutes, I was out. Thank fuck my men showed up. By the time I came to, the fight was over and Giovanni was gone. But I'm determined to hunt him down.

Tonight's goals were to get the women to safety, get Donovan medical help and hope his injury isn't life threatening, and then go back out and not come home until I watch Giovanni take his last breath.

But the order of things is out of whack at home, too. Elena not only refused to leave, but she was also ordering the men around. Liam was allowing it. God, seeing her when I walked in was like a stab to the heart. It hurt like hell that she'd kept the pregnancy a secret even as I know why. I can't blame her. In fact, I agree with her. She and the babies are safer without me.

I was coming to the city because I chose this—I chose you. I was under the mistaken impression that you wanted me to stay. Now that I know differently, I'll go.

Her words start to fall in place. By the time they make sense, she's leaving. Panic claws through my chest. If she leaves, she takes a piece of me with her. A piece I didn't know I had until her.

I reach out, my hand encircling her arm, a mixture of anger and something close to desperation seeping into my grasp. "I never said I didn't want you or the babies."

She scoffs, and I'm wondering where this part of her has been hiding. She's strong. Bold. Brave. "The minute you found out about them, you had Liam preparing to send me away."

My brain is still slow on the uptake. After a moment, I say, "You're the one who didn't want me to know about them. You said you didn't want this life. You wanted to be free."

"Because you didn't give me a chance!" Her hands clench at her sides. "I was leaving the compound for you—"

"Leaving? Or running?"

She exhales sharply. "Once again, I'm telling you that I was on the way here to tell you I wanted to stay and let you know about the pregnancy, but my father kidnapped me and handed me over to Romeo."

The image of Romeo, with his dick hanging out, dead at Elena's feet flashes in my mind. The terror of that moment. The recognition that she had become as essential to me as air.

"When you found out, though, you were angry, telling me to leave. What was I supposed to think?"

The silence between us stretches. This time, words are tumbling through my head but they're not her words. They're words that express my feelings. Words that I'm a coward to release.

"Why?" I ask.

Her brow furrows. "Why, what?"

"Why did you decide to stay?" Now I'm thinking she sees me as her protector. Her decision to stay is only because I can keep her and the children safe.

She looks away. "Because I'm an idiot."

I close my eyes, my heart cracking.

"Can I go now?"

When I look at her, something has gone dead in her eyes. I did that. That's the reason I need to let her go. I'm *Il Soldato Della Morte*. I bring death and destruction. Keeping Elena would only diminish her, a woman filled with life.

"No."

"First, you didn't want to see me, and now you won't let me go?"

My gaze locks onto Elena. "I've already promised you could go. But you've told me you wanted to stay. Has that changed?"

"You forget, Niko, that I have no power here. Whether I stay or go is in your hands."

My chest constricts. I'm losing her. "Don't you get it, *cara mia*? You have all the power. From the moment I saw you on the stage at my club, I've been under your spell."

Her eyes soften slightly as she studies me.

I realize that I need to find my balls and tell her what I want. It's the only way she'll stay.

I reach out my hand to cup her cheek. "I love you, *cara mia*, my Elena."

She stares up at me, and I feel like my world has stopped, waiting to see whether it will turn again or not.

"I love you too, Niko."

And just like that, the world spins and my heart beats. I tug her to me and cover her mouth with mine in the sweetest kiss. She's life and love, and I drink her in. Her fingers clutch my shirt as her mouth joins with mine. I realize that there haven't been many kisses between us. Just the one time? What the fuck has been wrong with me? All I can think about is kissing her from now until the end of time.

Except... even as her fingers tangle in my hair, pulling me closer, the soldier within stirs to life. The threat is still out there. Giovanni made a bold move tonight. One that nearly destroyed me and my family. I can't let him get that close again, especially to Elena and our children. He must pay for the turmoil he's sown.

I pull away, looking into her lovely face. "I have to finish this tonight so we can move forward. So you and the babies can be safe."

"No," she counters, her grip on me both firm and gentle. "You need to check on Donovan first. If it's okay for him to travel, we'll all go to the compound and regroup. Together."

The resolve in her eyes steadies me, grounding me when all I want is to unleash the violence roiling inside. It's strange how she can both make me feel terrified at what it could cost me to lose her, and at the same time, tether me to the world. Make me feel stronger. Take away the emptiness. Bring light to the dark.

"You and your sister, Donovan, and a few of my men will go. But your father won't see tomorrow's sunrise if I have my way. I need to strike now."

"Which is exactly what he anticipates." Her fingers brush against the stubble on my jaw. It's a little gesture that packs a big punch as my chest fills with emotion. "Wait. Regroup. Then go after him."

I want to stay here in this room forever, but I can't. Not with Giovanni still a threat to all I hold dear.

"He'll think he won." The idea of him gloating on how he pulled one over on me grates on me. Granted, he didn't succeed. But still, he got way too close for comfort. And he injured Donovan. My friend. My brother.

"Let him think he's won—for now. It will give him a false sense of security which will make him vulnerable."

There is some sense to her idea, but... "We're talking about killing your father. Maybe you don't want him dead."

"He's not my father. Maybe biologically, but he's never been a father in the sense of the word. Me and Lucia have only been assets... or liabilities. Besides, he caused a car accident and then handed me over to Romeo. You can't possibly think I have any feelings for him."

I smile, my thumb gently rubbing the outline of her bottom lip. "I had to ask."

"My father is going to feel like the king of the world for beating *Il Soldato Della Morte*."

I growl at the idea that he beat me.

"But that will be his downfall. He'll underestimate you. I have no doubt that you could end this tonight, but your top *capo* is injured and it's late. Don't risk being blinded by your own vengeance and go after him with less mental and physical strength."

I want to reject her theory, but then I consider the lives at stake. Not mine or my men's, necessarily, but hers and the babies growing inside her.

"Alright. We wait," I concede, my voice a low growl tangled with the reluctance of a predator being caged.

Her eyes hold mine, and I see the reflection of a man who is more than the Soldier of Death, a man driven by vengeance alone. Now I see a man who loves and is loved in return.

"Good." She smiles, her gaze going to my lips again. My own curve up in happiness and amusement. My little virgin likes kissing. What a fucking idiot I've been to deny her. I dip my head, capturing her mouth again.

When I pull away, I stare at her, my mind rewinding the weeks to the day I took her from that altar. The woman before me now is an enigma. She's not the same. Where there was once compliance, now stands defiance. Where there was fear, now is courage and determination. The transformation leaves me breathless.

"Just so I'm clear on everything... things have been a little fuzzy since I hit my head—"

"What?" Her eyes narrow in worry and her gaze seeks a wound.

I take her wrists, kissing her hands. "Just a little bump. It's okay. But to make sure, I want to clarify that you love me and plan to stay."

She purses her lips at me in feigned annoyance. "Are you sure it's a head injury and not that you're hard-headed? I told you earlier that I planned to stay."

I laugh. "Maybe both." I gather her to me. "You know what this means, don't you?"

"I have no clue."

"It means you're going to have to marry me."

Her smile is stunning. It's like the sun has lit the world. "You seem to be under the impression that you can boss me around. You need to ask me."

I laugh. "Of course." I regret not having a ring as I kneel on one knee before her. "Elena Fiori, *cara mia*, will you marry me?"

"Yes." The giddy laugh she lets out is musical. I rise, and she launches herself into my arms, her lips finding mine with a fervor that ignites every cell in my body. I feel renewed. And hard. She's right. I don't need to kill her father tonight. I need to love this woman. I need to show her with every touch, every kiss, that she is a part of me and that I'm nothing without her.

A knock comes on the door, and I growl at the interruption. I break away from Elena, a string of silent curses threading through my thoughts.

"Come in."

The door creaks open, and Liam appears. "Doc's on his way. Until then, Lucia's playing nurse for Donovan."

I can't help but smirk at the image, picturing Donovan's smug face, even beneath the haze of pain.

"He'll be in heaven," I muse aloud, thinking how the tough-as-nails *capo* has a soft spot for Lucia, despite the fact that she's married and clearly dislikes him.

Elena tilts her head. "Why would he love that?"

"Because he's smitten."

Liam barks out a laugh, the sound echoing against the walls. "Must be a masochist, then, because Lucia clearly can't stand him."

Elena's lips twitch into a smile. "She seemed worried about him. And... well... Giuseppe died."

"What?" I ask.

"Today, or maybe it was yesterday. I'm confused about the time. You know, he was good to her. It sounds like they were close companions."

"I'm sorry for her loss," I say.

"I wonder what Luca is doing?" Liam says.

Elena glances at me. "You know them?"

I nod. "Yes. Not well, but enough to be on good terms."

"I have the start of the paperwork you asked for. I just need to know where Elena wants to go."

She threads her arm through mine. "I'm not going anywhere."

Liam arches a brow.

"We're all going to the compound as soon as Donovan can travel. Elena and Lucia too, unless she needs to get back to Italy... although...?"

"She's staying for now. Luca said she's still a part of the Family, but until things settle down after the Don's death, he says she should stay here."

Liam looks between the two of us and shrugs.

"We're pulling back to the compound. We'll give Giovanni a moment to think he's won and then bring him down."

Liam's eyes flicker with surprise. Restraint isn't my usual MO.

"Regroup, then?" he asks.

"Exactly. Then we remove the scum from the earth."

"Understood."

"I'll be down in a bit," I tell him.

He nods and disappears, leaving Elena and me alone once more.

"You're okay with that, aren't you?" Her voice, soft yet certain, wraps around me.

"Absolutely." It's the truth. Not that I'm not itching to kill Giovanni, but I like the idea of catching him off-guard. Like I did with Tiberius.

"Good."

My chest swells with pride. I've underestimated her resilience, but I'm seeing now that she's going to be a formidable partner in life. With her, I'm going to be stronger, but also happier, even as I'm aware that my love for her will make me vulnerable. So will the children.

I pull her to me once again, but this time, I'm aware of Donovan's blood on me and the scent of gunpowder lingering on my clothes.

"I need to wash off this night." I give her a sexy smile. "Want to help?"

Her smile is sweet, showing her innocence despite the number of times I've had her.

I walk with her to the bathroom, turning on the shower. I realize that I'd much rather spend this time lost in her body over killing Giovanni. I strip, all the while watching her do the same.

"Come, *cara mia*." I reach out my hand and draw her into the shower. Then I drop to my knees, my hands resting on her hips as I run kisses over her belly. "Two. You really must have been turned on at the club to have two "

Her fingers run through my hair. "I must have been. But then again, maybe it was you."

I grin up at her. "I was turned on. Holy hell, my dick was so hard." I stand. "Sort of like now." I press my dick against her. "You do this to me, Elena. You make me feel. To want. To feel love."

"Niko." Her hands press against my cheeks. "You are loved. By so many. Not just me."

I drop my forehead against hers. There's no denying the pull, the need to feel something other than revenge. Her touch ignites something primal, something that's been simmering beneath the surface since the moment I laid eyes on her at the club.

In the shower, steam curls around us and water cascades over our bodies, washing away the violence and fear of the day. But this isn't just a cleansing. It's an affirmation. A vow. I'm hers, and she's mine.

Need coils tight inside me, but when her hands roam my body with a boldness she hasn't shown before, I temper my desire.

"I bet you've had lots of women." Her voice is soft.

I hook my finger under her chin. "None of them I've loved. Elena... how can I make you see that you've changed my life? Changed me?"

"I just don't want you to be disappointed."

My hands massage her tits, gently, but with purpose. "Are you kidding? You're the first woman my dick can't seem to get enough of. He's got a mind of his own."

She smiles like it pleases her to hear that.

"In fact..." I press her against the tile wall and lift her thigh over my hip. "He's desperate to be inside you now."

"I'm desperate for him."

I watch her eyes as I slide in, taking my time. Inch by inch, I enter her, and it feels like heaven. Once I'm as deep as I can go, I still, savoring the feel of her around me, tight, hot, home. Then I kiss her, completing the circuit. Our bodies, our hearts, our souls are now one. I want to stay like this forever, but nature has other plans. My hips rock, slowly, gently at first. We find a rhythm that's sweet and hot, tender yet desperate.

"Niko." Her voice, speaking my name, is the final straw.

"*Cara mia*... I'm coming."

"Yes..." Her fingers dig into my shoulders and her head arches. She's so fucking beautiful as her pussy tightens and her orgasm rolls through her. I wish I could watch it all unfurl, but my dick has reached the limit. With her pussy pulsing around me, I come, rocking my release into her. Even when the tempest is over, I kiss her, wanting this moment to last as long as possible.

When we finish, we clean each other and emerge from the shower. We're not speaking, but no words are needed as I help her dry off. As we dress, our eyes are unable to look away from the love filling our hearts.

As we descend the stairs, side by side, I feel the shift complete. She is my love. My other half. But she is also my partner. My queen.

When we enter my office, my men look at us, and I know they see it too. There's a slight dip in their heads, like showing reverence to their new queen.

"Donovan?" I ask as I guide Elena with me to my desk.

"He'll live," Liam says. "Unless Lucia kills him."

There's a snicker in the group. I smile in amusement, as does Elena.

"Orders are to lay low, recover, and regroup." I list out who is staying and who is coming to the compound. I add extra security to my assets but tell them to not be obvious. "We want Giovanni thinking he's won."

"And then we show him he hasn't," Lou says.

"That's right."

I pause, holding Elena's gaze. She stands by my side, nodding her encouragement.

"Before we face what's ahead, there's something I need to let you all know." A smile tugs at the corner of my mouth. I'm fucking giddy. "Elena has agreed to be my wife."

Murmurs ripple through the room.

"Smart move," Lou says. "Once Giovanni is gone, you can take over—"

"This marriage isn't about that. It isn't business." I bring Elena's hand to my lips and kiss it. "This woman has stolen my heart."

"You have a heart?" Liam jokes.

I laugh. "Taking Donovan's role?"

Liam shrugs. "Since he's not here, I figured someone should."

"Congratulations," my men say, and I believe they mean it. I think they can see it.

With Elena, I'm more than *Il Soldato Della Morte*. I am love. I am a father. And together, we are a force to be reckoned with. We won't just take on Giovanni. We'll take on the world and win.

LOVED NIKO AND ELENA? *Great news! Donovan and Lucia's story is available now and you can get your copy here. (Link coming soon).*

ABOUT THE AUTHOR

Ajme Williams writes emotional, angsty contemporary romance. All her books can be enjoyed as full length, standalone romances and are FREE to read in Kindle Unlimited .

Books do not have to be read in order.

Heart of Hope Series
Our Last Chance | An Irish Affair | So Wrong | Imperfect Love | Eight Long Years | Friends to Lovers | The One and Only | Best Friend's Brother | Maybe It's Fate | Gone Too Far | Christmas with Brother's Best Friend | Fighting for US | Against All Odds | Hoping to Score | Thankful for Us | The Vegas Bluff | 365 Days | Meant to Be | Mile High Baby | Silver Fox's Secret Baby | Snowed In with Best Friend's Dad | Secret Triplets for Christmas | Off-Limits Daddy

The Why Choose Haremland (Reverse Harem Series)
Protecting Their Princess | Protecting Her Secret | Unwrapping their Christmas Present | Cupid Strikes... 3 Times | Their Easter Bunny | SEAL Daddies Next Door | Naughty Lessons | See Me After Class

High Stakes
Bet On It | A Friendly Wager | Triple or Nothing | Press Your Luck

Billionaire Secrets
Twin Secrets | Just A Sham | Let's Start Over | The Baby Contract | Too Complicated

Dominant Bosses
His Rules | His Desires | His Needs | His Punishments | His Secret

Strong Brothers
Say Yes to Love | Giving In to Love | Wrong to Love You | Hate to Love You

Fake Marriage Series
Accidental Love | Accidental Baby | Accidental Affair | Accidental Meeting

Irresistible Billionaires
Admit You Miss Me | Admit You Love Me | Admit You Want Me | Admit You Need Me

Check out Ajme's full Amazon catalogue here.

Join her VIP NL here.

WANT MORE AJME WILLIAMS?

Join my no spam mailing list here.

You'll only be sent emails about my new releases, extended epilogues, deleted scenes and occasional FREE books.

Printed in Great Britain
by Amazon